THE SWOOP
OF THE CONDOR

Andrew Gibson-Watt

The Book Guild Ltd.
Sussex, England

The Book Guild Ltd.
25 High Street,
Lewes, Sussex.

First published 1991
© Andrew Gibson-Watt 1991
Set in Baskerville
Typesetting by APS,
Salisbury, Wiltshire.
Printed in Great Britain by
Antony Rowe Ltd.,
Chippenham, Wiltshire.
British Library Cataloguing in Publication Data
Gibson-Watt, Andrew 1925-
The swoop of the condor
I. Title
823.914 [F]
ISBN 0 86332 599 8

*'Then was seen with what a strength and majesty the
British soldier fights.'*

*Twenty percent of all sums due to be paid by the
Publishers to the Author will be paid by them on the
Author's behalf directly to the charity 'The Weston
Spirit', Registered No. 327937.*

CONTENTS

MAPS

End paper maps of the Falkland Islands and South America by Transmedia Graphics, Birstall, Leicester.

AUTHOR'S PREFACE

This book is a work of fiction. For the avoidance of doubt, let us repeat that in capital letters – FICTION. The envisaged circumstances are purely hypothetical. Apart from certain named political figures, all the characters in this book are fictional. In particular, I want to make it clear that I am sure no Argentine officer would ever behave in the wrong-headed way depicted, either in the council-chamber or in the bedroom.

It would be idle to deny that there is some serious import behind what I have written, fictional though it may be. In the years before the Great War, two books were published, *When William Came* by H.H. Munro, and the better-known *The Riddle of the Sands* by Erskine Childers: the aim of both books was to alert the British public to the possibility of a successful surprise attack being mounted by Germany on Great Britain. I understand that although both those books received a lot of publicity, they caused no great offence in Imperial Germany, touchy though the Germans were at that period. I hope therefore that this book will cause no resentment in Argentina. It is, let me say it yet again, a work of fiction.

I am sure that, among the many failings of which I may be accused, improbability and inaccuracy as to detail may be prominent. As to the first of those possible charges, the reader must make up his own mind how improbable my scenario is: the author can only point out, in the words of the world's oldest cliché, that truth is many times stranger than fiction. As to the second, I am no Tom Clancy: let the master of technical detail reign undisturbed. But I have a more important disclaimer to make on this point. I have never been to the Falkland Islands, and I have no knowledge of the layout of the British base at Mount Pleasant, or of the arrangements for its defence and that of the islands. Any similarity between those arrangements as

9

they actually may be, and as they are depicted in this book, is therefore purely coincidental. Were this not so, the book could not have been written, because I am not in the business of giving aid and comfort to Her Majesty's potential enemies.

I am grateful to Simon Crisp for his help and advice over certain aspects: I also want to thank my sister, Ann Dearden, and her daughter, Celia Campbell, for some helpful suggestions: Celia also typed the manuscript with skill and patience. Finally I want to thank my wife for putting up with a more than usually boring husband in the long winter evenings.

ANDREW GIBSON-WATT
Wyecliff, Hay-on-Wye

1

It had been a long day. The Prime Minister was very tired.

He had at last managed to get up to the private apartment at the top of No 10 Downing Street, and was relaxing in an armchair, a whisky-and-soda at his elbow. Never a great consumer of alcohol, he nevertheless looked forward to and enjoyed this one drink at the end of the day. His wife had started to produce supper and had taken her gin-and-tonic into the kitchen. He sat quietly and reviewed the day's events.

The day had begun as usual, after not very many hours in bed. The previous night they had left the constituency after his own result had been declared, and had then been driven to Party headquarters in Smith Square where, amid scenes of mounting tension and excitement, the results were coming in one by one on the big television screen. It had always been clear that, if they were to win, it would be by a narrow margin; earlier in the evening there had been an atmosphere of some despondency as one Labour victory after another had been announced. Later, things got better, and as midnight approached the late surge of Conservative support had started coming through; it became clear that they were going to have an overall majority of nearly twenty seats.

It had very nearly been a straight contest between the Conservatives and Labour: the parties of the centre had been virtually wiped out. The Greens, not really organized as a proper political party, had won a good many votes but no seats. Former members of the Social Democratic Party, standing as Independents, had won a couple of seats. The Democrats (or were they the Liberals?) had not done well, despite the rhetoric and the statesmanlike pronouncements of their leader: their electoral chances had not been improved by a continuing discussion over what their party's name should be. There were two Scottish Nationalist successes, and one Plaid Cymru.

Apart from these peripheral elements, Labour had been the significant foe, and Labour had been widely tipped to win.

Now the disappointed face of Neil Kinnock, speaking from his constituency in South Wales, appeared on the screen conceding defeat – well, not exactly: he had not been beaten, but somehow the other side had won. At Smith Square there was much cheering, and a number of bottles were opened. The Prime Minister made his rounds, thanking everyone individually. Finally, they got into their car and were driven back to No 10, to be greeted by a number of staff members who had waited up to give their congratulations. In the General Election of 12th May 1992, the British electorate had, for the fourth consecutive time, put the Conservative Party into power.

In the morning he had driven to the Palace. The Queen had been gracious. Ever since the traumatic events of November 1990, when Margaret Thatcher had been forced to surrender the seals of her office, the Prime Minister had been struggling to unite the Conservative party under his leadership and to haul it back into a position where it could win an election. He would always remember with pleasure the kind things which the Monarch had said to him that morning.

His reverie was interrupted by the telephone. 'President Bush on the line, Prime Minister' said the duty operator. A short pause, and there he was.

'John, I was out of town this morning: I just got back here and had lunch, and I thought I'd call to congratulate you on your victory. Four times in a row is quite something. You must be feeling very pleased with yourself.'

'George, you are kind.' (The 'George' bit was actually quite new: it had been 'Mr President' for the first year or so.) 'I am indeed pleased, and I am looking forward to continuing to work with you on all the things we have to do.'

'Yes. Now will you forgive me if I ring off? I have a difficult afternoon with a lot of Senators who don't like me. I just thought I'd call to say well done, and welcome back.'

'Thank you, George. I do appreciate your calling.'

'Goodnight, then, John. Oh, and do remember that if there's ever anything I can do for you, but anything, you have only to ask. Your country, and you personally, are of the highest importance in our eyes.'

'Thank you, George, I will. Goodnight, then, and thank you

again for calling.'

'That was nice of him,' said the Prime Minister as his wife came in from the kitchen, 'He said he would do anything for me, but anything, and I had only to ask.'

'I hope he meant what he said,' she said. 'One never knows with politicians. Now, how's that drink going? Cod Mornay will be *à point* in about three minutes, and tonight I really do think – dare I say it? – that we should have a fairly early night.'

This they did. But towards five-thirty next morning, the Prime Minister was half-awake. Outside in the May morning the dawn chorus of birds was in full voice. He lay dozing, one half of his mind still struggling to continue a strange dream in which two cats and an ice-cream van figured largely. He was fully awoken by the telephone beside his bed.

'I'm sorry, Prime Minister,' said the night duty operator, 'but it's the Minister of Defence. He says it's essential he speaks to you.'

'Put him through.'

'Prime Minister,' said Sir Henry Jones, 'I am sorry to wake you, but I must. We have a report from the Garrison Commander, Falklands, that there has been an aerial incursion at Mount Pleasant airfield, and there has been shooting: he is treating it as a first-class emergency, and proposes to deal with it at first light, which will be in just over four hours by our time.'

'What do you mean, an aerial incursion? Explain.'

He listened with mounting incredulity to what the Minister told him.

'How could your duty officers do a thing like that? How could they?'

'They are very experienced officers, Prime Minister. They did what they thought they should do.'

'Don't be so loyal. Did they refer to you?'

'No, they didn't. Actually they probably wouldn't have got me.'

'I see.' A pregnant silence followed. 'Well, what do you think about it?'

'Actually, I take rather a gloomy view of it, Prime Minister. There could be a lot of them there. I think we have to take it seriously.'

'Oh, my God,' said the Prime Minister. 'I see. Get hold of

Admiral Higgins, and bring him round here as soon as you possibly can.'

2

When Admiral Tomas Alfredo Vasquez entered his office in the Ministry of Defence in Buenos Aires on that fateful morning in October 1990, he had no idea that by nightfall he and his opposite numbers in the Army and the Air Force would have taken the first steps towards initiating a chain of events which would reverberate round the world.

Vasquez was the Commander-in-Chief of the Argentine Navy. At fifty-two, he was nearing the end of his career. Since the conflict of 1982, in which he had commanded an elderly ex-American destroyer, his rise to the highest post had been steady. He was a quiet man, not given to showing his emotions. Only his closest friends, and his wife, knew that beneath his quiet exterior lay a complex make-up, of which the principal components were anger and shame – shame at the ineffectual part played by the Navy in 1982 – the Navy whose then commander-in-chief had been the principal moving force in the whole adventure, and which had then chickened out after the sinking of the *General Belgrano*.

What a cock-up it had all been, he thought for the thousandth time as he stood at the tall windows in the first-floor office, looking down the wide city avenue. The plane trees were in full leaf now, and the crowds thronging the side-walks were in shirt-sleeves and light frocks in the early summer morning's warmth. What did they expect the British to do? What was the point, in a situation where you knew your anti-submarine capability was inadequate, of manoeuvering fruitlessly as Lombardo had done? Above all, why give up at the first serious reverse? It had taken years for the Navy to recover anything like its old place in popular esteem, and perhaps it never would recover it fully.

And now there was this steady and apparently serious move towards reaching a permanent accommodation with the

British – an accommodation which seemed likely to put the vital issue of the Malvinas' sovereignty on the shelf forever, so that it would become something to be ignored and glossed over, not to be spoken about in case the speaking caused a rift in the fatuous friendship which practically everyone except himself seemed to think was a good idea. He did not think it was a good idea at all. He would like to see the issue of the Malvinas settled once and for all, in Argentina's favour. It was something he thought about quite a lot.

The rapprochement which so annoyed the admiral had effectively begun the year before, with the holding of the centenary celebrations of the Inter-Parliamentary Union. The Argentine delegation to the celebrations, which were held in London, had been led by Senator Eduardo Menem, the President's brother. The Senator had received a lot of publicity in the British Press. He had somewhat bemused his hearers by stating that, as hostilities between Argentina and Britain had effectively ended with the end of the fighting, a formal declaration of a cessation was superfluous: this seemed to some people to be what is sometimes known as 'chopping logic'. Nevertheless, his remarks had made on the whole a good impression. He had shaken hands with the Queen. He had stated that he hoped Britain and Argentina would soon resume relations, and that once that had been done a number of urgent issues must be addressed. After that, the question of sovereignty over the Falklands must be tackled. Finally, he called for a reduction of forces in the area, saying, 'I think there is a consensus that the South Atlantic should be an area of peace, and conflict is no longer a problem, so there is no reason to keep the region militarized.'

The British, who three years previously had reduced their garrison from 4,000 to about 1,800 men (on grounds that the Mount Pleasant airfield had been completed), were at first inclined to view this last idea with caution; but they fairly quickly came round to it.

The Inter-Parliamentary celebrations in London were followed, just over a month later, by talks between officials at Madrid. Over the months that followed, very considerable progress was made towards the re-opening of normal relations. The issue of sovereignty was, throughout, studiously ignored – as was the formal question whether any state of hostilities still

existed between the two countries: there seemed to be a general consensus that it did not, but this was unspoken and the Argentine side carefully refrained from giving any formal admission to that effect. Still, in the prevailing atmosphere of goodwill and steady if cautious progress, this aspect did not seem to matter very much.

A further round of meetings in Madrid resulted, in February 1990, in the virtual abolition of the British 'protective zone', an agreement that no state of hostilities existed, and in the re-establishment of full diplomatic relations. Special channels of communication were established to minimize the risk of incidents occurring. An agreement was reached on fishing rights, including joint arrangements for monitoring and regulating fishing by vessels of other nations. Also, it was agreed that British Airways should be allowed to restart operating between London and Buenos Aires: this service began in the month of March 1990, and was soon well patronized by business travellers, of whom there were an increasing number because of the swift re-establishment of trade links. Finally, later in 1990 the British Government decided to reduce still further its garrison in the Falklands. The principal component of the garrison had, since the previous reduction, been a complete infantry battalion: this was augmented by some hundreds of Royal Artillery personnel manning the Rapier anti-aircraft surface-to-air missile launchers, Royal Engineers (still looking for mines) and administrative and supply personnel. The Garrison Commander, who at one time had been of Major-General's rank, was now a Brigadier. The Royal Air Force maintained on Mount Pleasant airfield a force of six Phantom F4 heavy fighters, and an RAF Regiment defence detachment.

Belize (formerly British Honduras) had of late also been a battalion station. The main purpose of this was to protect the territory from possible aggression by Guatemala, but there was also a useful spin-off in jungle warfare training. Now the Guatemalans had shown real evidence of willingness to abandon their claims. The Treasury economizers, always on the look-out for a break, suggested that the Belize situation might now be sufficiently covered by a force of two infantry companies – and that they could come, on a short-stay basis, from the Falklands battalion. This was therefore put into effect, as was a reduction in the Phantom fighter force from six to four. It was not done without misgivings, which were voiced in the more responsible British newspapers and in the House of Commons itself; but it was done, and the doing of it was well received in Argentina.

Half a battalion, mused Admiral Vasquez as he stood at the window. Only half a battalion and a few missile batteries, and four fighters. How typically British. How typically over-confident – in fact almost insolent. How sure they must be that they were now dealing with a genuinely friendly people who had recognized that the only way forward was by peaceful negotiation.

Shaking off these disturbing reflections, the admiral went back to his desk and started dealing with the work of the day. His secretary came in and took his dictation of several letters. After that was finished, the secretary said, 'General Gonzalez just called, and asked whether you might be free to meet with him and General Romera for lunch today. There is nothing in your diary.'

'Why not?' said the admiral. He was indeed conscious of having not very much to do. In truth, there was little to do in the Navy these days. He had envisaged a quiet lunch at home with his wife in their city apartment, and a return to the office at half-past four in the afternoon: summer routine was now, in May, generally accepted.

'Yes.' he said, 'Will you call my wife and tell her I will not be home. Where does General Gonzalez suggest we lunch?'

'At the Jockey Club lunchroom at the racecourse, Sir,' said the secretary. 'Two o'clock.'

This was a surprise. On race-meeting days, of course, the luxurious premises reserved for Jockey Club members were always full of the great and good; but this was not such a day. The course would be deserted, and lunch in the club lunch-room a matter of special arrangement with the steward. How strange. His opposite numbers in the Army and the Air Force must have something special and private to communicate to him. He was on very good terms with them both: they did all sometimes meet together to discuss things they thought impor-tant. On these occasions, his wife would sometimes ask him, 'How did the Junta business go today?' The admiral had never quite managed to persuade his wife that he and the other two service chiefs were by no possible stretch of the imagination a

Junta – or that in present-day Argentina it was the height of bad form to suggest that they were: the very use of the word 'Junta' was inadvisable in public, and not really very funny in the bedroom.

'Very well,' said the admiral, 'have my car here at one-thirty, would you? Now let's get on. Captain Varela is to see me, I gather. Is he there?' So the work of the morning, consisting today mainly of interviews with officers taking up or leaving service posts, began.

☆   ☆   ☆

The Jockey Club lunchroom, like the large anteroom leading to it, had huge plate glass windows which looked out over the wide expanse of the racecourse, deserted on this non-racing day except for a few workers on tractors mowing the grass and doing other things necessary for the upkeep of the course. It was a pleasant room with light-coloured chairs and pictures of horses and jockeys on the walls. Only one table was set for lunch, in the far corner next to one of the big windows. The two generals were already sitting at it: they rose to greet Vasquez as he came in. When he had arrived on the premises he had been greeted warmly by the steward, a retired naval petty officer whom he knew well.

'I am sorry, Tomas,' said General Jaime Gonzalez, the Army Chief-of-Staff and the senior of the two other officers, 'It was unforgivable not to arrange this well in advance. I am so glad that the unlikely happened and you were able to come. The fact is that Romera and I decided to lunch on the spur of the moment, and then we decided to ask you too.'

'Never mind,' said the admiral, 'It was a good thought, and luckily I was free. Yes, I'd like a glass of sherry – dry, please. Will anyone else be here for lunch?'

'No,' replied General Gonzalez, 'I have arranged that we are to be entirely private. What is more, your friend Luis the steward assures me there are no bugs here. He checks this room out personally every week, and did it this morning just to make sure. As you will remember, he is a highly-qualified electrician.'

Admiral Vasquez laughed in agreement. He did indeed remember that his former petty officer, trained as an electrical

19

artificer, had become something of a specialist both in the planting and in the elimination of eavesdropping devices: he had personally employed him in order to de-bug various offices on more than one occasion. He had sometimes wondered whether senior officers in the British Ministry of Defence found it necessary to do this. Argentine senior officers, if they were wise, did.

'Good,' he said. 'so we can be as indiscreet as we like. What are we going to talk about?'

There was a short silence before General Hector Romera, the Chief of Staff of the Fuerza Aerea Argentina, said, 'We think we ought to talk about the state of our country.'

3

This was by no means the first time that senior officers in the Argentine armed forces had felt the need to talk about the state of their country. Although Argentina has a long history of parliamentary democracy, authoritarian tendencies are never far below the surface, and even when properly-elected civilian administrations have been in office, much power behind the scenes has historically been wielded by the Army councils, of which the principal members have been the corps commanders in charge of the various military regions of the country: in late years the Navy and Air Force have also become involved in political affairs.

In 1976 the armed forces had actually seized power, the country being at the time seriously affected by economic depression, galloping inflation, and also by urban terrorism which threatened the very fabric of the state. General Jorge Videla was installed as President, with a three-man Junta from the three services. He had considerable success at first in tackling Argentina's financial problems, and by the use of very ruthless methods indeed there was also success in suppressing internal terrorism. However, by the end of 1981 the economic difficulties were again becoming serious. Videla resigned, and General Leopoldo Galtieri, the Army member of the Junta, assumed the additional appointment of President. This led almost immediately to the fatal decision to take the Malvinas by force.

It is traditional in Latin countries to embark on foreign adventures when internal problems become unmanageable. It is thought to encourage the population. However, for the effect to be at all lasting, the foreign adventure has to be successful, and the adventure of 1982 was not. The discredited armed services were quickly swept from power and, amid much international goodwill, Raoul Alfonsin took over the govern-

21

ment of the country.

President Alfonsin was a good man and a genuine democrat, but he proved powerless to get Argentina's economic affairs into any sort of order. The country was crippled (like many other South American countries) by a huge burden of foreign debt, a considerable proportion of which had been advanced during the brief period when the Videla administration seemed to have established monetary order, temporarily giving Argentina respectable international financial status: most of that money had been badly invested, and now it was difficult to keep up the interest payments on it. Inflation roared away almost unchecked and apparently out of control, so that when Alfonsin was defeated at the polls by Carlos Menem, who took office early in 1989, things had got so bad that serious riots were occurring due to people being unable to afford to purchase food. Menem had done his best to stabilize the situation and had met with a certain amount of success; but there was still a long way to go.

This was the background to the lunchtime conversation of the three service chiefs, in their private room overlooking Buenos Aires racecourse.

'The most disappointing thing about this man Menem,' said General Gonzalez as the steward Luis discreetly left the room for the last time, having placed the coffee and brandy on the table, 'is his total inability to get the economic thing right. He just doesn't seem able to get anywhere. We need a financial genius like Dr Schacht in Germany in the Thirties, and he doesn't seem to exist.'

'I agree,' said Admiral Vasquez. 'One must however say that we are unlikely to see much improvement until the foreign debt question is settled. I don't see that happening until Argentina enjoys more genuine international respect. I believe we are despised in the world at the moment, and a principal reason why we are despised is the weak way we are handling the Malvinas issue. How can the government go on making concession after concession to the British, leaving the matter of sovereignty on one side as if it didn't matter? I personally believe we might win next time, and even if we don't it might bring the British to their senses. Long-term, their position is untenable, and well they know it.'

The other two men nodded thoughtfully, General Romera

saying, however, 'Of course, there is a case for saying that we are not in a position now to engage in military adventures, and should concentrate on building up international goodwill. Personally I do not take that view: I think we should get more respect by acting. And if we failed, Menem would no doubt pardon us, as he pardoned Galtieri and all those others last year.'

'He had to do that,' said Gonzalez grimly. 'He was under enormous pressure.' The General was in a position to know about that, having played a leading part in the army councils' pressure on the unfortunate President.

'I think, gentlemen, we ought to get down to real business,' remarked Gonzalez next. 'May I explain to you in general terms how I see our objective in the Malvinas?'

The other two officers nodded their agreement as they filled their coffee cups and brandy glasses.

'First of all,' General Gonzalez began, 'I do not think there can be any question of any actual coup to remove the government, as there was in 1976. Public opinion in the country would be outraged – the people just do not want military government. Besides, I do not believe that in the short term we should be able to do any better on the economic front than Menem and his lot. That improvement will come later, when we by our actions have restored our country's international standing. Meanwhile we need those politicians. If our operation succeeds as we intend it to, the politicians will be glad to jump on the bandwagon of our success. If by any chance it fails, the country will need them to pick up the bits. We have to do the job behind their backs.'

His listeners nodded their agreement: Major-General Romera selected a fine Havana cigar and lit it.

'We may have to restrain Menem and a few other people for a day or so while the operation is actually going on,' went on General Gonzalez, 'if only to preserve their innocence. I see it as being most desirable that, in the eyes of the world, Menem is seen to have had no part in the preparation of the operation or in the decision to carry it out. In any event, if he did know about it, he would not agree to do it – that I know. It has got to be our show.

'Now, my friends, may I come to another point which I consider to be of the first importance? I am sure that we have to adopt an entirely different attitude to the Malvinas from that adopted in 1982. Let me explain what I mean.

'In 1982, from the islanders' point of view, we went in in a most heavy-footed way. We occupied Stanley and all the other places where people lived. We billeted soldiers everywhere and we didn't even feed them properly, so that there was constant trouble with sheep, pigs and chickens being killed. We laid mines everywhere and people are still being blown up by them. In short, from the outset we were looked on as invaders who simply wanted to absorb the islands into Argentina and blot out every vestige of their independence. So the people just hated us. I think we have to do it very differently this time.'

'Thought-provoking stuff,' interjected Admiral Vasquez, 'But surely there was no other way we could have done it in 1982? We had to expect an attack and, if you remember, we got it. We had to occupy the whole of the main island, at least.'

'Yes, you are right. I agree with you. But this time will be different. If we take Stanley, the British will be hard put to it to mount the sort of attack they made last time. Details have yet to be worked out, but from my discussions with one officer I think should be involved in the detailed planning, I am fairly clear that this operation can be a much lighter affair. We have to occupy the main seat of British military power, by which I mean the new airfield, and perhaps Stanley itself. But once we are there in charge, we do not have to expect an attack from the British.'

'Why not, for God's sake?'

'Well, lots of reasons. First of all, I'm not sure if they are now in a position to mount that sort of Task Force. Secondly, Romera's aircraft are in much better shape to fight them off – improved types, better range, and above all, this time the bombs will have some proper fuses; they will actually go off when they hit a ship. Furthermore, I don't believe that the British will get international support, UN support, I mean. I just don't believe the international community will support them again, like they did in 1982, whatever the technical rights and wrongs may be. They won't do it.'

'Let's suppose you are right about that. Where does that get us?'

'It gets us to a very light occupation of the Malvinas. We have to be in secure control of the new airfield and perhaps also of the old Stanley airstrip. But that's all. We don't have to flood the place with useless conscripts, if we're not going to be attacked. And that will enable us to make an effective effort to win hearts and minds of the islanders. They can go on running their affairs: they can be an autonomous territory within Argentina, and we won't interfere with them. They can go on keeping their sheep and thinking of themselves as Brits, and at the same time they can have all the privileges of Argentine citizenship, except that of being conscripted into the Army at age eighteen. We shall be in a position to make a real effort to win these people over, and that is what we must try to do. As soon as we are established there we must make an announcement that that is how we intend to proceed – a large degree of autonomy for the islands, their own courts and police, no troops stationed there once the British have acccpted the situation, and privileged status as Argentine citizens. Not only will that make an impression on the islanders, but it will also be seen very favourably by international public opinion, which is going to be so important to us.'

'I must say,' said Admiral Vasquez after a brief interlude of silence, 'I think it is very clever. I agree with you all the way, Jaime. What is your reaction, Romera?'

'I too agree with the thinking.' replied the Air Force general. 'I am wondering about some of the details. Presumably full action by the Air Force will be required? It really boils down to this – do you intend to go by sea or by air? If the latter is intended, I see formidable difficulties with the British radar. They will pick us up in plenty of time to scramble their fighters, and although there are only four or five of them, they are most formidable planes. The Rapier missiles are also most efficient. If you are going to try to fly in the attack force by transport aircraft, I see C-130s being knocked out of the sky in all directions.'

'Yes,' said Gonzalez, 'I follow you. But I think we must await a planning report before we decide on any details of the attack. Having said that, you should certainly envisage mounting a full-strength effort with the Air Force. I suppose, Tomas, you are going to ask me what I think the Navy's role should be?'

'I am, indeed.' replied Vasquez. 'As you both know, my service has been severely criticized for its failure to act effectively in 1982. The trouble is that the fundamental situation has not changed: once we leave the shallows of the continental shelf and get into deep water, we are very vulnerable to submarine attack. It is my impression that the British have one hunter-killer nuclear-powered boat of the *Conqueror* type permanently on station. We have limited anti-submarine capability, although there has been an improvement lately. I am not being negative, but I must point out that these aspects will have to be considered.'

'I take the point,' said Gonzalez, 'we must indeed consider them with care. Now, do you both agree with my suggestion that we must have a joint planning staff to study the operation in detail, and then make detailed recommendations to us?'

The two other officers nodded their assent, and then Vasquez said, 'The operation must of course be kept deadly secret. Even if it were known that planning sessions were taking place involving staff officers of the three services, it could be fatal. The staff detailed for this job must be very small – could we keep it to three men and a typist, do you think?'

'Yes,' said General Gonzalez, 'three wise men. The man I have in mind for the Army is Colonel Mario Hernandez. He is chief of staff to the Third Military District at Cordoba. I suggest the meetings can take place there: it's a long way away, and life is leisurely. He hasn't got much to do, and his district commander is a solid man, completely in my confidence: he won't ask any questions if I tell him he mustn't. Furthermore, he has a personal assistant whom I know well: she is a super-efficient girl, and her discretion is assured: I would trust her with my life.'

Vasquez smiled to himself. He was one of the very few people in whose knowledge it was that the Army Chief of Staff did indeed know the young woman officer in question extremely well. Until her transfer to Cordoba she had been his mistress for several years. However, he agreed with the General's assessment of her professional qualities, so he merely said, 'I quite agree: the typing of the report should be safe with her. As for the Navy representative, I have a Captain Varela in mind: he came in to see me this morning on giving up command of a ship, and he has not yet been found a new post. He is a first-class officer, dedicated to the service and loyal to me personal-ly. He comes from near Cordoba, and his visits there will

26

attract little attention.'

'Good,' said the General, 'Romera, what about you?'

'To be frank, no-one springs instantly to my mind at the moment,' replied General Romera, 'but it won't take me long to find someone suitable. When I do, I'll give him one of those nice little HS 125 jets – it might make life easier for all of them.'

'Handsomely said, my friend,' said Gonzalez. 'And now, have we said enough? I will give a detailed verbal brief to Hernandez, and you no doubt will also brief your nominees. Shall we ask them to report in, say, three months?'

On this note the meeting broke up, and the three heads of service went their separate ways. It was already half-past four, and they went straight to their respective Ministry offices to begin the evening work-spell customary in the summer months. Nothing had been written down. Nothing had been overheard. Only Luis the steward, as he cleared up the table and made ready to return to his suburban home, said to himself, 'I wonder what those three are up to?'

4

The city of Cordoba lies some three hundred and fifty miles north-west of Buenos Aires, in open pleasant countryside, on the fringes of the Andean foothills. To the west of the city rise some quite considerable mountains, forerunners of the mighty cordillera of the Andes, the snow-bound peaks of which are visible on a clear day. It is a pleasant city with broad avenues. On the southern outskirts lies the military base in which the local district headquarters are located. Lieutenant Alicia Nunes had not been pleased at being posted to Cordoba. An unmarried young woman of twenty-three, she was keen about her chosen profession and also very keen about her love-life, which in her last posting in Buenos Aires had been exciting. A tall, raven-haired beauty who wore her perfectly-tailored uniform well, she had attracted the attention of no less a personage than General Jaime Gonzalez, the Army Chief of Staff. Being happily married with three teenage children had not seemed to the General to be any impediment to an affair with this enticing young woman officer. Accordingly there had been many afternoons when the general had found pressing reasons for not going home for lunch and the customary siesta. The siesta period had on those occasions been spent in a discreet apartment in a street not far from the Defence Ministry.

It had lasted for two years, and then there had come this sudden posting to Cordoba. Alicia had begged her lover to get it changed, but in the end he had professed his inability to do so: there had been a tearful scene before she had accepted the situation. She was now just beginning to realize that the general had probably decided that enough was enough, and that prudence and the continuance of his happy marriage demanded that an end be made. Grudgingly she was beginning to admit to herself that he was probably right, and that she herself had needed a change of scene and of lover – which latter change had not proved too difficult to arrange once she had settled in her new appointment.

The new appointment itself was an agreeable one. Colonel Hernandez was chief staff officer to the district commander, a brigadier-general. The latter liked a quiet life, and here in Cordoba he had it. He left most of the day-to-day work to his chief-of-staff. Hernandez was known to be one of the most able officers in the Army. Alicia's job was to be his personal assistant – a good assignment, and one which she was enjoying a lot. No romance was to be expected from Hernandez – he was a serious-minded officer who also happened still to be head-over-heels in love, after five years of marriage, with his wife. From the start, however, he had given Alicia his friendship, and had been open with her about all aspects of the job.

There were not very many women in the Argentine Army. In this far southern corner of the Western Hemisphere, ideas of sex-equality which had become commonplace in Europe and the United States were only now beginning to be accepted. Women soldiers were objects of curiosity and, South American man being what he was, of ribaldry. Women officers were an especial curiosity: they were few in number, and only three or four years previously it would have been unthinkable for a woman officer to hold the sort of post that Alicia held now. Still, it was beginning; and, as so many people have found out, the step from 'secretary' to 'personal assistant' is one of the most important steps of all.

Now there was this new and intriguing joint-service planning assignment upon which her boss was to be engaged. Captain Varela of the Navy had already arrived, and had been assigned quarters in the base. Estranged from his wife, and therefore for practical purposes a bachelor, his official posting was 'on attachment to the Army for development of ideas of joint interest'. Such attachments were not unusual in the Argentine services, but usually involved less senior officers. Captain Varela, however, was understood to have been in poor health: he had elderly parents and other relatives in the Cordoba district, so that the posting was seen to be of a compassionate nature.

Major Juan Carbona, the Air Force nominee, was to arrive tomorrow. His marital status was unknown, but he would no doubt prove to be an interesting addition to local society.

As to the assignment itself, Colonel Hernandez had told her little, but he had told her how the matter was to be handled. He himself would be largely employed in the planning sessions: they would take up the greater part of his time for the next three months. She would not, for the time being, be involved, and would be fully employed in doing the work that he would otherwise be doing, in collaboration with the staff-captain. At the end, however, she would be very much involved, because she would be entrusted with the typing of the final report which the three planners were to make to higher authority. Lest she think that such a reversion to her former secretarial metier was inappropriate to her status, Hernandez emphasized to Alicia that the job was one of the utmost importance to the State, and one where the highest degree of security and confidentiality was required. He gave her to understand that at that final stage, when she was typing the report, he would be ready to talk to her at length about all aspects of its contents. To Alicia, this seemed sufficient confirmation of his trust in her and of his confidence in her abilities.

The Argentine Army was not at a high peak of efficiency, but it was doing its best, against some handicaps and difficulties, to improve. Conscription at age eighteen was still in force: the period of service was two years, so that there was a continuing turnover of soldiers, most of the energies of the regular cadre of non-commissioned officers and senior enlisted men being devoted to the training of these birds of passage. The British Army had been in this position in the years after the Second World War, and its men had been only too glad when National Service ended and they were able to spend their time being fully-professional soldiers. In Argentina, it had not yet been found possible to abandon universal conscription – for various reasons which no-one, even if pressed, would have found very easy to explain. What had happened since 1982 was a determined effort to upgrade the place of conscript soldiers in the military effort. Everyone still remembered the image, caught in the world's media coverage, of the miserable young conscripts under General Menendez' command in the Malvinas, shivering in inadequate uniforms, underfed and undermotivated, only too ready to surrender to the formidable combination of Royal Marines, Paras, Guards and Gurkhas moving in against them. It had been an easily-appreciated lesson, and one which the parents in Argentina had not been slow to rub in. It was generally appreciated that the regular non-commissioned officers had culpably neglected their young conscript soldiers, and that the officers had let them do it. Thereupon, the energies of the Army high command had been directed to ensuring that a different state of affairs would prevail in the future.

In all stations, therefore, including Cordoba where the garrison consisted of an infantry battalion and an artillery regiment, a great deal of time was spent on training, and a large part of the chief-of-staff's job consisted in arranging field exercises, sometimes in conjunction with the troops of neighbouring garrisons. 'Neighbouring' is a relative word in a vast country such as Argentina, and these joint exercises involved much transportation work. Also in the garrison was located the newly-formed School for Non-Commissioned Officers; for the first time in history the regular sergeants of the Argentine Army were receiving specialized training in their profession, man-management being a principal item of that training. Until a year or so previously, all this activity had been gravely hindered by a shortage of money. Now, however, President Carlos Menem, aware of the growing current of discontent in the services and under heavy pressure from the still-powerful army councils to upgrade the standing of the services in the public eye, had agreed to a considerable loosening of the purse-strings. Ammunition and petrol were suddenly available for exercises; the Air Force had been given the green light to modernize its ageing fleet of aircraft, and the Navy also were authorized to purchase, not indeed any additional ships, but a wide range of anti-submarine and anti-aircraft equipment which had previously lain outside the scope of its budget.

Alicia Nunes therefore found herself busy, now that most of her chief's work had been delegated for the time being to her and to the staff-captain, a most competent officer with whom she found it easy to work. As a beautiful and unattached girl her free time was also filled: she was much in demand among the young officers of the garrison, and was able to enjoy both an agreeable social life and (by picking and choosing carefully) the delights of a satisfying sex-life.

To this tasty cocktail of life, Major Juan Carbona was now

added as an additional ingredient.

He arrived in style in the small Hawker-Siddeley business jet promised by his chief. A sergeant-pilot came with him: the aircraft landed at the Cordoba airport, which was mainly used for civil flights but also by the military. Major Carbona then reported himself for duty at Colonel Hernandez' office: it fell to Lieutenant Nunes to arrange the details of his accommodation and to inform him of the arrangements under which he would confer with his two colleagues.

Carbona was twenty-nine years of age, very fit, and with the looks and attitude to life of a top-class professional polo-player; that is to say, he was very handsome and knew it, and he intended that every possible moment outside the time allotted to the exercise of his profession should be spent in bed with an attractive woman. Alicia Nunes, who was no fool, became aware of this as soon as he came into the office: like most other women, she was immediately attracted by the handsome flier, but she was also aware of another factor, one that she instinctively disliked – Carbona was a 'macho-man', a man who, she judged, liked to domineer women and might well be expected to ride rough-shod over them. For the moment she suspended judgement: in the nature of things it was inevitable that, thrown together as they were, would get to know each other quite well. Whether this would lead to an enjoyable relationship was something which would have to be decided.

The three wise men conferred on most days each week. At a comparatively early stage, they found themselves able to agree upon the fundamentals. The brief which they had been given absolved them from any consideration of political factors – their task was simply to recommend how the proposed operation could best be carried out; but as to background policy they had been clearly instructed in the sense of General Gonzalez' suggestions to his fellow service chiefs at their Jockey Club meeting. It was thus easy for them to agree upon the basics; and it then became necessary for them to consider details.

The time-scale of the operation was obviously one of the things that they had been asked to consider. Their discussions led them to agree that certain purchases of equipment would be necessary, and it was clear that a span of time might be necessary for those purchases to be effected. It was therefore agreed that these intermediate conclusions should be notified to their superiors, in order that they should be able to organize what was needed within the projected time-scale. The time-scale itself was also agreed in principle by the planners, and would be communicated to the superiors on the same occasion.

So the HS 125, piloted by Major Carbona with the sergeant-pilot as co-pilot, took off from Cordoba Airport and within the hour was cleared for landing at Buenos Aires. From the airport there, the 'three wise men' were taken by an Army car to the racecourse, where a lunchtime meeting had been arranged on the Jockey Club's premises.

'I must say,' remarked Admiral Vasquez when Colonel Hernandez, as senior planner, had finished the intermediate presentation, 'there is one thing I like about this idea. It lets us out of being mass murderers. I have been worrying about that a bit.'

'Casualties in any kind of war are inevitable,' said General Gonzalez, 'but in principle I agree with you. I see it as being central to our case that we take a moral initiative from the start. As we are all agreed, we are not going to enslave the inhabitants of the Malvinas, or make exactions of any kind on them, such as taking over property or even billeting troops. As for the British, they can look out for themselves: they didn't mind how many of our chaps they killed in 1982. But if your idea works, and we can avoid actually killing them in large numbers, and point out publicly from the start that we have not done so, then I think that will help us get the international support we need.'

'Where do we go,' asked the admiral, 'to get what we need?'

General Romera coughed apologetically. 'As a matter of fact,' he said hesitantly, 'I have to tell you that my procurement branch happened to make some enquiries in this general field about nine months ago. I don't quite understand why they did that: when I got to know about it, I told them to put it on the back of the shelf. But some interesting facts emerged. Briefly, the weapon is available and my chaps know where to go to get it. I need hardly say that it is extremely expensive.'

'We shall have to decide on quantities,' said the Army

33

General. 'Will the Navy join in?'

'Definitely, yes,' said Vasquez. 'As you all know, our old carrier *Veintecinco de Mayo* is not big as carriers go, and cannot fly off many planes compared with the Air Force; but every little helps, and I have it in mind that, as well as doing that, she could perform a valuable function by decoying the resident British Navy away from the immediate area of the operation. Will you work on that one, Varela?'

The Captain nodded his assent. 'I have actually got quite a few ideas about that, Sir.'

'Very well,' said General Gonzalez, 'it seems that we are agreed this idea must be pursued. Now, what about timing? When are we going to go? I think we must assume it will take us a little time to get what we want, so that affects the timing. What do you say, planners?'

'Sir,' said Hernandez, 'we have come to what you may think is a rather strange conclusion. We believe that the operation should be timed to take place as nearly as possible simultaneously with the British general election. May I ask Major Carbona to speak on this as he knows about the British political system?'

'Go ahead,' said General Gonzalez, 'this is interesting.'

'The British system, gentlemen,' began Carbona, 'is that a general election may be called at any time by the government in power. The British Queen, as you know, is a constitutional monarch, and in this, as in almost all other things, she has to accept the advice of the Prime Minister. But the longest period allowed between general elections is five years. This means that the present government must call an election by, I think, the end of October 1992. In, practice, unless there is an absolute emergency, the British find it very difficult to hold general elections in any other periods than September/October, or April/May. Usually it is October or May. To hold elections at other times of the year is thought to annoy the voters.

'This British government is in trouble on many fronts. They have a bad balance of payments situation, and they have managed to make themselves unpopular with the electorate in many ways. Labour is at present comfortably ahead in the opinion polls. The Conservative government would lose if it went to the country now: its only hope is to hang on until the last moment, in the expectation that Labour will shoot themselves in the foot as they usually manage to do – over some issue like unilateral nuclear disarmament. But some people think that to wait until the last possible moment would be a sign of weakness: so it is likely they will go either in October 1991 or May 1992. We should be ready by the first date. We could, in theory, get only three weeks notice, but in practice it is always a month. We think it would be possible to fit in with that.'

'Thank you, Major Carbona,' said Gonzalez, 'but now I must ask – why do you want to coincide with the British election?'

'We see it this way, General,' replied Colonel Hernandez. 'If we were to go well before the election, then we should have to deal with a Conservative government desperate to win the election, and quite prepared to play the patriotic card in order to do so, as Mrs. Thatcher did with such success after the 1982 war.

'If we go on election night, or a day either side, the British government machine will not be at its best. If Labour wins, then no newly-elected Labour Prime Minister is going to try to do a 1982. It will be a perfect opportunity to acquiesce in what we shall present as a reasonable settlement of the Malvinas problem, and they can have a field day blaming the previous government. If on the other hand it is the Conservatives who have just been elected, they will be in a difficult position. If they can get the green light for a task force, well and good; but our guess is they won't, either from the British people or in New York. There will be strong pressurre on them to accept a fait accompli, and one must always remember that the present prime minister, although no doubt a patriotic man, does not have the historical personal commitment that Mrs. Thatcher would have had if she had remained in office. In any case, it will be a serious humiliation for them, and I think that's what we all want.'

'Yes,' said General Romera suddenly. 'It's what I want. I think of all those young men, my colleagues then, who died; how brave they all were; and the British shouldn't have won – they only won because of those damned fuse-settings. It will stay with me all my life – I can't forget it. I want to beat the British, and I hope I live to see the day when I do. The Air Force will pull out every stop, and give of its best: we shall no doubt have casualties, but it will be worth it. Yes, let's humiliate the British if we can, and beat them down into the mud.'

There was a silence throughout the room, until finally Admiral Vasquez said, 'Yes, General Romera, you are right. This is what we have to do. It is a good plan, a plan which gives us the best chance of success. I vote that we adopt it.'

'Very well,' said General Gonzalez, 'we shall have to get on with the purchasing. I thank the planning officers for coming to us today with such clear ideas, which we are able to adopt. You, Romera, must be responsible for the weapons purchases: finance, as you know, will not be a difficulty, within reason, that is. As to timing, unless my colleagues and I have second thoughts, that also is agreed, and the planning officers will now please proceed to the preparation of their final detailed report.'

As Luis the steward cleared up before going home, he again smiled to himself: this is getting interesting. The bug which he had concealed in one of the power-points was no bigger than a collar-stud, but every word of the conversation in the room had been recorded on tape.

5

There is a quiet street in Geneva, not far from the lakeside esplanade in the old part of the city, where businessmen who like to conduct their affairs under a cloak of secrecy live and work. The solid houses have solid front doors, with peep-holes through which callers can be scrutinized. When the bell is rung this scrutiny takes place, and then either the entry-phone tells the caller that Monsieur X cannot see him, reason unexplained, or a bolt is slid back and the caller is admitted. It is generally agreed in Geneva that many of the occupants of these discreet offices-cum-residences are engaged in the international arms trade.

To one of these houses came, on a grey day in January 1991, two men. Both wore overcoats and broad-brimmed trilby hats, and scarves against the damp chill of the day. One of them was Major Paco Suarez of the Argentine Air Force: the other was an acquaintance with whom he had long done official business for his service's procurement branch, an Argentine businessman with whose surname we need not be concerned. It was this latter man who possessed the personal credentials necessary to unlock the front door of the house in the Rue des Orfèvres, the bell of which they now rang.

When the formalities of admittance had been carried out, the visitors were shown by a uniformed maid into a dark room on the ground floor, where they were asked to wait. A few minutes later, they were joined by the man they had come to see, a dark-haired person of quite unremarkable appearance, on whose fingers however glittered several large and clearly valuable rings.

'Ah, my dear Julio,' said this man, 'how pleasant to see you again. On the last occasion, I remember, it was a good deal for us both. Now, who is this gentleman you have brought with you?'

The businessman whose Christian name was Julio intro-
duced Major Suarez. The dark man smiled, saying, 'It is
always a pleasure to do business for the Argentine Air Force.'
And he asked after the health of several retired officers whose
names were known to Suarez: a few moments of small-talk
ensued.

'Now,' said the arms-dealer, 'let us get down to business.'
They sat down round a dark, polished mahogany table. 'What
is it that you want?'

Major Suarez told him. The dealer whistled softly. 'That's
not too easy,' he said, 'but it's not impossible. I suppose you
realize it's going to be very expensive? How much do you
need? Are you fighting one battle, or a long war?'

'One battle,' replied Suarez, 'in fact one air strike by, say,
ninety planes.'

'Only one? Four bombs per plane?'

'Yes, only one strike, and I think four one-hundred kilogram
bombs per plane.'

The dealer did a quick sum on his pocket calculator, and
then wrote a figure, denominated in US dollars, on a sheet of
paper which he pushed across the table to his two visitors.
'Unless my friends in Tripoli have become more rapacious of
late, that is the sort of money you are going to need,' he said. 'It
is a large sum, as you see; but it includes my own modest
commission.'

The businessman Julio knew from past experience that the
dealer's commission was very far from being modest, and that
it represented a sizeable proportion of the seemingly astronom-
ical figure written on the paper: he also knew that the figure
contained a useful cut for himself. He merely nodded, saying to
Major Suarez, 'I take it this is within the budget?'

'Yes, I suppose it is,' replied Suarez, 'in fact I think it will
have to be. Is this a firm figure?'

'Not yet,' said the dealer, 'but I don't think it will be far out.
I shall have to negotiate the deal in detail. If the suppliers are
greedier than I think they will be, you will either have to pay a
bit more or get a bit less. Frankly, I don't anticipate problems.
The terms when I do settle them, by the way, will be 'f.o.b.
Tripoli, buyer collects'. In other words, you will have to
arrange shipment. As to payment, I anticipate that they will
ask for an irrevocable bank Letter of Credit, opened through

and confirmed by a major Italian bank, for the main sum.'

'Your reference to 'the main sum' leads me to suppose you may require something up front, my dear Yves?' enquired Julio.

'Yes,' replied the dealer. He gestured, almost apologetically, with one be-ringed hand. 'Half a million US dollars.'

The two Argentinians had not come unprepared for such an eventuality. There was no arguing to be done, only paying. Major Suarez took from his wallet a number of cheques, made out to bearer and drawn on a leading New York bank by The Central Bank of Argentina. He handed one over: the dealer scrutinized it, folded it up and put it in his pocket.

The rest of their conversation concerned details – the packaging of what they were buying, when it should be ready for shipment, and so on. It was arranged that the dealer would confirm the full details, including the final price, through the businessman Julio. Finally, they were ready to leave.

'Where do they get these things?' asked Suarez as they were rising to their feet.

'Oh, the Soviet Union.' replied the dealer. 'Originally supplied for use against Iran, and never so used. The Iraqis sold them on to Libya, after the end of the Iranian war, to raise some foreign exchange: also, I think, by then they had acquired something deadlier, so this stuff was surplus to requirements. The Libyans are always ready to acquire weaponry. I find them, I may say, a deeply unattractive people, but they are straightforward to do business with, I will give them that.'

He led his visitors to the front door. In a moment they were once more out in the quiet little street in the grey Geneva evening. The business was done, and it was time to return to Paris and tomorrow's flight to Buenos Aires: there, Major Suarez would report to General Romera, who in turn would inform his two colleagues. Some manipulation of the services' unused appropriations, so recently authorized by President Menem's government, would be necessary to meet the expenditure which had now been incurred.

☆   ☆   ☆

Five months later, a small freighter flying the Argentine flag moved on a blazing morning towards the entrance to Tripoli harbour. The pilot came on board, and with a tug's aid she berthed in a remote part of the harbour under military control. Loading of the cargo began immediately.

This cargo was in two categories. Category one was a large number of big packing-cases, marked 'Explosives' in Arabic, English and Spanish, with a plethora of skull-and-crossbones marks. Category two was a smaller number of cases marked 'Surgical Equipment'. On these cases markings in the Cyrillic alphabet could be seen.

When the loading was completed, the documents were brought into the captain's office for inclusion in the vessel's manifest. The special flag which denotes an explosive cargo was hoisted: the tug came, and the small, rusty ship was pulled out into the Mediterranean to start her long and slow journey to the South Atlantic.

The military-controlled part of Tripoli docks was not open to public entry, but even if it had been, no particular interest would have been taken in this shipment. There was however one person, a leading seaman aboard the tug, who carefully noted what he had seen being put on board, and the fact that the ship was flying the Argentinian flag.

In Cordoba, meanwhile, the planners were approaching the end of their task. Soon it would be time to begin to collate the mass of detail and give shape to the report.

Alicia Nunes, busy with the work that Colonel Hernandez was not doing, nevertheless found some time to play. She was a very keen tennis player, and had found to her delight that the garrison officers' club had excellent courts. The climate of Cordoba is by no means oppressively hot even in summer, and the siesta regime which entails an early start to the day, no work in the afternoon, and an evening work session, was not in force there. Alicia was therefore able to play tennis at the club most evenings in summer from about five o'clock.

She had many friends at the club by now, and encountered no difficulty in finding partners and opponents. It did not take long for Major Juan Carbona to discover that his duties as a planner sometimes enabled him to go to the club of an evening;

he also was a keen tennis-player. He found himself, from time to time, playing with or against Alicia, and in due course the sight of those long, bronzed legs and the image of what lay above them began to excite thoughts of what comes naturally to most men.

They became fairly good friends, but on Alicia's side there was no immediate prospect of a closer relationship. She was a modern, sophisticated young woman, a woman of her time. She knew in her heart that one day she would meet a man with whom she would want to live and sleep for the rest of her life, and whose children she would want to bear and bring up. Meanwhile, until he appeared, life was for living; and she grasped firmly the opportunities which modern medical knowledge, and (even in Argentina) modern moral thinking offered to liberated, intelligent and sophisticated girls like herself. She took lovers as she wanted to take them. The general had been a more serious interlude – more serious out of respect for his status. Now that was over, and she was free once more to do as she pleased – a freedom which she exercised with care and discretion. She was not yet quite sure about this handsome airman.

But he was becoming increasingly interested in her. He sought her company, on and off the tennis courts, as often as he could. There was something about those dark eyes and that soft complexion which spoke to him strongly. He had had many women in his life, and he was not accustomed to being refused: but he met in Alicia a cool, almost amused resistance, which began to arouse in him a proud anger. He would have her, he said to himself, and then he would teach her what a real man was, a real Argentine man. It would be a pleasure to see her humbled, and begging for his favours.

So matters went on for some weeks. They played and drank and ate together, and danced too, which he found a most exciting experience: and all the time he found his oblique hints and suggestions coolly turned aside. But towards the end of his projected stay in Cordoba he began to feel that the tide was turning in his favour: she was more responsive, warmer: her dark eyes flashed with laughter more often, and there was more than a hint of coquetry in the way she shook her head at his importunities. He began to feel desire rising in him as strongly as it had ever risen, and he became determined to press matters

41

to a conclusion.

In truth, Alicia had been trying to make up her mind. She found the handsome major fearfully attractive: she was for the moment without a satisfactory lover, and she was sorely tempted to start an affair with Carbona. And yet – there was that slight suspicion that had struck her the first time she met him. It seemed a difficult decision to take, but she found herself growing more and more inclined to take the risk, and plunge into the unknown waters.

It came to a head one night when they both attended a dinner-dance at the Comodoro Hotel in the centre of Cordoba. After dinner they had every dance together: he was an expert and so was she, and their bodies moved together in perfect harmony. When they danced closely together his obvious arousal could not be concealed, and she in her turn became excited. Finally he whispered in her ear, 'Alicia, my darling girl, you know I love you. I want you so badly and I guarantee I will make you happy.' She smiled brilliantly at him and nodded, but said nothing as they continued to move together around the crowded floor. He went on, 'I have a room booked in the hotel for tonight. The hall porter is a good friend of mine: he will have us woken early, with a taxi at the door, and we can be back on the base before anyone wakes up: what do you say?' She nodded again.

'Just let me say my goodbyes, and then I'll get my coat. What's the room number?'

So in ten minutes' time she was tapping on the door of Room 321, to be admitted by a shirt-sleeved Carbona: almost at the same moment, the room-service waiter arrived with a bottle of champagne in an ice-bucket, and they had to wait while he opened the bottle and poured out the wine: then they were in each other's arms.

They did drink some champagne while they were undressing each other, but their minds were urgently on other things. Between sips, he unzipped her dress and unhooked her brassiere: he had already pulled his shirt over his head, and soon his trousers were round his ankles: she stared with admiration at the olive-skinned beauty of his hairless torso, and then, when she pulled down his underpants to join the trousers round his ankles, at the strength and size of his manliness.

They were naked: it was time to go. Displaying his strength,

42

Carbona picked her up bodily and carried her over to the big double bed and laid her on it, where he at once joined her. There in their love play he proved skilful and considerate, and it was not long before she breathed, 'I am ready, darling.'

He murmured into her ear 'Will you go on your front, my love? Your bottom is so beautiful that I want to feel it against me,' and she acquiesced in this, having not much choice in the matter because he firmly turned her over and mounted himself between her thighs. In this instant of time she was was conscious, confusedly, of his fumbling with something unseen to her, something that he then seemingly put down on the bedside table because it made a clatter, and then the cheeks of her bottom were parted, almost roughly, by his fingers, and then . . . .

Then, in a flash of comprehension and instant rage she realized that the unthinkable, the unspeakable act by which some South American men seek to establish their manhood and their domination over their womenfolk, was being attempted and, with the assistance of lubrication, was well on the way to happening. Desperately she tried to close herself off: she cried out, 'No, no, for God's sake, no: I will not have it!' and she struggled to free herself from his grasp; but he had her firmly in his grip, and his weight was on top of her. He merely laughed, saying, 'Oh, yes, you will have it, you will have all of it up there, and you will enjoy it: everyone does in the end.'

Alicia was a brave and decisive girl, and anger and disgust blazed up in her. Swiftly and strongly, she reached behind her with her right hand. She managed to find his testicles, grabbed them, and gave them a sharp squeezing yank. The result was spectacular.

Carbona let out a cry of agony; the monstrous intrusion was at once withdrawn. He rolled off her, clutching himself and moaning in pain. He remained so, thrashing about the bed and moaning and crying, for some minutes; meanwhile Alicia, shocked and furious, and not yet beginning to be sorry for him, went at once into the bathroom and very swiftly did the washing she deemed essential: coming out, she quickly put on her clothes including her fur coat, which she had brought with her because the nights at that season were chilly. Now, he was recovering fast; he was sitting up on the bed, and was shouting at her.

'You bitch,' he yelled, 'you absolute bloody bitch!'

'And you,' she shouted back, 'are a pig! A bloody macho pig! How dare you insult and defile me like that? I should have known – you are just a bloody pig, and you ought to be kept with a sow in a sty where you could screw her how you liked.' Alicia, when roused, had a nice line in South American invective.

He glared at her, wounded male pride and hatred coming at her from his furious eyes like gamma-rays. He was, she saw with sudden alarm, once more in control of himself, and he could move, and he was going to move. 'I'm going to kill you, you bloody insolent bitch,' he said, levering himself off the bed and preparing to lunge across the few feet that separated them, 'and before I kill you I'll teach you a thing or two. Yes, I'm going to teach you all of it.'

But now Alicia had opened her handbag, and in her right hand glittered the small Beretta pistol which was issued as a matter of course to all women officers in the Argentine Army, a pistol which they did not usually wear when in uniform but which they were told, by the old-fashioned, concerned and paternalistic generals who ran the army, to keep with them at all, repeat all, times. How right the old granddads were, she thought, as she held the little hand-gun steadily pointed at Carbona's crotch.

'Stay right where you are,' she said. 'If you come one foot nearer I'll fix you so you won't be putting that bloody prick of yours up anyone, anywhere.'

He stayed. Her fury and determination were evident enough. He was reminded, absurdly, of a book illustration in the English class at his school, of Queen Boadicea 'bleeding from the Roman rods' and about to chop up the Romans with revolving knives on her chariot-wheels. Definitely no valour now, he thought, only discretion.

Alicia backed up to the door, still holding the little pistol steady. 'Goodnight and goodbye,' she said. 'I suppose we shall have to meet in the course of our duties, but not for longer than necessary, that I promise you.' So saying, she opened the door and went through it, making good time to the lift. Carbona had not thought of anything more to say or shout before she left: still in fairly great pain, he looked and felt the very picture of humiliated dejection. Alicia went straight through the lobby of the hotel and through the revolving doors, where she at once found a taxi to take her back to base. Her passage was observed with interest by Pepe the head hall-porter, who knew exactly who she was and where she had been. He was known as 'Pepe No-Sleep' because he seldom left his counter in the lobby. He seemed to be on duty at all hours: in consequence he was a very rich man, and of course much the best-informed person in Cordoba.

Upstairs in Room 321, order was being restored. Juan Carbona was still suffering, but the pain was receding to a more manageable level. When he was able to move, the first thing he did was to go over to the ice-bucket and drink the rest of the bottle of champagne, which meant more than half of it. That made him feel a great deal better, and he contemplated what to do next. Curiously, the assault on his most tender parts seemed to have made no difference to his desire, which had been running at a very high level. He found he very badly needed a woman. At that stage of the game, she could only be a tart. He rang Pepe No-Sleep, and asked him if he could find him one.

Pepe was not surprised by this request. Yes, he said, he knew a very high-class girl who might well be available. If he wished to stay the whole night, he could, and she would wake him early in the morning. No, she would not come round to the hotel, but her apartment was nice and it was only a hundred metres away. He could recommend her highly. She was not cheap, but you had to pay for quality these days. Very well, he would ring her at once. If the Major would come down to his desk he would let him have the address. If she was not available he could try someone else.

Carbona dressed. He was feeling a lot better: the pain had more or less gone, and he was uplifted by the champagne. He went down to the lobby.

Pepe, behind the counter, told him that the lady awaited him. Her name was Maria MacFarlane. The piece of paper on which her address was written lay on the counter, but Pepe kept his hand on it until Carbona realized that something was called for, and passed over a note which went straight into the hall-porter's waistcoat pocket. My God, thought Carbona, he's like an auction house, I bet he takes commission from both buyer and seller. Thanking Pepe, he went out into the street

45

and quickly found the apartment-block. He rang the appropriate bell and was admitted by entry-phone. Upstairs, the door was opened to him by Maria MacFarlane herself.

Maria's history was an odd one. Born of an Argentinian mother and an Irish father who owned an *estancia* about seventy miles east of Cordoba, on her mother's death she had been sent to finish her education in Paris at the age of seventeen. There she made the disturbing discovery that she had an insatiable and entirely promiscuous sexual appetite. She finally consulted a French friend, an elderly lady who had in her youth been a well-known *horizontale*: from her she received the practical advice that, if that was the way things were, she had better go professional. She did so, and was soon ensconced in a small Paris apartment. But competition was fierce, and she was homesick for her own country and for the *estancia* which (her father having died in a road accident) was now hers. She therefore returned to Argentina; not wishing to live in Buenos Aires, she set up in Cordoba, not on the face of things a likely place to find a high-class whore specializing in the top end of the market; but she soon became well-known, and clients came from all parts of Argentina to see her. Her apartment was very smart and comfortable: for holidays she went to her *estancia*, which was run by a manager and his family. She was entirely free of romantic entanglements, for, as she said sadly, if she had a man she would inevitably make him unhappy.

Tall and shapely in a long brocaded housecoat, she welcomed Carbona and led him into her sitting-room. The usual preliminaries were discussed in a business-like way: she established that Carbona wished to stay all night, and she promised to wake him early. Her price was named, and Carbona handed it to her in large-denomination notes. She then enquired whether there were any 'specialities' which he wanted, and was told that there were none. There then seemed no reason not to go straight though into the bedroom, another beautifully furnished room containing a large double bed with pink linen sheets.

Carbona, fortified by the champagne which he had drunk and much taken with Maria's looks and promise, was full of strength and desire. He now felt entirely relaxed, and he also found that he had that complete and blissful release from inhibitions which men often experience when in the company of prostitutes. He undressed quite methodically, placing his clothes neatly on a chair: as he did so he thought about what had happened earlier in the evening, and suddenly the pain and humiliation he had suffered seemed distant memories, and his strong sense of humour began to assert itself: he began to laugh, and when he turned round naked and erect to face Maria he was still chuckling.

She asked him why, and he told her how an attempted 'speciality' had gone so wrong.

She laughed at this and said, 'Well, you can't blame the girl, you know. You men are really silly sometimes. No tricks of that sort with me, is that understood? Good. *Alors, le petit chapeau. Mon Dieu, quel vrai canon!*' Deftly she rolled a French letter onto his erect penis. Two more sheaths lay ready in their little packets on the bedside table.

'Come, *cheri,*' she said, taking him by the hand: the house-coat fell open, revealing her beautiful naked body. 'Come, let us have a night of love.'

Even after a night so spent, Maria MacFarlane always woke early, and she responded at once to the faint bleep of the little electronic alarm clock under her pillow. Beside her Carbona was dead asleep, one arm flung out across the coverlet. Quite a man, she thought to herself. Swiftly and silently she got up and made her way over to the chair on which he had left his clothes.

Maria MacFarlane had one little trick which she had learnt from her old French friend. Men, that lady had stated, can usually be relied on to sleep very soundly – young men, that is. Furthermore, the sort of man who stays all night with an expensive girl usually has quite a few more banknotes of large denomination in his wallet, and often does not know how many he does have. It is almost always possible to abstract one more note while he is asleep: even if he does miss it later, he will invariably 'write it off to experience', especially if you have given him a really good time. Maria had practised this rather dangerous little trick, with excellent results for her income, for years. The small element of danger added a spice of excitement to her life. So she opened Carbona's wallet and took from the wad inside it one large note, which she put in the pocket of the housecoat which she had slipped on when she got out of bed: she then put the wallet back in his coat pocket. As she did so, she noticed that a piece of paper, apparently a page torn out of a small notebook, had fallen from the wallet onto the carpet. There was some writing on it.

She bent down to pick it up, but at that moment there was a stirring in the bed: Carbona was waking up. There being no question of replacing the paper in the wallet, she stuffed it up the sleeve of her housecoat, and was able to slip out of the room in the direction of the kitchen before he was properly awake. Shortly she emerged with a small tray bearing a steaming cup of black coffee and a croissant, which she took to him. 'You are awake,' she said, 'It is just six o'clock.' It was not long before he was dressed and gone, after thanking her for a night which, he politely said, he would long remember with pleasure.

When he had left she had her own small breakfast, which she took back to bed with her. When she was in bed she remembered the paper, and fished it out of her housecoat sleeve. She at once saw that the writing on it was of the greatest possible interest. It seemed to be brief notes of, or for, a conference; and there was absolutely no doubt what the subject was.

The first thing she did was to make a copy of the writing on a sheet of her own notepaper. Next she dropped the original paper on the floor, near the chair on which Carbona's clothes had been arranged. Then, she rang a number in Buenos Aires, the number of the man whom she knew only as Ramon. He answered, and the ritual identification exchange took place. She had heard from Alfredo, she said: he would be in Cordoba in two days' time: could he possibly come up and talk to him? Yes, of course, and a date two days thence was fixed. She put down the telephone with a smile of satisfaction: this was something big, something of importance, and the man she knew as Ramon would be generous: furthermore, he was a man with normal human feelings, and on the occasions in the past when he had come to her he had also been a client, and an enjoyable one, too. In view of the relationship, she had to allow him a discount on normal rates, but in this life you had to take the rough with the smooth.

Twenty minutes later, Pepe No-Sleep rang. Yes, he had been a very satisfactory and well-behaved client. No, she had

48

not forgotten Pepe, of course she had not. The client, Pepe then said, had just telephoned in a great state of agitation. He had missed from his wallet a bit of paper, an entirely unimportant bit of paper actually, on which he had made notes of an address he was to give shortly to the local military academy. Without it, he would be at a loss. Could this paper have accidentally fallen from his pocket, and could it still be there, on the carpet? Wait a minute, she would look. Yes, here it is, by the chair where he put his clothes. Can't make head nor tail of it, and don't want to try: presume he wants it back? 'Yes,' said Pepe, 'he does want it back. Put it in an envelope, seal it, and write my name on it. I'll send the boy round to collect it, if you don't mind. Perhaps it would be convenient if he also brought back – that little favour?'

6

It was typing time for the planners' report. Alicia Nunes was moved into a room in the suite of offices which the wise men had been using, and she started typing the main body of the report, while the three officers were still working on the appendices which dealt with the minutest details of the operation, and the respective contributions to be made by the three services. It did not take Alicia a moment to realize what it was all about, and she found it tremendously exciting. Colonel Hernandez, true to his word, came in at the end of every day's work and spent ten minutes discussing with her what she had been typing that day: then, before they went back to their quarters, he gathered up all the completed work, as well as the rough drafts, and put it in a big envelope which he locked in the office safe, of which he had the only key. He also gathered up the contents of the waste-paper basket and personally put them through the shredding machine which had been installed in the office. The same routine had been followed every day since they had started working – in fact twice every day, at lunchtime and at the end of the day. A sentry was maintained outside the office all night, in case anyone felt inclined to go in for safe-breaking.

Every time he participated in this security routine, on which they had all agreed at the start, Juan Carbona felt a twinge of mortification. How could he have been guilty of such an absurdly unprofessional lapse? The notes had in fact been made the previous evening, before he and Alicia went dancing, and were a sort of aide-memoire for the section of the report which he was due to write in working hours next day. It had cleared his mind to write the notes: his mistake had been in not burning the paper when he had got his thoughts in order: he had not liked to leave the paper in his quarters, so had simply put it into his wallet as the safest place. Still, things seemed to have worked out all right: according to Pepe, the girl Maria had scarcely given the paper a glance, and it had come straight back by hand in a sealed envelope. Put it out of your mind, said Carbona to himself.

He could not, however, put Alicia Nunes out of his mind. Now that she was working in their suite he saw her every day, and sometimes also in the club in the evening. It was clear that everything that had grown up between them was in irretrievable ruin, and that was his fault too: it had been extraordinarily stupid of him to expect a proud and independent-minded girl like Alicia to submit to his sudden surge of machismo. Well, what he had found was now lost forever. Try and forget it, and remember that there are plenty of other girls in the world.

As for Alicia, she had long ago seen the funny side of what had happened. That did not lessen her total and angry rejection of such antics, but it did mean that she did not really bear Carbona very much resentment. There was no need to do so; she had been the victor in the encounter: she had put him well and truly in his place, and he could stay there. So in their office meetings she was cool and correct and official, speaking to him as a lieutenant should speak to a major when on duty: in the club she simply avoided him, and he made no attempt to force his company on her.

So, in the office suite in the Cordoba garrison lines, all the threads were now drawn together, and the skein was complete.

☆   ☆   ☆

'1. We are instructed,' the report began under the heading 'BACKGROUND AND INFORMATION' 'to report in detail upon a proposed operation to be named 'Operation Condor', and to prepare detailed plans for putting the operation into effect and carrying it out.

'We are further instructed that the seizing from the British of the Malvinas Islands, which is the object of Operation Condor, must take a very different form from the occupation carried out in 1982. On that occasion the British armed presence in and around the islands was negligible, and we were able to carry out without interference or danger a well-organized and methodical seaborne assault. The thinking of our then government was that the islands should be wholly absorbed into

51

Argentina and be subjected to direct rule from Buenos Aires like any other province of our country, without any regard being paid to the feelings and wishes of the inhabitants, who were and are all of British stock. In the circumstances of 1982 it was to be expected that the British would attempt to retake the islands, which indeed they did with results which are well-known to everyone: it was therefore necessary to garrison the islands with large military forces, including necessarily a high proportion of young men carrying out their normal obligatory period of military service in the ranks. It would not have been possible, in view of the comparatively small cadres of regular soldiers in the Army and Marine units, to dispense with the services of the conscripts; but they were at a disadvantage when it came to fighting the elite units, entirely composed of professional regulars, which the British deployed against us. The occupation of all the centres of population by large forces, which was unavoidable, also contributed to the alienation of the inhabitants.

'In this operation, we are instructed, the political objective (on which we are not asked to comment) is different. It is envisaged that, although the Malvinas are to be seized from the British and thereafter denied to them, they will be accorded a high degree of autonomy within the overall framework of the Argentine State; and it is both hoped and expected that this understanding treatment will lead to a much greater degree of acceptance on the part of the inhabitants that their future lies with Argentina. As we shall show later in this report, this policy fits very well with the military situation as we see it and which we now briefly describe.

'2. Full details, so far as they are known, of the forces maintained by the British in the South Atlantic area are given in Appendix A to this report. Essentially they consist of the greater part of an infantry battalion, with attached artillery and engineer troops and administrative personnel. All these troops are high-class long-service regulars under competent and well-trained officers: they are virtually on a combat footing and are not accompanied by their wives and families: a high degree of readiness and fitness is maintained. The Rapiers, batteries of which form the main anti-aircraft defence, are efficient weapons already proved in action, and are fully served by radar installations.

'The Royal Air Force maintains, at high readiness, a force of four Phantom heavy fighters. These are high-performance, sophisticated modern aircraft which, working with modern long-range radar systems, constitute a formidable air defence. There are also a small number of RAF troops specially trained for airfield defence. All these forces are located on and around the modern airfield which has been constructed at Mount Pleasant about thirty kilometres south-west of Port Stanley, which is the seat of government. There are barracks for the troops with all modern amenities, as well as hangars and protected parking places for the aircraft. Permanent positions, in the form of dug and sand-bagged emplacements, lie around the airfield and are assumed to constitute a strong integrated defensive system. Besides these buildings in permanent occupation, there are quite large unoccupied sections, the declared British policy being to fly in reinforcements should any indication be received by them that attack is imminent.

'Besides the forces on land, the Royal Navy normally maintains one frigate based at Port Stanley. We understand from Intelligence that it also maintains in the area of the Malvinas at least one modern nuclear-powered submarine of the 'hunter-killer' type throughout the year. These boats are never seen because they are independent of shore facilities, but the Intelligence reports of their presence have been repeatedly confirmed by Navy sources.

'Finally, in this outline review of the forces available to the British we must include their surveillance and intelligence-gathering facilities. The British are known to enjoy regular access to the information gathered every day by two US spy-satellites: the orbits of these vehicles pass, we know, over some of the most important military, air and naval bases in our country, specifically over the airfields in Patagonia and Tierra del Fuego. Furthermore, we must point out that there are in Argentina many tens of thousands of people wholly or partly of British descent. It must be assumed (and the assumption is confirmed by Intelligence) that the British have widespread agent networks in place. The conclusion is that it will be very difficult for us to prepare and mount any operation against the Malvinas on the scale necessary to ensure success, without prior warning being given.

'In view of this conclusion, and of the professional make-up of the British garrison, the sophisticated equipment available to them, and their ability to reinforce quickly by air at short notice, it is our opinion that any operation to seize the Malvinas must be a difficult and formidable undertaking.

'3. Although we think that any operation must be both difficult and formidable, paradoxically the problem is in our view a very simple one in essence: the difficulty lies in how actually to solve it.

'The whole British system for garrisoning the Malvinas and for reinforcing them quickly in case of need is in fact fundamentally flawed – it has an Achilles Heel. This flaw lies in the fact that the entire garrison including the aviation and some of the radar components are effectively concentrated on, or very near, the airfield at Mount Pleasant. The garrison is very small as the British cannot justify the expense of keeping a large number of troops permanently there. It is British policy, declared and emphasized many times in their parliament and by ministers, that in times of serious tension, or if it appeared really likely that we were about to invade, they would reinforce very quickly by flying in more troops in wide-bodied jets, via Ascension Island. A 'spearhead' battalion is kept on permanent short notice to move in from the United Kingdom. The reinforcing procedure has been recently practiced, and must be assumed to be highly efficient. We do not know the minimum time in which such reinforcements could arrive, but in our opinion eighteen hours is the absolute minimum, and twenty-four may be more likely. During this short period, the garrison with its air and naval support and its very efficient radar warning systems may be expected to hold off any attack.

'If, however, the Mount Pleasant airfield could be captured and the garrison neutralized during this period, whatever it may be, then the factors which the British see as operating in their favour would be turned around and would start operating to their detriment: as soon as it becomes impossible for wide-bodied jets to land at Mount Pleasant, the whole reinforcement scheme falls to pieces.

'Strictly speaking, to bring about this result it is not necessary actually to capture the airfield: it is only necessary so to dominate the runway that aircraft cannot land by day or night. This would produce a stalemate situation in which, in the longer term, time might well be on the side of the British:

54

we do not favour such a situation, and mention it only to illustrate the vulnerability of the British position in its absolute dependence on rapid reinforcement by air. As a further illustration of this vulnerability, we ask that imaginative consideration be given to the dilemma which would present itself to the commander of a TriStar aircraft full of soldiers approaching the Malvinas, if he should learn on his radio that heavy fighting is taking place on the airfield and that the runway on which he expects to land is being swept by small-arms fire. We hope that no Argentine pilot would ever be placed in such an unenviable position – an unattractive choice between landing a totally vulnerable aircraft in the middle of the fire-fight, and seeking permission to land at Montevideo, with the international complications that that would entail.

'A further dilemma is bound at all times to confront the British: what state of tension, what degree of evident preparation by Argentina is sufficient to trigger the reinforcement procedure? The British armed forces are always stretched by their commitments in Germany and elsewhere in the world, and the last thing they want is to be always dashing off to the Malvinas on alarms which prove to be false ones. On occasion, perhaps, a British government could gain kudos at home by demonstrating its instant readiness and its resolution, but repetition will not improve the image. Therefore, if the present Argentine government was really in earnest about recovering the Malvinas, an indicated course of action might be to stimulate repeated false alarms over a period of years so that the British came to a state of constant reaction by reinforce-ment – and one day they would weary of it and drop their guard, and our invasion would then actually take place. It is of course quite clear that our government does not place a high priority on recovering the islands, which is why it has in the past two years embarked on a policy of rapprochement with Britain, in which the issue of Malvinas sovereignty is studiously ignored – so we are instructed.

'It is clear to us therefore that Operation Condor must take the form of a rapid seizure, without any warning being given to the British, of the airfield complex at Mount Pleasant by some form of coup-de-main.

'Political considerations are not in our brief, but we wish to state that we very much doubt whether, if the airfield was successfully occupied and the garrison overcome before reinforcements could reach them, the British would find it possible in today's circumstances to mount the sort of Task Force expedition which they mounted in 1982, to restore the position. The degree of international diplomatic support which the British were able to win in 1982, both from their principal allies and in the United Nations, might very well not be extended a second time to a British government which has consistently refused to discuss the question of sovereignty. The war option is not nowadays a popular one internationally: besides this, the British could now in our opinion find it difficult to assemble the necessary naval forces. Even if they succeeded in doing so, they might well hesitate to commit their ships to battle in the South Atlantic against the improved aviation resources now available to us (see Appendix B to this report for full details). The British admirals know very well that the margin by which they maintained themselves against air attack in 1982 was a very narrow one, which would have been fatally eroded if the bombs used in our low-level attacks had been properly armed and fused, or if one of their two aircraft-carriers or one of their large troopships had been put out of action.

'The question whether the British will find it possible and advisable to mount such a recovery expedition, and whether they will actually do so, is important because it bears on the number of troops we are to employ in Operation Condor. We conclude that they will not, and consequently we propose to employ initially only sufficient troops to occupy the airfield and to prevent reinforcement. If however the British do send an expedition, we think there will be ample time to increase our numbers and our defensive facilities to a state where, given the improved systems (particularly in the aviation sphere) now available to us, we will be able to beat off the sort of attack that we failed to overcome in 1982.

'RECOMMENDATIONS

'4. We have given consideration to the question whether the seizure of the Mount Pleasant airfield (which, as mentioned above, is our basic recommendation) should be accomplished by an airborne assault, or by a seaborne invasion as was done in 1982. We will deal with the latter possibility first.

'We do not feel that a seaborne invasion is advisable. Although comparatively small numbers of troops are to be

56

employed, we see no way of putting them ashore close to Mount Pleasant without their being detected and intercepted by the Royal Navy. It is true that the British have only two (or perhaps three) units on station, and that hunter-killer submarines are not designed to deal with a large number of small surface targets; but we do not think the idea of conveying our attacking troops in a number of smallish vessels operating out of Patagonian ports is a viable one. It would be almost inevitable that the British would gain prior warning of our intentions, in time to activate their reinforcement procedures. The alternative, of sailing from Buenos Aires or Puerto Belgrano in one or two larger vessels, is open to the same objection, and in view of the submarine presence would be too risky.

'Therefore, we recommend that the assault be made by air-landing.

'A prime difficulty here is that Argentina does not possess airborne forces on the necessary scale. As we all know, we have only one parachute battalion: it is very much under-strength, and is also short of jumping practice. We cannot even think of glider-borne troops as employed by both the Germans and the Allies in World War Two, because of the distance and weather factors involved. Our attacking troops, other than the parachutists, would have to arrive by troop-carrying planes, easily detectable by the British radar and highly vulnerable to fighter attack by day or night.

'We think therefore that the airborne assault must be accomplished by the use of unconventional deception tactics, and we give details below of our suggestions in this respect: a part of this recommendation has already been mentioned in our interim report made in December 1990.

'We further recommend that the troops to be employed should consist of the following units:-

1st Parachute Infantry Battalion
5th Marine Infantry Battalion

In both these units, conscript soldiers must be weeded out and posted away. If necessary, numbers must be made up to 300 rank and file in the Marine battalion, by posting in regular enlisted men from other Marine units.

'We envisage, it will be understood, a total strength of around 650 rank and file, excluding officers – all professionals.

'We recommend that the commander of the landing force should be Rear Admiral of Marine Infantry Carlos Ricarda: he is an outstanding officer with background and training suitable for such command.

'We proceed in the following paragraphs to give our detailed recommendations for the preparation and mounting of the attack.'

☆ ☆ ☆

It was quiet in the Jockey Club lunchroom. Outside on the racecourse, the tractors came and went in the sunlight, mowing and sweeping in preparation for the race meeting to be held on the following Saturday. Inside, behind the big windows, there was a light haze of blue cigar smoke.

Today, the three wise planners, piloted down from Cordoba in the little Hawker Siddeley business jet, had presented their report to their three principals. An early lunch, modest in scope, had been eaten, and then Colonel Hernandez had produced three copies of the report. They had been reading it.

'I must say,' said Admiral Vasquez, 'I think the planning staff have got it right so far. I am sorry that the Navy, apart that is from the Marines, has such a minor part to play; but I can see why.'

'You will see more, Admiral, from the later parts of the report,' interjected Captain Varela, 'the Navy, the floating bit of it I mean, will have a lot to do.'

'It seems to me,' said General Jaime Gonzalez, 'that the only service which really is not going to be doing very much is the Army. It makes me wonder whether I ought to be too outspoken in comment on this report.'

His colleagues disagreed with this remark, pointing out the participation of the parachute battalion: in any event, the Army must stand ready to pour in massive reinforcements if there was an effective response from the British. They were all in it together.

So they continued their reading and, as they did so, they began to discuss with the three planning officers various points of detail which now started to emerge. Their reading and the discussion continued for the whole of the afternoon and some way into the evening: by the time they had finished they were

58

all agreed what was going to be done, and how it was going to be achieved.

As they left the lunchroom, thanking the steward Luis for having looked after their needs and their privacy, General Gonzalez said, 'I don't think we should go on meeting here: it will soon become conspicuous. I will suggest a new venue in a day or two.' There was no disagreement with this suggestion.

So that's that, thought Luis as the officers left. Never mind, he said to himself. He had had a good run. A lot of today's work involved reading, so the record on the tape would be fragmentary. Interesting times lay ahead, he thought.

7

The following months were a time of quiet and meticulous preparation in Argentina, against a background of the strictest security. So far only seven people were privy to the conspiracy, and there were in existence six copies of the planning report. It was now agreed that nothing further at all should be committed to paper, so far as possible; those additional people who now had to be informed were to be spoken to, sworn to secrecy, told what they had to be told, and no more. Within these guidelines, the three service chiefs began to arrange and dispose their forces so that the normal routines of training and exercising could continue to be carried out without revealing that more was in preparation.

The operations were very much assisted by the decision that the attack, and the subsequent occupation, could and should be carried out by a very small number of ground troops. This meant that knowledge of the planned operation could be confined to a small number of unit commanders – outside the Air Force.

The Air Force was a rather more difficult problem in this respect. The plan called for an all-out strike by the full strength of suitable aircraft available. All would have to fly from the southern airfields which had been used in 1982 – Comodoro Rivadavia, San Julian, Santa Cruz and Rio Gallegos in Patagonia, and Rio Grande and Ushaia still further south in Tierra del Fuego. In the past few years a comparatively small number of strike aircraft had been kept at these southern fields: any appreciable increase in numbers down there would be quickly spotted by the British and would tend to cause alarm, something the conspirators obviously wished to avoid at all costs. It was decided therefore that the main body of the aircraft to be involved would be flown to their destination airfields only one or two days before the attack was to take place. Meanwhile the squadrons, one by one, were to be sent down in rotation on brief visits, to familiarize the pilots with the surroundings from which they were to operate on the great day. This process, it was thought, could be represented as normal training exercises, and would not therefore be likely to arouse British suspicions in the increasingly relaxed climate between the two countries.

Different considerations had to apply in the sphere of logistics. Apart from bringing up to full strength and efficiency the repair and maintenance facilities at the southern airfields (not an easy thing to do without sending more technicians, who were in short supply, down there), the two main problem areas concerned fuel and bombs.

In the 1982 operations, a tanker full of fuel had been stationed in Patagonia. Then, however, the air operations were expected to be (and actually were) protracted: a very large number of sorties were to be flown, involving huge amounts of aviation fuel: on this occasion (unless indeed it proved necessary to defend the islands against a regular British riposte), only one all-out air strike was envisaged. It was therefore decided that the fuel storage facilities at the various airfields should be topped up to full capacity, and in some cases discreetly expanded. If the worst came to the worst, there would be time enough to send down a tanker.

As for the bombs, the Air Force's stock of them had fallen low in 1982 and had not been fully replenished. As was all too well known, the fuses and arming mechanisms used in 1982 had not functioned well, owing to the exceptionally low altitude at which most of the attacks had been carried out. Most of the bombs used in 1982 had been of 250 kg or 500 kg, suitable sizes with which to attack ships. On this occasion, however, the attack was to be against ground installations in support of an air-landed attack: smaller bombs were called for. Purchases were made in several foreign countries to bring the Air Force's stock of bombs up to the numbers required. This had to be done more or less openly, and it was then necessary to transport the bombs down to the southern airfields rather less openly. Various stratagems were employed in attempts to conceal these movements. In the end, General Romera and his staff were able to feel fairly sure that the increase in traffic down to the southern airfields, although certainly perceptible, had not been so great as to endanger the security of the operation.

The part, moreover, which the Air Force had to play in the operation meant that the pilots had to receive training in what they were to do. Although precise information about the layout of the airfield complex at Mount Pleasant was hard to come by, in the end it was found possible to construct a passably accurate sand-table model of it and of its immediate surroundings. It was also found that one remote airfield in the centre of the country could be adapted for target-training purposes, and all the squadrons in turn practised attacking it. As in 1982, very low-level flying was to be the order of the day, in order to minimize the risks of detection by radar and also to put the defenders' radar-predicted missile systems at some disadvantage. All this specialized training meant that the Air Force commanders had to take their pilots into their confidence at quite an early stage. The same applied to the pilots of the 3rd Naval Attack Squadron who were to fly from the carrier 25 *de Mayo*. This produced the paradoxical situation that, while very few people in the Army were informed about the proposed operation, a high proportion of Air Force officers were, as well as an appreciable number of Navy and Marine officers. The Army, of course, was to be entrusted with certain internal-security tasks in the capital, and this meant that several unit commanders, as well as the commander of the 1st Parachute Infantry Battalion which was to be part of the attacking force, had to be in the know.

The planners and their superiors had accepted the suggestion originally put forward by Major Carbona, that the attack should be timed to coincide with the forthcoming British general election. It was assumed, therefore, that October 1991 or May 1992 were the likely times, and that in either alternative a four weeks' period of notice would apply. All arrangements therefore had to be made in accordance with this timetable: in the unlikely event that the election took place at some other time in the existing British government's last year of life, some rapid adaptation would have to take place.

At the highest level, places were found for all three planning officers on the immediate staffs of their respective commanders. Lieutenant Alicia Nunes was also brought back to Buenos Aires, still as personal assistant to Colonel Hernandez. There was a slightly awkward official interview between her and General Gonzalez at which the General did his best to explain to her that, yes, she was a most valued and trusted officer and she had a vital part to play in the intended operation, of which she was one of the few people who had knowledge; and, no, there could be no revival of the relationship which had formerly existed between them. Alicia was quite ready to accept this: she had never been really in love with the General, and she knew perfectly well that he now had another mistress – not a female officer, she was glad to know, but a quiet and beautiful young woman towards whom she felt no jealousy, and who was installed in the apartment near the Defence Ministry which she remembered so well. Also, she herself had made the acquaintance of a handsome young Navy flier with whom, she was becoming increasingly certain, she was on the point of falling seriously in love in a way she had never done before with anyone. This one, she was beginning to think, was the real one, the one she would marry if he asked her.

They had met when she had accompanied Captain Varela on a briefing visit to the aircraft-carrier 25 *de Mayo*. Her captain, who had an important part to play in Operation Condor, had already been briefed in outline by Admiral Vasquez: this visit was made in order to fill in details. Alicia found herself accompanying the briefing officer on quite a few such visits. Her presence achieved two objectives: one, in the situation the conspirators were in, it was desirable for a second person to be present in order to be able to corroborate what had been said: two, the decision to commit nothing further to paper had thrown a heavy burden of detail on the briefing officer, and two heads were better than one.

At lunch in the carrier's wardroom afterwards, there he was. Tall, dark and handsome, a naval lieutenant in the air arm, pilot of one of the planes of the 3rd Naval Attack Squadron embarked in the carrier. Their eyes had met across the table, and at once it was different.

Alicia Nunes was a modern, liberated young women. Passionate by nature, and freed by modern medicine and morals from the constraints of the past, she had enjoyed love-making with men of her choice: so far, Juan Carbona had been her only serious error of judgement. But she had never confused sex with love. One day, she knew, she would truly love someone:

her married friends had all told her that when she met that man, it would be different. She would experience a new sensation, something far transcending mere casual sexual attraction. It happened to her at lunch that day in 25 *de Mayo*.

Since that day they had met several times. She was herself extremely busy, spending much time away from Buenos Aires on briefing visits to Navy and Army commanders (fortunately, she was not called on to accompany Major Carbona on such visits, because the whole business of Air Force briefing was on a quite different plane, and General Romera had had to involve his entire staff), and so her free time was limited. Lieutenant Carlo Martinez, for his part, was busy too: the squadron, which had not done very much flying of late owing to restrictions on fuel-consumption, now found those restrictions lifted and was able to embark upon a concentrated course of low flying from the carrier, over selected areas of upper Patagonia. They also trained for some days with the Air Force, at the up-country location. So there was not too much time for poodle-faking, especially because the carrier, when not out exercising, was based at the main Argentine naval harbour of Puerto Belgrano, many miles to the south of Buenos Aires. Still, they had managed to meet on two more occasions since the first, and there was no doubt on either side about what they felt for each other.

Carlo Martinez, in common with all the pilots who were to take part in the operation, had been briefed and knew in outline what he was going to have to do. Like all the other pilots, he was enormously excited and elated, as indeed was Alicia; but as time went on and the first probable date of the operation approached, their growing love for each other began to cast a shadow over those enthusiastic emotions, and Alicia for one could not help wondering whether her beloved would survive. So in the autumnal weather of the first half of 1991, when on their snatched meetings they held that close commune which only lovers have, they were aware that the happiness which they had both found could end in sadness for Alicia and sudden and violent death for Carlo Martinez.

In a quiet room off Whitehall in that summer of 1991, a high-level intelligence committee held one of its regular monthly meetings. Such occasions are of a routine character: the participants all know each other well, and business proceeds briskly. As usual, this meeting was mainly concerned with the everlasting game still played out, despite the manifestations of perestroika, glasnost and so on, between the Western intelligence agencies and the KGB. When, however, the meeting approached its end and the last agenda item, 'Any Other Business' was reached, one man spoke up.

Yes, he said, he did have some other business. A number of facts had recently come to light, which led his department to think that Argentina was in process of making some preparations of an abnormal character. Since at that particular moment there was a lull in the country's perennial quarrel with Chile over the disputed islands in the Beagle Channel, one could only wonder at whom these preparations might be aimed.

The committee chairman asked the speaker if he would given them some details of the items which had come to notice. Yes, said the man who had spoken. Principally, the items concerned purchases by Argentina of arms and equipment from foreign countries. Suddenly they seemed to have a lot of money to spend. In particular, they had been buying bombs.

'Where have they been buying bombs?' asked the Director of Naval Intelligence, 'and what sort of bombs? Big ones, or small?'

'Both,' was the reply, 'but mainly small ones. The biggest purchase was made in Libya a few months ago. It was done quite openly in an Argentinian ship which flew all the proper flags. Our agent there got quite a good look at the packing-cases: besides the bombs, which were all crated up – a very big shipment – there were also a large number of cases marked 'surgical equipment', and those cases at least seemed from their markings to originate from the Soviet Union. Probably the bombs did too.'

'I don't see why they shouldn't buy some bombs,' said the DNI reflectively, 'they must have used most of their stocks in 1982. It may be this is the first time they've had any money to do some normal stocking-up.'

Most people round the table nodded in agreement, but the original speaker went on.

'The trouble is, chairman, that we also have reports from all over the country, confirmed by what the cousins kindly give us from their satellites, of an abnormally large amount of Air Force flying activity. For years they haven't done much with the strike aircraft – I mean the old Skyhawks, and the Mirages they have recently got from Israel, and the old Mirages and Daggers. By the way, the Daggers have been upgraded: they've got some radar stuff now. As you know, gentlemen, the Argentines have now got a lot of Pucaras, the short-range aircraft which they describe as 'counter-insurgency' planes, of a new improved pattern. Most of the flying training in recent years has concerned them, in the up-country stations like Mendoza and Cordoba. But now, in the past few months, they have been rotating the Skyhawk and Mirage squadrons, taking them down to Patagonia one at a time – and why Patagonia, if they're peaceful with the Chileans? Taking all this activity with the purchase of bombs abroad, and other things, I'm afraid we must consider whether they have designs on the Falklands. And, I may say, we have one more piece which makes the jig-saw puzzle almost complete.'

'I've never heard you make such a long speech as it is, John,' said the chairman. 'You'd better tell us the last bit.'

'There has been a slightly suspicious conflab, an inter-service conflab, going on in Cordoba. You know, gentlemen, that's a big provincial city, up-country towards the Andes. It's a military base, the headquarters of a region, but they've had an Air Force officer and a naval captain there for weeks. The Argies do a lot of inter-service research, that's quite normal, but the trouble with this bit is that one of these officers dropped a nice piece of paper into one of our people's laps, literally into her lap if I may say so, and the paper comprised some sort of short notes, headings you know, about what could have been a training exercise but what we think is fairly clearly a projected attack on the Falklands.'

This caused a mild sensation round the table. Thoughts of lunch at Boodle's, with time for a leisurely gin-and-tonic first, were beginning to recede.

'Is the agent reliable?' demanded the Director of Military Intelligence.

'Yes, she is wholly reliable, and she is also intelligent. She had to make a copy, and then pretend she hadn't read the original. I'm afraid there's very little doubt what is under discussion: the party in Cordoba seems to have been some sort of joint planning session. There was even a name on the paper – 'Operation Condor'. I stress, 'Operation', chairman, not 'Exercise'.

'A fairly flagrant lapse of security,' said the naval captain.

'Yes, most flagrant. I'm afraid the whole circumstances of the encounter were indiscreet. Our agent is that sort of girl.'

Everybody laughed, then the DNI said, 'But why, why, are they thinking of this sort of thing now? It's all going so well. The whole thing is getting friendlier and friendlier. Why should they want to take military action now, when relations are so rapidly returning to normal?'

'That we cannot tell. We can only report what comes to us, and the inferences which we draw.'

There was a pause in the room, a temporary silence. Outside, the traffic roar was muted. The chairman spoke.

'Gentlemen, in my view we have no option but to take it to the Prime Minister. With your agreement, I will do that as soon as possible.'

The conference in the Prime Minister's room at the House of Commons was attended by the Foreign Secretary, the Minister of Defence and the Chief of the Defence Staff, Admiral of the Fleet Sir Thomas Higgins: the joint intelligence committee was represented by its chairman, the DNI, and by the representative of the security services who had spoken at the committee meeting. He now said his bit again, to an attentive audience.

When he had finished, the Prime Minister asked the Foreign Secretary whether he had any information which might tend to support the inferences drawn by the security services. No, said the Foreign Secretary, nothing whatever. Absolutely the reverse. Relations in Buenos Aires were extremely cordial. The work of carrying forward the return of British-Argentine relations had now of course been transferred from the sphere of special conferences meeting in Madrid to the normal diplomatic sphere. The ambassador in Buenos Aires was constantly involved in this continuing dialogue, and he had recently reported that, in his opinion, the time had almost arrived when the impossibly difficult area of joint sovereignty, in one form or another, might be cautiously approached.

'Not until after the election, please!' interjected the Prime Minister. 'We can't even think about that now.'

'Quite so, Prime Minister,' said the Foreign Secretary, 'but that's how good it is at the moment. To be brief, we have absolutely no indication that the Argentine Government and all its representatives are not negotiating and discussing with us in perfectly good faith.'

'Well, thank you. It seems to me that we have first of all got to decide whether these reports (the accuracy of which I think we must accept) produce a situation where we think we must take some action. If the answer to that is yes, then we have to decide what that action must be, and that may be much more difficult. All agreed?'

They were all agreed. 'Right,' said the Prime Minister, 'Admiral Higgins, give us your view of the Argentine military position, and what they could do if they were minded to try something on.'

'They are very weak, Prime Minister,' Admiral Higgins began. 'Their chief weakness is that, in an intelligence sense, they are in a box. As these reports show, we have such good information from a number of sources that, effectively, once they begin to do any of the things necessary to mount a military adventure, we know about it very quickly. As for mounting the sort of operation they did in 1982, that's quite out of the question, I mean quite inconsistent with keeping it secret from us.

'As for their armed services, essentially they are much the same as they were in 1982, except that most of the ships and aircraft are nine years older, and that's a long time in today's world; also most of them were not very new then. All the services have been starved of money for the last nine years: only last year did they suddenly get some surprisingly big allocations of money, so that they could start some long-overdue modernization.

'To take the services separately, the Navy has hardly changed at all. They still have the old carrier, and the Type 42 destroyers, and a couple of good modern submarines. The carrier, one must presume, can now fly off the Super Etendard aircraft, which carry Exocets. Also we think they have made some progress in anti-submarine warfare technology. The Army – no change. The same mixture of professional NCOs and short-term conscripts, though we are told they have been trying to improve the conscripts' role and standing a bit. Now the Air Force. They have still got some of the aircraft which they used against us in 1982, the ones that were left, and they're very long in the tooth now. They tried to buy twenty-four modern-version Skyhawks from Israel, but the US embargo bit and the planes are still in Israel. They did manage to get some new Mirage IIIs, and they have updated the old Daggers by giving them some radar. In the main they have been concentrating on their home-grown Pucaras, which are excellent planes for short-range work but no good for a Falklands adventure.

'To sum up, Prime Minister, they are very weak all round. I personally don't think they would have any chance of getting a 1982-style thing off the ground. With the forces we have there, including the nuclear sub, we could break it up easily; and, as I say, they can't even prepare such an operation without us knowing about it and being able to get the reinforcement procedure (which, as you know, is constantly at a high readiness state) going.'

'Then what do you think they are up to? What do these reports indicate? Should we take no notice of them?'

'No, Prime Minister,' replied the Admiral slowly, 'I don't exactly think we should take no notice of them. It may of course be that the Argentines are simply taking advantage of the purse-strings being loosened, to stock up their depleted arms inventories and do some overdue contingency training, to see if the old Skyhawks and Daggers can still fly without the wings falling off. But it also may be that they think the rapprochement process is going a bit slowly and that they could push it along a bit by reminding us they can still bite. Like a police interrogation, where you get Mr Nasty taking over from Mr Nice. They may be trying to embarrass you and your colleagues in the run-up to the election. An actual operation, no, I frankly don't believe it. But I think they are testing us: they know perfectly well their every move is monitored. They may be combining necessary stocking-up and training, with an exercise to test our reactions. If we do nothing, they may feel it safe to go on one stage further – Grandmother's Steps, you know. I think we have got to react a bit, let them know we're not asleep.'

'Does anybody think,' asked the Prime Minister, 'that this could be an indication that the military are pushing the civilians, that they are getting the upper hand over Menem, and that we might find ourselves faced one day by another Junta?'

'I don't actually think so, at this moment,' the Foreign Secretary said. 'We do know that Menem and his government are under fairly strong military pressure on a number of matters. For instance, their release of Galtieri and Co, and the pardoning of most of the so-called 'dirty-war' criminals was certainly the result of pressure.

'But there's not much indication that the services might take over: the country simply is not ready for such an idea. I agree basically with the Admiral: we cannot dismiss the reports, but we have no way of knowing what lies behind them. I assume the Admiral is right and that a real operation is not in contemplation: apart from anything else, it would be a gross breach of faith on the part of the Argentine Government, in which I for one simply do not believe. I can't believe Menem would be going along with us in progressive discussions, and all the time be preparing to stab us in the back. He simply is not that sort of man. Things are going reasonably well for him anyway: he's struggling to get his economic act together, and he must be anxious for world opinion to continue to approve of him and all his works. No, I think some sort of kite is being flown to test our reactions: so we must react somehow. If history tells us anything, it is that non-reaction to South Atlantic developments is fatal.'

There was a general murmur of agreement in which the Prime Minister joined. 'Well, then,' he said, 'how do we react? That's the difficulty. If we react publicly there will be a media sensation. I shall be accused of making a war scene in order to win the election. After all, it's June now, and we might go to the country in October. We're well behind in the opinion polls. I can just see the headlines – "P.M. Manufactures War Scare". I don't fancy that.'

'They don't use words like 'Manufactures' in headlines,' said the Defence Secretary. 'Much too long. But I agree with you:

at this particular moment it could be highly counter-pro-
ductive electorally. Perhaps they really are trying to embarrass
us. But first, I would like to explore what we are actually going
to do. Perhaps we really ought to think about a modest beefing-
up of the garrison? As you know, a lot of members were not
very happy about the last reduction, and perhaps they were
right.'

'I have a proposition,' said the Chief of the Defence Staff,
'which may just fit. May I explain it?

'The Belize situation has taken a pronounced turn for the
better. The Guatemalans have really backed down, and it
looks like they mean it. Why not simply take back the two
companies to the Falklands? That would restore the battalion
there to full strength. Belize could just be used for training: for
instance, the Gurkhas at Aldershot could go out in relays. I
think the two companies' being restored would be quite a
substantial reinforcement, and be seen as such. If there are
questions here, and if we don't want to offend the Argentines
publicly, we can link it to a training commitment. But the
Argentines will know we have sent them a signal. Actually, the
training bit is genuine: I understand that the Garrison Commander, now that his infantry force is so small, has definite
qualms about any proportion of it being away from base. This
means the men get a bit unfit, as well as bored. This way, he
could afford to have a few off training in the sticks at any one
time.'

'How about aircraft?' asked the chairman of the intelligence
committee. 'Would you propose to restore the two Phantoms
we took away?'

The Admiral made a small face. 'Well,' he said, 'actually
that's not too easy at this precise moment. I discussed fighter
strengths with the Chief of the Air Staff only three days ago:
he's slightly fussed because, for various technical reasons with
which I won't bore everybody, there's a temporary shortage of
pilots. They've been leaving in greater numbers than desirable.
The RAF are dealing with the problem, and they think they
will succeed in containing it; but for the moment there is a
definite shortage – Meredith can't even man all the fighters he
has, and he wouldn't take kindly to sending two more, and four
more pilots, to Mount Pleasant at this moment. It's not a
satisfactory situation, and both the CAS and I are determined

that it must be dealt with, and it will be dealt with – but can we look at the idea again in six months' time?'

'I certainly agree with you that it's an unsatisfactory situation,' the Prime Minister remarked rather tartly. 'It costs millions to train these boys, and then they don't stay ten minutes. I insist that the RAF gets this one right, and quickly. However, having said that, I suppose we must accept what you say, for the moment. As for the infantry reinforcement, does everyone think that will be sufficient?'

'I don't think we can answer that question,' said the Foreign Secretary, 'until we settle how we are going to communicate the news to the Argentines. If we are all agreed, and I sense that we are, that we are being tested and that we have to make an appropriate response to show that we are alive and in business, then the problem is to make the reaction adequate but not excessive – adequate so that the Argentines get the message, but not so strong that they take offence, so that all the progress we have made is jeopardized. That's the problem, and it's one I'd like to think about.'

'May I make a suggestion?' said the Defence Secretary, 'Clearly we have to do this through their ambassador here. It must be done very tactfully, and we must emphasize that we are not making any public announcement, and that if questions are asked in this country, the answer given will be that there is a need for training facilities. His government will no doubt understand that in making such a modest increase in the islands' garrison, HMG is acting in accordance with its perceived duty to the inhabitants, and it is HMG's earnest hope that before long, circumstances such as a reduction in flying activity in Patagonia will make it possible for the garrison to be once more brought down to the lower level, and perhaps even lower still, etc. etc. etc.'

'Yes,' said the Prime Minister, 'that ought to give them the message, without giving them cause to make a song and dance. I really can't run the risk of having the 'warmonger' label stuck on me, unless, that is, there's a real war, in which case I'll make a virtue out of it. Now, are we all agreed? Right, you two get on with it, please. I trust that the security services will continue to monitor the situation? In particular I think we'd all like to know whether the delivery of our message has any apparent effect.'

At this point the division bell rang. 'For once the timing is right!' remarked the Prime Minister as he rose to leave the room. 'Let matters proceed, then,' he said, 'but we must keep our eye on this one.'

8

The Argentine Ambassador in London had been appointed as soon as diplomatic relations had been restored in February 1990. He was an experienced diplomat and politician. A Peronist, he had served as Deputy Foreign Minister in Carlos Menem's government. The appointment of so senior a man as Argentine representative in London had been a clear indication of the importance attached by the Argentine government to maintaining the pace of rapprochement with Britain.

Now he was being shown into the presence of the British Foreign Secretary, with no idea of the reason why he had been sent for. As it was the Foreign Secretary himself, it could be something really important.

The Foreign Secretary rose and greeted his visitor cordially. After a brief exchange of small talk, they moved to deep armchairs round a low coffee-table, and the business of the meeting began.

'As you know, Ambassador,' the Foreign Secretary began, 'Her Majesty's Government attaches very great importance to the restoration of full and friendly relations between our two countries, and it is very pleased indeed with the progress which has been made in solving the problems arising from those islands which we call by different names. Unfortunately it is not only a question of names.'

The Argentine ambassador smiled. 'More a question of sovereignty, perhaps?' he asked urbanely.

'Yes, indeed,' the Foreign Secretary said, 'and one day our two governments will have to stop putting that issue on one side, and discuss it seriously. But that is not a very easy thing for H.M.G. to do at this particular moment, with an election coming up. The Falklands are still an emotive matter with the British people: it would be unthinkable that they should become an election issue. No doubt, if we are re-elected with

74

a comfortable majority, it may be possible to address the question.

Where is this leading? The Ambassador wondered; but he said nothing, so the Foreign Secretary continued.

'I hope that what I now say will not be misunderstood,' he said, 'but I have been asked to tell you that, in view of certain developments, my government has decided that it must restore the strength of the British forces in the islands to the level at which it stood before the reduction which took effect last year. This rather modest increase will however apply only to ground troops: there is no immediate intention to restore the aircraft numbers.'

'I must say that this comes as something of a shock, Foreign Secretary,' said the Ambassador. 'May I ask why your government proposes to take this action, which is bound to cause disappointment to my government, and which can only be regarded as a retrograde step in the dialogue between our two countries which has made such enormous progress lately?'

'Ambassador, I will be frank. You must be aware that Her Majesty's Government, by various means, is exceedingly well-informed about military dispositions in your country.' The Argentine inclined his head without speaking. The Foreign Secretary forged on. 'Since those very unfortunate events in 1982, we have had no cause for concern, even during the early period when your government declined to say that no state of hostilities existed between us. Now that you have done so, basically we have even less cause for concern. But we are bound to take note of what our service chiefs say: they were opposed to last year's reductions in strength, and now they have made some representations which we feel we cannot ignore.'

'I thought your service chiefs were, unlike our service chiefs in the bad old days before democracy was restored, wholly devoted to serving the government of the day? Do they really make representations so strongly that your government feels obliged to reverse, for no reason apparent to us, a conciliatory trend which has given so much hope to us all?'

'Well, of course, Ambassador, you are quite right. Our service chiefs are strictly generals and admirals, and they have no politics. But they do have opinions, and they do have contacts, continual contacts I must say, with Conservative Members of Parliament. If the service chiefs are unhappy about something, then as well as advising their minister of their unhappiness they do pass it on also to those Conservative members who are interested in defence matters: so the minister gets attacked from that direction also. The service heads are quite close to those sections of the Conservative Party: it is really a question of class,' the Foreign Secretary concluded, rather lamely.

'Ah, class!' said the Ambassador with a smile, 'So important in Britain and not unimportant, may I say, in Argentina. But let us stick to the point. May I ask, what sort of representations have these class-conscious generals and admirals made, and what are the circumstances which have caused them to make them?'

This is the difficult bit, said the Foreign Secretary to himself. This is where I could get it wrong.

'Ambassador,' he said, 'I hope I can speak very directly. Our service chiefs are alarmed by what they see as a sudden increase in Air Force activity in Patagonia. We know that you have certain, ah, differences with Chile, but those differences do not seem to be to the fore at the moment. Therefore our service chiefs find this sudden increase in the activity of aircraft, long-range aircraft I must say, somewhat alarming, and they have communicated their alarm (which is no doubt unjustified) to the Members of Parliament, who have in turn impressed their concern on the responsible ministers. It is, as you know, possibly an election year: everyone is rather sensitive. As a result my government has, with reluctance, decided that it must make a gesture of reassurance to these influential people. I hasten to say that no public announcement is to be made, and in the unlikely event that the move becomes public knowledge, we will say that it is in the interests of military training: on no account do we wish to affect the so-rapidly improving relations between our countries, or jeopardize in any way our progress towards final solutions.'

The Ambassador thought this speech over for a bit before replying. He was genuinely astonished by the statement about increased flying activity in Patagonia; he knew nothing about any such activity. He did know vaguely that the President had been forced to allow the services, after many years of austerity, a bit more money. Perhaps the Air Force had had a rush of flying training to the head. But maybe the British knew a bit more than he did: he would find out very soon; meanwhile he must make the right diplomatic noises at this embarrassed but not inexpert Englishman.

'Foreign Secretary,' he finally said, 'I can do nothing but tell you that my government will be both alarmed and offended by the action which your government is taking, an action which as I have remarked is of a most retrograde nature in the present improving climate of relations between our two countries. I must also protest that the premise on which the action is apparently founded, which is that some form of offensive action is contemplated by my government, is, I am sure, mistaken, and can only be a particular cause of offence. The only mitigating factor which I do however see is that you do not intend to make any announcement about what you are doing, and so you seem to have no intention of bringing baseless charges against Argentina at the bar of world opinion. I am sure that my government will be appreciative of this considerate attitude on your part. But I must repeat that my government is bound to be very concerned at this development.'

These were strong words for an ambassador to use to the Foreign Minister of the country to which he was accredited. They were, however, spoken with perfect courtesy and with a smiling mein, as if to indicate that the words had to be said, the matter being a serious one; but that the speaker, at any rate, had no wish to exacerbate the matter. The Foreign Secretary, who had listened attentively to the ambassador, now spoke once more.

'Ambassador,' he said, 'I did not expect you to react in any other way. In foreign affairs, it is sometimes necessary to take unpalatable actions, and in so doing to take the risk of causing offence. I am glad that you accept and recognize that we wish this matter to remain an entirely private one between our two countries. I have explained to you the reasons which have led us to take this step, and I ask you to communicate them to your government. I also once more ask you to stress to them that we have absolutely no wish to embarrass them in any way. Our only desire is to see this small hiccough, if I may so describe it, in our friendly dialogue, smoothed out so that we may continue in the steady normalization of our relations.'

'To be practical, Sir,' the Ambassador now remarked, 'I am, tomorrow, due to fly to New York. My Foreign Minister is making one of his fairly frequent visits there. He likes personal contacts with his overseas representatives, and he hates air travel. To minimize that activity, he sometimes ask me and other Argentine ambassadors to join him there for consultation. I shall of course take this opportunity to deliver the message which you have just communicated to me. On my return I shall, if I may, inform you or perhaps one of your officials of his reaction. If I may be permitted a final personal observation, I am perfectly sure that the circumstances which have given rise to this action on your part will prove to have an innocent explanation.'

'Thank you very much,' said the Foreign Secretary, rising to his feet to indicate that the interview was at an end. 'I am grateful to you for your comprehension of our position. Your country is well served. I wish you a safe and pleasant visit to New York.'

When, two days later, the Ambassador met with his Foreign Minister in New York, he found him just as surprised by this unexpected development as he had been. The Foreign Minister knew nothing of any markedly increased Air Force activity in Patagonia. Of course, all the services had had some money pushed at them lately. They had been getting a bit restive, and it had really been time to loosen up a bit with the defence allocations: the marginally improved economic situation had allowed this. So perhaps the Air Force had actually been able to spend some money on aviation fuel. But as for the British taking alarm at this – that was incomprehensible. The two men agreed that the British, who as they knew were very well informed, must have found something to alarm them. But, there again, perhaps they had misinterpreted a perfectly understandable renewal of ordinary flying training after a period of inactivity enforced by financial stringency. In that case, they were being both stupid and heavy-handed. They were those things, sometimes.

The Foreign Minister left New York as planned: he clearly had to make some enquiries of his colleague the Minister of Defence; but he was inclined to think that the whole thing might be a storm in an Earl Grey teapot.

The Defence Minister of Argentina was an elderly retired general. In former times there had been separate ministries for the three services, but in the administration of General Videla the three portfolios had been combined as an economy measure, under one minister with a new title. The same thing, let us note, had happened in London a few years previously.

The Defence Minister, when invited to confer with his colleague the Foreign Minister, was perfectly mystified. About the only thing he had to do as a minister was to establish the spending levels allowable to the three services. What a thankless task this had been for so many years! He had always been under pressure from the service chiefs to get more for them, but had never been able to do so. Then, only a couple of years ago, President Menem had relented: well, of course the Air Force had started some long-overdue flying training: he knew that well, but that was all he knew. He would investigate, and report back.

When he got back to his office, the Defence Minister called Major-General Romera, the Chief of Staff of the Air Force. He was informed that Romera was away, on a tour of the airfields in Patagonia. His second-in-command? Alas, he was accompanying the general: they were not expected back for another three days. For the moment Colonel Alfonso Jones, the Director of Flying Training, was in charge of Air Force affairs. Could he perhaps assist the Minister? Yes, indeed he could, he was just the right man. Yes, right away.

Colonel Alfonso Jones, the great-grandson of a Welsh immigrant to Patagonia in the last decade of the nineteenth century, was a capable officer. He was in every way privy to the service leaders' conspiracy. He went to the Minister's office in some trepidation.

Meanwhile, General Romera and his deputy were making a final check-up tour of the southern airfields. They found all in order. The fuel dumps were sufficiently stocked: the bombs, many of them newly-acquired and transported secretly by long-distance lorries travelling by night and resting under the trees by day in order to escape the all-seeing satellite eye, had arrived and had been stored: the maintenance technicians, some of them grumbling at being exiled for no apparent reason to this windswept southern province, were there in sufficient numbers: to placate them, it had been necessary to tell them that many more squadron visits would take place over the next few months (which was not in fact the case); and to give them a special 'hard-lying' allowance. All in all, the general was pleased with what he found: the nests were ready to receive the birds when their migration southwards was due: the familiarization phase was over, and now there was nothing to do but await the date, and try to keep the technicians happy in the meantime.

Colonel Jones, when he went to the Minister's office, knew most of this. He was able to assure the Minister that the course of flying-training, which had indeed been undertaken as the result of a sudden affordability of aviation fuel, was in fact completed. From now on there would be very little activity in Patagonian airspace. The old Skyhawks and Daggers, and the old and new Mirages, would for the most part return to their normal bases up-country and be once more placed in semi-storage. The course of training had been necessary to make sure they could still fly, and the pilots could still fly them in the only environment in which they were ever likely to be employed.

'Yes,' said the old minister. 'That's all very well, and I quite understand what you say. But meanwhile you have managed to alarm the stupid English. They think we're going to attack the Malvinas again. So upset are they that they are going to increase their garrison to the levels of two years ago. Not a big increase, it's true, only another two or three hundred men; but they're upset and it's a bit of a setback. Can you absolutely assure me that Patagonian skies will be quiet from now on?'

Colonel Jones nearly fell off his chair.

'Yes, Minister, I can assure you that. This increase in the Malvinas garrison – will it be public knowledge?'

'No, it won't, at least the English won't be making a fuss about it. Well, Colonel, I'm glad to hear what you say. I'll speak to General Romera about it next week, if I remember, which is doubtful. Have a glass of sherry?'

Alfonso Jones left the Minister's room, after two glasses of excellent sherry, in an agitated state. An increase in the garrison! That was not what the doctor ordered at all: it was not the numbers involved that mattered, but the fact that the English were awake and aware, and informed. He was certain that all possible precautions had been taken to avoid alerting them, but here they were, alerted as could be, and increasing their forces as a warning signal. This would have to go to General Romera at once, if he could find a telephone line. There was in fact a secure line in a neighbouring building occupied by the Air Force – it bypassed the Ministry switchboard.

He did not see the taxi which, braking to avoid a dog and skidding out-of-control over the pedestrian crossing which the pre-occupied air force colonel was using, knocked him down, breaking both legs and causing multiple internal and head injuries. In hospital he did not wake up for two days: when he did wake, it was apparent that he was suffering from amnesia, and he stayed that way for several months.

The Defence Minister, quite unaware of what had happened to Colonel Alfonso Jones, sought out his colleague the Foreign Secretary a day or two later.

No problem, he said, they've only been training, glad to have some fuel for once, and now they've stopped doing it. No, there would be no more special activity. It seems to me the British have over-reacted: it's only two hundred men anyway, and they're not making a public thing about it. Why don't we just forget it? The British will think they have impressed us, and we know it is all rubbish.

The Foreign Minister, after giving the matter a little concentrated thought, decided this was a sensible approach: he did mention the matter in Cabinet, and found the Prime Minister and his other colleagues in agreement with his approach. All were incredulous that the British had jumped to such a conclusion; but they accepted that, as the British were not going to make a public fuss about it, neither should they. President Menem, when the Prime Minister duly reported to him, took the same line. Far from being outraged, he was rather amused that the British should be so stupid.

When General Romera and his deputy returned from Patagonia, they were very upset to find out that Colonel Jones had suffered such a serious accident. They visited him in his hospital bed, but he was making no sense and would make none for many weeks. Romera telephoned the Minister's Secretary, to be told that the Minister had found out all he needed to know from Colonel Jones: meanwhile he had gone off on holiday to visit his only daughter, a married woman living in Lima.

General Romera went back to his desk. It was a shame about poor Jones, but there was already too much to do. He settled down to his work. He was not closely acquainted with the Foreign Minister, and their paths seldom crossed. They did not cross now. Meanwhile in London the Argentine Ambassador, in an interview with the Minister of State at the Foreign Office, had reported that the increased air activity complained of had been of an innocent character, arising as it had out of loosened purse-strings and the necessity of carrying out some concentrated training: his government, he added, was pained at the drawing of so wrong a conclusion by the British, but in view of the absence of publicity it was not disposed to make a serious issue of the matter.

9

As the months of 1991 went by, and winter in Argentina promised to become spring, the conspirators began to experience in earnest the tension of uncertainty and of waiting. There was still no sign from London of the General Election with which they were resolved Operation Condor should coincide. There was discussion among them as to whether they should drop this condition, and proceed with the operation regardless of the British election programme.

It was however finally agreed to adhere to the original plan, mainly because it was thought that not to do so would add greatly to the danger that the British might strain every nerve to mount a Task Force expedition. It had not been found possible to beat off the British Task Force in 1982, and although the conspirators expressed to each other their confidence in being able to do so in 1991, privately they were all of the opinion that it would be much better if they did not have to do that. The British Government would be obliged to react, or at least to try to, if the operation was to take place now. If on the other hand the operation was postponed until the election had just taken place, there was a good chance (at present much better than even odds because Labour were well ahead in the opinion polls) that the new government would be one which would almost certainly not even consider an expedition. Even if the Conservatives won, they might be less keen to fight if there was no electoral mileage to be got out of doing so. It was therefore decided that the original reasoning had been sound.

An added advantage of adhering to the original plan was a psychological one. To go now, without regard to election dates, would be to go in cold blood. It somehow seemed a much easier thing to do if they were acting under the compulsion of 'one month's notice to move'. So as the month of September drew to a close without the awaited announcement in London, the service chiefs resigned themselves to waiting another six months. In May it would be late autumn in the Malvinas, almost winter. Perhaps that was a pity: there might be a spell of absolutely impossible weather, but it could not he helped; that was a risk which simply had to be accepted. Everything was as ready as it could be, and only the order to go in four (or conceivably three) weeks' time was lacking. When the moment came, everyone knew what had to be done: meanwhile life had to go on for another half-year.

For Alicia Nunes, who was fully aware of these consider-ations, this respite was a blessing. She now now very strongly in love with Carlo, and so was he with her. Owing to the exigencies of their respective services, they had not been able to meet very often, but when they did manage to meet they found they were entirely happy in each other's company. They were in love, and the question now arose, what should they do about it?

What they did, of course, was what every other young couple in love did in 1991. When Carlo got leave, he moved into Alicia's small apartment in Buenos Aires. She had had many lovers in her life, but she found that with him it was better, many times better, than it had ever been with anyone else. What was more, she truly loved him as a person, not just as a lover. This was it: he was the man, and she began to long for him to ask her to marry him. One day, he did.

He had a week's leave and had arrived late the night before, tired out from the long drive in his small Fiat car from Puerto Belgrano. He had fallen into her bed, and breakfast in the morning had been a late affair. Now in mid-morning (for it was a Saturday, with no work to be done) they were strolling, hand in hand and perfectly happy, in the park. A convenient seat beckoned: small boys whizzed about on bicycles, and pigeons cooed.

'I suppose you know, my darling,' Carlo said as they sat down, 'that I truly love you as I have never loved anyone else, and I would like to ask you to be my wife?'

Alicia's response to this suggestion was to burst into tears and embrace him tenderly. She then told him he had made her the happiest girl in the world.

'We are in a funny position,' he said when things had calmed down a bit, 'because we both know I have to go to war in six months' time. I might not survive. You would be a widow. What do you think? Shall we wait and see if I do survive?'

This led to quite an animated but also thoughtful discussion; and to the decision that no, they would not wait, they would get married just as soon as they could.

So they made their plans and worked out how and when to tell their respective families, from whom indeed no objections were to be expected: two young lovers in the first bliss of their declared love for each other – a love which was given particular intensity and poignancy by the special circumstances of their situation.

In Belize (British Honduras, that had been) it was hot. Never mind whether it was winter or summer, Belize was hot.

When the former British colony had independence granted to it, the Guatemalans who inhabited the next-door Central American country decided to press a claim which they had not ventured to put forward with any strength in the days of British empire. They said the whole territory was really part of their country. As their spokesmen were generals with sky-blue caps covered with gold fruit salad, it was clear that they meant what they said; and the rulers of the newly-independent country asked the British to continue to maintain some troops there, to discourage the Guatemalans. This was done, with entire success as to that main objective: a secondary objective, that of providing a training-ground in tropical warfare for soldiers who might otherwise have got bored or restive in Aldershot or Tidworth, was quickly invented; and that also was a success.

Until 1990, a 'battalion group', that is to say an infantry battalion with, under command, some Commando gunners, some Sappers, and a troop of armoured cars, comprised the British force in Belize. Formed into two so-called 'Battle Groups', this force occupied several jungle camps in the interior, facing the frontier (or what was presumed to be the frontier, because its exact line was unknown) with Guatemala. It was an ideal training situation, because the threat from Guatemala was a real one: there were incidents of varying significance all the time: training under such conditions was rather like fox-hunting: it was like war without most of the danger.

Now, in 1991, the 'battalion group' was a memory. Guatemala having, for the time being anyway, resiled from its position as a claimant of the Belize territory, the British force was progressively reduced until it formed only two infantry companies, on a four-months training tour. These two companies were now the only residents of the up-country jungle camps. The Guatemalans knew they were there, and that was a good idea because it was not inconceivable that the generals in sky-blue caps, faced with some crisis of confidence at home, might change their minds. Finally, when the process of rapprochement with Argentina had progressed to the point where a reduction in the Falklands garrison seemed a possible idea, the economizing genius of the Treasury came up with the idea that the two companies could be drawn from the resident battalion which was the principal component of the Falklands garrison. So two birds were killed with one stone – an exercise dear to the Treasury's heart.

This was why C and D companies, 1st Battalion The Royal Mercian Regiment, found themselves in Belize in September 1991. Major Julian Wilkins, as the senior of the two company commanders, was in command: he was in fact dignified by the title 'OC Troops, Belize'.

Two months previously, C and D Companies had been in the Falklands with the Headquarters of their battalion, while A and Support Companies (B Company was in suspension due to slow recruiting) were in Belize. They had relieved A and Support Companies, and had been enjoying themselves, so far as it was possible to enjoy oneself in a country with such a population of big insects and snakes both large and small, ever since.

Major Wilkins, on this tropical morning of September 1991, was sitting in a long cane chair on the verandah of his up-country headquarters bungalow. He took very little notice of the jumping pit-viper curled up in the corner of the verandah. He was quite well acquainted with this particular viper, and had some confidence that it would respect him, if he did not go out of his way to annoy it. Potentially a difficult customer, the viper justified its existence by keeping the verandah area free of mice and other small rodents.

Major Wilkins took a sip from his long glass of fresh lemonade and reflected how nice it was to be there, even allowing for pit-vipers and spiders as big as saucers, rather than in that boring bloody Mount Pleasant airfield camp on East Falkland.

Granted, it was a comfortable camp, but the boredom was extreme, as was the climate, in respect of wind and rain if not of frost. Here, he reflected, the soldiers were sweaty but happy. They quickly got used to turning out all their clothes and boots, on getting up in the morning, to dislodge the scorpion which might have crept in during the night. They did not really mind the sweltering humidity which caused many of them to break out in prickly heat. They greatly enjoyed their time off down on the coast, where they could swim off Caribbean beaches, and scuba-dive and water-ski: they were even able to play a little cricket. Mostly, however, they spent their time up-country in one or other of the old battle-group camps, learning from resident instructors the tricks and routines of surviving and fighting in a jungle environment.

Clatter, clatter, clatter came the helicopter: it landed on the pad, and as the rotors slowed, the door opened and a figure in khaki-drill fatigues ducked out. He came over to Major Wilkins, halted, saluted, and handed over a message. This was a Dispatch Rider, 1991-style.

Major Wilkins read the message, which was from the services attaché at the British High Commission. His face fell. At that moment one of his subalterns came out onto the verandah.

'Hello, what's up?' he enquired.

'What's up, Tony, is that we're off back to the Falklands, leaving by air on Friday. John Evans doesn't say much, just that there's a tightening-up down there: apparently the Argies have been making nasty faces. So the system is being reorganized. This will continue as a training station, for short tours by troops stationed in UK. I must say it's not the most welcome news: I was just beginning to enjoy it here, and so were most of the men, I think.'

'Yes,' said the subaltern, 'they'll be really cheesed-off. Oh dear, there'll be some broken hearts too. 'Oh, what will the ladies of Camberley say, when we pack our bags and march away?' That's one department where Belize is far and away ahead of most of the field, and the Falklands isn't even a runner at all. Oh, dear me.'

'You sound personally distressed, Tony, but it can't be helped. Ours not to reason why. Right, DR, take this back, will you?'

He wrote carefully 'WILCO, with some regret but WILCO all the same' on the bottom of the message pad, signed his name, folded the message and gave it back to the Dispatch Rider, who saluted and returned to the helicopter: in a moment it was lifting away over the jungle towards Belize City.

'Right, let's get cracking. We've got a lot to do and only four days to do it in,' said Major Wilkins, hoisting himself out of his cane chair, but gently, so as not to alarm the pit-viper. 'Get on the blower to Alan, would you? Tell him the bad news, and will he please get D Company back here as quick as he can.'

In London the winter passed fairly uneventfully. In reversal of the trend of the previous few years, it was a fairly cold winter, with three weeks of really icy weather in January. Politically, too, there was mostly cold comfort for the Conservatives. But very slowly they were beginning to lever themselves out of the pit which they had dug for themselves in the second half of 1989. The resignation of Mrs. Thatcher, and the leadership contest which at one time had seemed likely to tear the Conservative Party apart, were now but memories. The poll-tax had come, and the unpopularity and the upheaval which it had caused were not yet memories – it was still a most unpopular innovation, and people were only just beginning to get accustomed to it. The original objective of the tax had of course long been forgotten: owing to the very numerous classes of exemption which the government had been forced to concede, in the end very few more individuals were paying poll-tax than had paid rates in the past, and most of them found that they were paying more than they had paid before. Still, there were signs that the storm was beginning to abate: this poll tax upheaval had been a principal factor in the Cabinet's decision not to go to the country in the autumn of 1991. In other sectors too, factors which had seemed difficult in autumn 1991, such as the continuing conflict between the

Minister of Health and the doctors, now seemed to offer more hope. Inflation was down to six percent, a welcome improvement; and it had been found possible to lower interest rates by a couple of points. The housing market was on an upward trend, as was the Stock Exchange.

Above all, the eyes of the electorate, instead of seeing only domestic problems and not much liking what they saw, were now increasingly turned on the extraordinary events which were continuing to take place in Europe. The certainty that Germany would once more be a united country, and a very powerful one at that, had of course caused considerable anxieties to the military establishments of both West and East. The very continuance of NATO and its establishments had at first seemed in doubt, and as the two Germanies moved by headlong steps towards reunification the question of German neutrality began to loom large in many people's minds. The demise of NATO had not yet come about. A far more pressing problem was the determination of the European Commissioners, and of the governments of France, Germany and Italy, to force the pace of monetary integration, which most thought must shortly be followed by political integration.

This had, on the whole, worked well for the British Government. The British electorate, always cautious about integrating too fast and too fully with the rest of Europe, seemed to feel that their cause was, at this juncture, in good and safe hands. The efforts of the Prime Minister and Foreign Secretary to slow the pace of European integration, and to preserve for Britain more of the immemorial features of her independence, now attracted favourable media and public comment, on the whole, and Labour's unceasing criticism began to seem increasingly shrill and unreal. Even the issue of unilateral nuclear disarmament, which at one time had seemed to be one of diminishing importance (a development which could do no electoral good to the Tories: after all, they had won the last three elections largely on the issue), had assumed fresh prominence owing to the political developments in Europe and in the Persian Gulf. If there is a chance that NATO will no longer exist and that there will be no American forces in Europe any more, perhaps we had better keep our nukes a bit longer, people said.

So it had turned out to be in the Conservatives' interest to play out their time to the full. They were in better shape electorally than they had been in the preceding summer. But now the die had to be cast. There was no more time in which to manoeuvre. In the second week of April 1992 the long-awaited announcement was made: a general election would be held in the United Kingdom on 12th May 1992. On the other side of the Atlantic, at the other end of the world, a small number of resolute men knew that now all their plans would be put to the test.

10

When the news was received in Argentina that the British general election was to be held in one month's time, on 12th May 1992, the conspirators experienced a sense of relief: the waiting period was over. This was quickly succeeded by apprehension – they had to do it now, and it might not come off: something unexpected might turn up and wreck everything, and then what trouble they would be in. But there was no escape – it had to be done now, and it was going to be done.

So well had they prepared the way that very little in fact remained to be done until a day or two before the operation. The principal remaining task, in fact, was the assembly of the strike aircraft on the Patagonian airfields. They would have to fly down two days before at most, and in some cases the very day before: to assemble sooner would expose the planes (for there was no means of dispersing them invisibly on those bleak southern airfields) for too long to the all-seeing American spy satellites. They would be seen, as it was, and the only hope was that if the information was passed on to the British (as the conspirators had no doubt that it routinely was) the routine was usually a leisurely one, not geared to the fact that instant action had to be taken on it at the London end: in this, as it turned out, they were correct. The three hundred men of the understrength 1st Parachute Infantry Battalion, and their troop-carrying aircraft, also had to be assembled in Patagonia: they posed no problem, as they could fly down on the very day, on the evening of which the operation was to begin.

For Alicia and Carlo this was a time of intense happiness; however, the dark shadow of the impending operation was looming increasingly over them. They had married, but were in fact living in much the same way as they had before the ceremony. For most of the time Carlo was on duty with his squadron at Puerto Belgrano, the 25 *de Mayo's* base, and it was not often that he was able to get away to Alicia's small apartment in Buenos Aires, which was their home for the time being. Clearly some better arrangement would have to be made in due course, but nothing could be done until after Operation Condor: then it might be possible, given the powerful friends Alicia now had, to arrange a posting for her within reach of her husband's station: if the worst came to the worst, she might have to leave the army and become a housewife, and she had made up her mind to do that if it became necessary.

Meanwhile, neither of them was under any illusions as to the dangers which Carlo might encounter. The plan with which she was so familiar called for the 25 *de Mayo* and her two attendant Type 42 destroyers to leave port a couple of days before the operation and steam south towards the edge of the former 150-mile 'protected zone', and then turn east, sailing round the zone's edge until she reached a point roughly east of Port Stanley. It was considered certain that she would attract the attention of the Royal Navy's resident fleet submarine, and perhaps also of the resident frigate, and that she would be shadowed, thus drawing the naval opposition strength away from the immediate vicinity of the islands. Just before dawn on the chosen day, unless very bad weather intervened, she would launch her attack squadron and they would go in to attack Mount Pleasant, timed to reach the target a very few minutes before the Air Force planes were due to come in from the west. They would be detected first, and be the first to receive the attentions of the British fighters and air-defence missile batteries. When the survivors did get back to the carrier, they might find nothing to land on because the British might have sunk her. The opinion in fact was that they would feel unable to do this in their presumed state of uncertainty about what was happening on the islands: if the sinking of the *General Belgrano* in 1982 (an entirely legitimate hostile act in the opinion of the Argentine Navy) had attracted such violent and continuing criticism, how much less likely the British might be to sink this large ship in the very much more uncertain circumstances which would obtain for many hours on this occasion. Nevertheless, the Navy fliers had been given the most dangerous job to do: it had been explained to them that this was a great honour, and so indeed they all saw it.

Alicia had always managed throughout her busy life to keep

92

a shell of protection to prevent herself getting hurt by any of the numerous lovers she had encountered. As she reached across under the sheet for Carlo, sleeping soundly beside her, she knew that shell had gone. The barriers were down, and she was happier than she had ever felt in her life. His very presence made her skin tingle with anticipation. She had a moment of intense anguish when she let herself imagine that he might never come back from the forthcoming operation. She cursed fate for putting them in this agonizing position. And yet it was the very operation which had brought them so closely together. She knew that she must put aside her negative thoughts and immerse herself totally in enjoying her new husband. After they had made love and slept and made love again, they showered and ate a large breakfast. They laughed a lot, and talked over plans for a bigger house when Operation Condor was over. It was a bright cold day, so they left the breakfast things, put on warm coats and went out hand in hand into the April sunshine. They looked at the shop windows, and when Alicia admired a pretty gold pendant, Carlo rushed into the shop and bought it with Alicia remonstrating weakly and laughing as he put it round her neck.

'A beautiful woman deserves a beautiful present', he said, kissing her firmly on the nose.

'You'll spoil me to death,' she said, and then wished she hadn't said that word. They walked for over an hour down back streets, along windy shopping arcades, and then home to their small flat. Even the dreary domestic chores were fun together. Carlo put some music on, and they washed the breakfast dishes. Carlo had some writing to do, and Alicia had still not thanked everyone for their wedding presents.

The days slipped by with scarcely a harsh word spoken between them despite the growing tension inside. Soon Alicia would be sleeping alone, waking alone and breakfasting alone, and Carlo would be fighting for his country.

The evening before his departure they both felt so forlorn and speechless that they went to see a film. Here they could not see the sadness or worry in each others' eyes, but only sit with hands entwined, shoulder to shoulder with their thoughts.

☆   ☆   ☆

It was nearly time for the passengers to begin boarding. In the brightly-lit, echoing passenger terminal at Buenos Aires International Airport, an announcement had just been made from the British Airways desk that Flight BA 244 for Sao Paulo, Rio de Janeiro and London would be boarding within the next fifteen minutes and that first-class passengers would be called forward shortly.

In the big 747, the captain and his co-pilot were making their instrument checks. The food had come on board and had been stowed in the galley by the chief steward and the cabin staff under his control. The weather report was good: moderate westerly winds should help them make good time to Sao Paulo and then to Rio, and thereafter on the much longer stage to London. Soft music was playing on the internal loudspeakers. The captain indicated to the airport staff member who was on board that, so far as he was concerned, boarding could start.

At that moment a number of uniformed men came up the aircraft steps and spread out throughout the aircraft. Their leader, a captain in the Air Police, went in to the cockpit and told the astonished pilots that the aircraft was being requisitioned and that they were under arrest: elsewhere in the big plane, police were rounding up the cabin staff. They were allowed to bring their coats and flight bags with them, and were escorted down the aircraft steps and ushered into a closed and heavily-guarded bus. There was no explanation, and no real possibility of argument: in a country like Argentina, it is not advisable to argue when you are told by a man in police uniform that you are under arrest.

In the terminal, exactly the same thing happened to the half-dozen British Airways staff, most of whom were of Argentine nationality. An announcement was then made over the loudspeakers to the effect that British Airways much regretted that, owing to unforeseen technical difficulties, Flight BA 244 was delayed for a minimum of twelve hours. Passengers would be accommodated overnight, and they would find their transport awaiting them outside the terminal: their baggage would be unloaded and brought to them as soon as possible; meanwhile would they kindly proceed back through, from the departure lounge into the main terminal hall, outside which they would find their transport.

The flight would not have been full, but there were over two hundred and fifty passengers. The announcement, which was repeated twice in both English and Spanish, was unwelcome but had to be obeyed. Once in the main terminal hall, a good many passengers made for the British Airways desk with their expostulations and complaints, to be met by a young Argentine lady in British Airways uniform, who, if they had realized it, had not been there when they had checked in. No, she was very sorry, there was no more information: yes, it was hoped the flight would leave about eleven am next day: no, it was not possible to send messages from the airport – facilities for that would· be available at the overnight accommodation (this turned out to be not the case until the following morning): yes, your baggage will certainly find you: now, will you please go to your transport, which awaits you. She was flanked by two stalwart members of the Air Police: the passengers went, and got into the string of buses drawn up outside the terminal. They were driven for some thirty minutes to a large Army camp, where some trouble had been taken to provide acceptable civilian standards of comfort for members of both sexes, but from which, in the morning, they found that they were not allowed to stray. Their baggage did join them, and they were fed, and (eventually, next day) they were able to send messages: that they were so treated, in spartan but adequate comfort, was largely due to the organizing ability of Alicia Nunes, whose special task this had been.

The cockpit of the 747 was not left empty for long. As soon as the British Airways staff had left, two Argentinian Air Force officers in combat fatigues came on board and occupied the pilots' seats. A third man also came in and took over the seat allotted to the flight engineer. Both pilots had worked as such for American airlines, spoke perfect English and were familiar with 747s of this pattern. Their first task was to remove the details of the course, which had been pre-set, from the inertial navigation system, and to substitute details of a different course: the second pilot then went back to the galley to check up on the feeding facilities, and also to make sure that the alcohol was stored in a way which would forbid casual access.

During this brief interlude, the baggage-trains came and the passengers' baggage, together with whatever cargo had been embarked, was unloaded from the holds. Then, in response to an affirmative from the control tower, the stairs were pulled away, the engines were started, and the big plane taxied slowly away, round the perimeter track to a large hangar in the airport's maintenance area.

There, in a guarded perimeter outside the hangar, the 747 parked. Steps were brought forward and placed against the opened doors. From the hangar, the three hundred officers and men of the 5th Marine Infantry Battalion, together with some thirty specialist personnel and Rear-Admiral of Marine Infantry Carlos Ricarda and a small staff, emplaned. The Marines, in full combat gear, carried with them their small arms. Their kitbags, together with the battalion's mortars and machine-guns and a supply of ammunition for all weapons, was loaded into the baggage holds. The Marines also brought with them into the cabin of the 747 a number of rope-ladders with end-staves of suitable length to fit behind the aircraft's regular doors. The Marines took off their helmets and equipment and put them into the overhead lockers, together with such weapons as would go in: those that would not were laid on the aisles beside the seats. The soft music played. The Marines produced their reading matter, fastened their seat-belts, and began looking forward to eating the meal which would have been eaten by the British Airways passengers – but which would be served to them without alcohol. Rear-Admiral Ricarda, in combat uniform, moved slowly with the colonel of the Marine battalion, down the aisles of the 747, greeting Marines he knew, chatting to others, and wishing them all a safe flight. He was a much-admired figure in the Marine Corps, and known personally to most of these long-service, professional soldiers. They were off to a happy start as the big plane taxied round to the take-off position: exchanges took place with the control tower, and they were cleared for take-off: the senior officers returned to their seats in the first-class section, and fastened their seat-belts: the 747 opened its engines and thundered off down the runway, up into the star-studded sky. Once away from the airport, and over the wide expanses of the River Plate, shining in the moonlight, a course was followed for the south.

The Argentine President and his beautiful wife returned to the presidential palace, the Casa Rosada, at ten minutes to midnight. They had been to dinner with the Spanish Ambassador: it had been an agreeable evening. When they entered, the President was surprised to be told by his head butler that General Gonzalez and Admiral Vasquez were in his office, and that they insisted on seeing him on a matter of most pressing importance. Damn them, said the President to himself, whatever can be so important at this hour? But he had a high regard for both his service heads, and realized that he must see them: while his wife went up to bed, he went through to the office where he found the Admiral and the General in uniform: they stood up and bowed as he entered.

'Gentlemen, I did not expect you tonight,' said the President. 'What is your business?'

'Mr President,' General Gonzalez began, 'I have to tell you of a very important development which is taking place at this moment. The Argentine armed services are in process of reoccupying the Malvinas.'

The President looked at them, speechless for a moment. What a totally impossible country this is, he thought. What the hell do they think they are playing at? Finally, he said in a voice of exaggerated calm, 'How extremely interesting. May I enquire whether this exercise has the blessing of the Argentine government? My impression is that the President, at least, has not signified his approval. Explain yourselves, please, gentlemen.'

'I will explain, Mr President,' the general replied. 'Admiral Vasquez and I, and our Air Force colleague, have for long been convinced that the intolerable humiliation heaped upon our country by the British in 1982 must be expunged. We have watched with incomprehension the government's discussions with the British, in which the question of sovereignty has been deliberately left on one side. We see Argentina a pariah nation in the international financial world: no other country will take us seriously and give us the debt rescheduling agreement we need, while they see us pussy-footing with the British, making concession after concession, agreement after agreement on this and that, while the only important thing is put on one side. No-one, including the British, will respect Argentina until the sovereignty question is settled. When it is settled, we shall be able to start solving our problems. May I go on, Mr President?'

The President inclined his head. 'I think you are totally and utterly mistaken, but yes, by all means go on.'

'You may not realize it, Mr President, but the British position in the Malvinas is now very vulnerable. They have few troops and only a handful of fighter aircraft, and they are all concentrated on that new airfield of theirs. All their eggs are in that one basket.'

'And is it not an impregnable basket?'

'No, Mr President, it is not. A little ingenuity, a little original thought, and the basket can be broken and the eggs can be pushed off the wall. And once the eggs are smashed, not all the Queen's horses nor all the Queen's men can put them together gain. We have devised a method of doing this. We are landing a small force on the Mount Pleasant airfield tonight, by deception. In the morning, our Air Force will attack with all it has, and the Navy planes too, and if all goes as planned the British garrison will be neutralized and our force, which will already be there, will walk over them; and once we are in control of that airfield, we have won. The British will not be able to reinforce. All we have to do is sit on the airfield and call for international arbitration on our plans, which are revolutionary: once sovereignty is conceded, the Malvinas will have virtually complete autonomy within Argentina: that's why we are not going beyond the airfield. We don't have to, and we mean to begin as we intend to go on.'

'Given that I still think you are mad,' said the President, 'I begin to see that you have given the matter some thought. But where do I come in, in all this?'

'You don't, Mr President.' Admiral Vasquez spoke for the first time. 'Although you may not immediately believe me, we happen to think you are a valuable person in this country. We have to face the fact that something may go wrong with our operation, and that a damage limitation exercise may become necessary. Furthermore, we don't intend to become involved in running the country. General Gonzalez is not Videla or Viola or Galtieri. I am not Massera or Anaya. The government is going to go on running the country, whether it likes it or not: it will like it, once we have explained matters to it. But Argentina must have one man in reserve, one man who is unstained by what we are doing, one man who will be able to come back and pick up the bits, if the bits have to be picked up. If they don't, that man can eventually become re-associated with us and with the government, and he will then reap the fruits of our success. That man is you, Mr President. We are going to take you into protective custody tonight, and we are going to keep you (in comfort and honour, I may say) in custody until the dust has settled and the international community of nations has accorded Argentina its approval: then you will emerge once more, and resume the supreme direction of the country. And we, Gonzalez and I and Romera, we seek nothing: we seek no power: we do not think military government is the right thing for our country, and we do not imagine the people think so either. If we win, as we are quite sure we are going to do, we will be prophets of honour in our country. If we lose, you will be there, uncompromised, unsullied, to restore the situation, and you will have the pleasure of placing us under arrest. That is why we are going to arrest you now, and take you off to your temporary home.'

'Most eloquent, Admiral Vasquez. But what if I refuse to co-operate? What if I arrest both of you instead? There is a guard in this palace, you know.'

'The captain of the guard, Mr President, and both his officers, and the sergeant I may say, are under our direct command. I am afraid you have no option.'

'What about my wife: are you going to arrest her too?'

'Do we understand she has gone to bed? May I ask, does she expect to see you again tonight?'

'A most impertinent question, but yes, she does.'

'Then, Mr President, our suggestion is that you tell her, through the bedroom door, that you are detained by most urgent matters of state and will have to leave town tonight. Then, in the morning, my own wife will wait on yours and, if she is agreeable, will bring her to your temporary home. I may say, we see no necessity for your wife to be placed in protective custody with you: she will be accorded complete freedom.'

The President stood up. 'You seem to have it all worked out, gentlemen. I am tired: I have an overwhelming desire to go to bed. Do as you suggest, in the morning, with my wife: she also deserves some rest. I must make it quite plain, without any qualification, that I am acting under duress. God help you if you fail, gentlemen.'

☆　　☆　　☆

On that Wednesday night, Flight-Lieutenant John Dickinson was duty air controller at Mount Pleasant military airfield on East Falkland. He was not anticipating an active tour of duty, as no aircraft were expected in from the United Kingdom or intermediate places until the following afternoon. In fact no aircraft at all were expected, if one discounted the possibility of hostile intruders. That remote possibility was the main, almost the only, reason why he was there.

Just before midnight, however, when Dickinson was dozing over his book, he was awoken by a message from the radar controller, to the effect that the apparatus had picked up a very large aircraft approaching from a north-westerly direction. Dickinson quickly double-checked with his written instructions that no TriStar or other large aircraft was expected that night: next, he alerted the duty Phantom crew to stand by for immediate take-off: he then set about trying to make contact with the incoming aircraft. He tried the likely UHF frequencies used by military planes, and then several likely VHF frequencies. He finally switched to the VHF International Aeronautical Emergency Frequency on 121.5 MHz, and received a clear message at once.

'Mayday, Mayday, Mayday, GXYJQ 747 British Airways calling Mount Pleasant control request permission to land as fuel endurance now limited thirty-five minutes over.'

Dickinson replied at once, with 'GXYJQ Mount Pleasant roger but explain your presence in this sector over.'

The reply came, 'GXYJQ 747 I am Flight BA 244 Buenos Aires to London via Sao Paulo and Rio. I am under control of hijacker repeat armed hijacker wishing land at Punta Arenas in Chile. Punta Arenas advises airport closed repeat closed by fog and will not accept. Fuel limited as we normally mainly refuel at Sao Paulo for Atlantic crossing. See no alternative to landing with you, over.'

Help! said Dickinson to himself, why did this have to happen to me tonight? He did lots of things fast. First he said to the aircraft,

'GXYJQ roger wait, repeat wait, will revert shortly, out.'
Then he spoke to the Phantom crew who, cursing and swearing, were struggling into their flying gear: he told them to take off as soon as they could without further contact with or instructions from him, proceed on the appropriate bearing and

make radar and then visual contact with the incoming aircraft, discover whether or not it was a 747 in British Airways livery, and report back: no, don't shoot it down, not yet anyway, and get on with it. Then he spoke to the Force Headquarters duty officer, and asked him to get the senior available officer up to the control tower at once. Finally, he picked up the special red telephone and found himself speaking to the night duty officer at the Ministry of Defence in London, where it was nearly four o'clock in the morning.

Dickinson explained the situation and the actions he had taken so far. The duty officer, a lieutenant-colonel not so far exposed to such situations, woke up quickly and applied his mind. They agreed that the story was not a very likely one: the South Atlantic just was not a hijacking area: why should any hijacker want to seize an airliner and head for Chilean Patagonia? they asked themselves. Then Dickinson reminded the colonel that there were terrorists in Argentina, under pressure from the police and military: just conceivably, the story could be true. Yes, said the colonel, just conceivably it could, but wait, let's check with British Airways whether their London-bound flight is off course. Hold on.

Within two minutes the MOD colonel was back on the line with the information that British Airways were concerned about their Flight BA 244. It should by now be in Sao Paulo airspace and in touch with ground-control: it was not. Furthermore, it had not been in radio communication with the Brazilian ground stations which it would normally have contacted. In short, it was about to become a missing aircraft. Finally, British Airways said their office in Buenos Aires had simply said the flight had departed an hour late and they had had no more news of it. According to British Airways, there were two hundred and fifty-plus passengers on the flight.

'Well,' said Dickinson, 'what do we do at this end? Do we believe this unlikely story, and let it land? I'm checking on it, of course, whether it looks like a British Airways plane. I will also further question the pilot on the hijack story. Oh, and yes, is it the case that the Buenos Aires to London flights normally only carry enough fuel to reach Sao Paulo, with a margin of course?'

'Hang on,' said the colonel, 'I can check that one quickly.'

Within a minute he came back with the answer, 'Yes, that's true; for good and sufficient reasons they take on the main

101

amount of fuel for the Atlantic crossing at Sao Paulo. So that stacks up. Ring me back in ten minutes' time, would you? This is too big for me: I must try and mention it to someone more senior.'

At this point, Lieutenant Colonel Makins, CO of the 1st Mercians, came into the control room in his pyjamas and dressing-gown: he was, in military parlance, 'captain of the week' – a duty which rotated between senior officers for standby duty. The Garrison Commander, he told Dickinson, was still out to dinner with the Governor in Stanley, and was expected back at any moment. Dickinson quickly filled him in, and they discussed the unlikeliness or otherwise of the pilot's story, given that two points in it had already been practically confirmed by London. A problem was that communication with Punta Arenas was difficult: there was no direct radio link, and telephone calls had to be routed through Santiago: delays of up to one hour were commonplace. The fog story was therefore not easily to be checked; but Punta Arenas was known to be a very foggy place. Meanwhile the fuel endurance of the intruding plane ostensibly filled with more than two hundred and fifty civilian passengers, was going down by the minute. It was decided to make contact with Argentina via the military 'hot-line' which had been established in 1990. It had not been frequently used. When someone sensible finally came to speak on the Argentine end, he was only able to say that he was absolutely certain no Argentine military or naval aircraft was involved: civilian airliners were outside his ken.

The commander of the RAF Regiment squadron in immediate command of the airfield defence came in, also in his pyjamas. He quickly agreed with Makins' suggestion that his duty flight should be activated to take due measures on the airliner's landing – an event which all in the control room now thought must inevitably be allowed to take place.

Dickinson now called London again: Makins spoke to the duty officer. The latter had managed to contact his immediate superior in the emergency schedule – a rear-admiral who had been peacefully asleep in his suburban home. The Admiral, once awoken, had taken it all in very quickly. After asking all the right questions, such as enquiring whether it was possible to check with Punta Arenas, to which he received the answer that it was not possible to do so at all quickly, he said he was quite sure the aircraft must be allowed to land, due precautions being however taken against some unspecified form of trickery. He personally did not see, he said, how three hundred and fifty men, which was all that a 747 could carry, could be much danger; but clearly the precautions must be taken.

'So we let them land, keeping a close watch on them?' asked Colonel Makins. He received an affirmative answer from the duty officer, and then continued, 'On the assumption that the story is true, we shall then have to deal with the hijacker. Thinking out loud, I suppose we'll have to give him fuel to go on to somewhere in Chile, which is where he wants to go. Of course he may give up, in which case we shall have to ask you what to do with him.'

'Do so,' said the Colonel in London. 'Presumably you can feed the passengers. I don't think they expect to be given beds in these circumstances. Let's hope the fellow isn't too tiresome. In the last resort, remember you have an SAS section in the Islands, but I trust you won't have to use them. Keep in touch, will you? Let me know the form when it's landed. This is of course subject to interception confirming that it really is a British Airways plane. If it isn't we shall have to think again.'

'Roger and Wilco,' said Colonel Makins. 'Thank you for your help. To recapitulate, if our fighter reports it's a BA 747, we'll let it land, taking the precautionary measures. Out, for the time being.'

Just as he replaced the receiver, the Phantom pilot came through on his UHF radio. He reported that with the aid of ground radar and their own, they had quickly made contact and had approached from astern on their radar: then the four jet exhausts were seen and suddenly there she was in the moonlight, a 747 in British Airways livery, the letters on her fuselage corresponding with her radio call-sign. The blinds were mostly drawn down as they crept up her side: when they drew level with the flight deck the two pilots could be clearly seen: a third man, his face not discernible, was standing behind them, holding something in his hand.

'Right,' said Makins, 'I think that's it: tell him to come home and land, and then remain with his aircraft until stood down. Now we'd better put this chap out of his misery: tell him he can land. Your duty flight,' he added, turning to the RAF Regiment squadron commander, 'to embus and escort the plane onto the apron; maximum readiness for action.'

Flight-Lieutenant Dickinson went to the radio.

'GXYJQ,' he called. 'You are cleared to land at Mount Pleasant,' and he went on, after receiving a requested acknowledgement, to give normal directions for a landing. The big 747, now only fifteen miles away, prepared to carry out the landing procedures.

Fifteen minutes later the giant airliner, descending from the east, made a perfect landing and thundered past the control tower towards the western end of the runway. The RAF Regiment flight, in its weapons-carrier vehicles, motored quietly after it: shortly it would slow and turn onto a slip roadway, and they would escort it back to the apron as ordered.

By this time the officers had put on some day-clothes, and the Garrison Commander had returned from his dinner-party: he was quickly put in the picture. All the officers stood waiting, in some degree of tension, for the 747 and its escorting weapons-carriers to arrive back on the apron. When, after five minutes, they did not arrive, all except Dickinson went down onto the apron. Immediately on their arrival there they heard, borne upon the westerly wind, the sound of small-arms fire. Then there was silence: they stood there in some dismay, but in a moment the RAF Regiment duty officer came out to them, saying that he had had a radio message from the young officer in command of the duty flight, saying he was under fire from the vicinity of the 747: the message was then cut short, and it had not been possible to re-establish contact with the duty flight. Should he take the rest of the squadron down there and investigate?

The consensus, pronounced by the Garrison Commander, was that he should not. In the darkness he and his men would be at considerable risk if, as now seemed certain, the 747 had carried armed men instead of ordinary passengers: they would be unlikely to be able to achieve much in the dark: the indicated action was to wait until daylight, the situation being meanwhile treated as a major emergency and steps being taken to place the whole garrison on full alert. The possibility of ordering an attack with missiles by one or more Phantoms (which aircraft have complete night-time operational capability) was discussed but almost immediately dismissed. Apart

104

from the likelihood of hitting such members of the duty flight who might still be in circulation, it seemed a too early stage in the proceedings at which to write off one of British Airways' expensive airliners. The squadron commander was told to send out foot patrols in the direction of the runway end with the object of making contact with the duty flight if possible; but they were not to go too far and should not on any account attempt to approach the 747. Wait for daylight, was the decision, London being so informed meanwhile.

The 747 had made a good normal landing, but when its speed had dropped it made no move to slow to taxiing pace or to turn off onto any of the slip-roads leading back to the apron. Instead, it continued to roll along the ground for another seven hundred yards, until the lights which marked the end of the runway loomed up. Then the 747 finally halted and switched off its headlights, and things began to happen fast. The emergency doors were all unfastened and the escape chutes quickly activated: the regular doors were opened and rope ladders lowered. Swiftly and as quietly as was possible, the Marines left the aircraft: sorting themselves out on the tarmac, they ran out in a semi-circular inverted arc facing down the runway and inwards, and assumed firing positions: several machine-guns were set up.

There came three sets of headlights, advancing towards them down the runway. The Marines waited steadily in the darkness until the vehicles began to slow down, and then on their Colonel's order opened a withering fire. All the headlights went out: after a moment the Colonel ordered fire to be stopped, and the sections in the enveloping arms of the arc went forward from the flanks.

The British duty flight had no chance. One moment, it was going forward to see what had happened to the plane: the next, heavy-calibre machine-gun bullets were plastering all three vehicles with fire. The officer in command just had time to radio his headquarters before he was shot and killed. The soldiers leaping out of the weapons carriers, in an attempt to take up positions from where they could fight, were rushed from the sides of the runway by many times their numbers of armed men. For a few moments there was a confused shooting match, and then the British soldiers were physically over-whelmed and disarmed. Leaving a number of dead and wounded on the tarmac, they were led aft under guard to a place under the tail of the aircraft.

The Argentine position was now consolidated. A strong screen was thrown out some distance down the runway to guard against any further British approaches. The dead of both sides were collected and laid out on the ground, and the Marine doctors and medical orderlies began the process of bringing in the wounded, both British and Argentine, and doing for them whatever it was possible to do in the circumstances. Two squads of Marines set off in the direction of two Rapier ground-defence posts, the locations of which were known to be each about half a mile from the runway end. It was not of course possible to knock out all the Rapier posts or even a majority of them; but if these two could be dealt with it would be a step in the right direction.

There was no further British approach. The main body of the Marines settled down in the cold and breezy night to keep watch, sleep as much as they were allowed to and, like the British in their camp, to await the coming of dawn.

When the call came through to the Ministry of Defence in London the duty colonel, roused once more from an uneasy sleep, listened with incredulity and dismay to what he was told by the Garrison Commander.

'So what are you going to do, Sir?' he finally asked.

'Nothing tonight. It's too difficult. I've already apparently lost one platoon, and I don't want to risk losing any more. It seems like an armed attack, in fact it must be, but we don't know how many hostiles are involved and it can't be more than 350. I am treating it as a first-class emergency: in the morning we'll see what it's all about. I'll call again if there's any more news.'

The duty officer put the telephone receiver down. There was a nasty sinking feeling at the pit of his stomach, which seemed unlikely to go away for a long time. He called his immediate superior on duty call, the suburban-sleeping Rear-Admiral, and told him the tale. The Rear-Admiral experienced the same sort of sinking feeling, only with him it was worse, because on this occasion the buck stopped with him. But he had laid particularly strong stress on the adoption of precautionary measures. Damn those stupid soldiers, he thought ruefully: can't they do anything properly? He told the duty officer not to fail to pass on any more news received, and meanwhile not to worry too much. Then he called the Secretary of State for Defence, Sir Henry Jones.

The Minister was also sleeping peacefully, in his flat in Ashley Gardens. He too listened with dismay to what he was told, and he too experienced a distinct sinking feeling. He told the Rear-Admiral not to fail to pass on any more news received, and meanwhile not to worry too much.

Then he called the Prime Minister at No 10 Downing Street.

At General Romera's advanced headquarters at Comodoro Rivadavia, anxious listeners on the arranged high-frequency wavelength heard the awaited message. 'Condor landed, repeat Condor landed' bounced via the ionosphere from the 747's radio transmitter. Due acknowledgement was sent, and was itself acknowledged: henceforth silence prevailed on the airwaves.

11

In the hour before dawn, that cold hour in that near-freezing but mercifully dry night, with the west wind blowing steadily from West Falkland over the bleak moors and mountains, there was much activity in the Mount Pleasant airfield camp. The Mercian battalion had all been stood-to since four o'clock: breakfast had been eaten, and now the trenches and sand-bagged emplacements were manned. Weapons-carriers and half-tracks were ready to move. In the Rapier positions surrounding the camp, a similar state of alertness prevailed.

In Garrison Headquarters, Brigadier Charles Gresham conferred with the Mercian commanding officer, Lieutenant Colonel Humphrey Makins, and his second-in-command and three company commanders. Wing-Commander Price, the senior RAF officer on station, was also present. His three serviceable Phantoms were being readied and fully armed for take-off. To his great chagrin the fourth plane, which had been undergoing a major maintenance overhaul, could not be ready for a dawn take-off with the others. Although the Phantoms, with their very sophisticated systems, were perfectly capable of operating at night, the uncertainties of the situation had convinced all the senior officers that no further action should be taken until the problem could be properly appraised in daylight.

'Well, gentlemen,' said the Brigadier, 'it is pretty clear that we have an armed incursion, but on what scale we do not know. They have come, whoever they are, in the British Airways jumbo, and those planes carry 300 or more, we know. So there could be 300 or more: on the other hand, they could be very much fewer in number. All we know is that the duty flight went off up there, that there was shooting, and that they haven't come back. There is also the problem that numbers 3 and 4 Rapier positions have gone off the air, I understand, in the last few minutes. It looks as if they have been attacked and perhaps overrun. What bothers me is that we don't know the scale of this incursion and what its purpose is. Conceivably it could be a demonstration by a gang of hotheads: on the other hand, it could be a serious attempt to overrun our positions and capture the airfield. To do that, they would have to bring in more than 300 chaps: they know perfectly well our positions are very strong. What do you think, Price?'

'I think, Sir,' replied the wing-commander, 'that a demonstration by a few people is hardly likely. It is bound to end in surrender and capture, and they have shed blood, we must assume. No, I think it's a serious attack and they must be expecting reinforcements in the morning. Radar search, I understand, shows nothing at the moment, but I think it significant that we don't hear from those two Rapier posts. I think they've been attacked and put out, and that means that transport aircraft will come tomorrow.'

'But won't you knock them down,' asked the brigadier, 'irrespective of Rapiers? I don't know how many transport aircraft they've got; surely not more than a dozen?'

'Yes, of course we'll knock them down with the greatest of ease,' the wing-commander said, 'but we have to reckon on also having to knock down a large number of strike aircraft before the transports come.'

'You think they will attack at low level, as in 1982? Have they got enough planes to do that effectively?'

'Well,' the RAF officer said reflectively, 'we know they've still got twenty-four of the old A4 Skyhawks in flying order. They've also got twenty-two of the Daggers, that's Israeli-built Mirage types you know, that they used in 1982: those planes have been modernized – they've given them some radar. Finally, we know they recently acquired nearly fifty Mirage III's. That's a total of about ninety bomb-carrying aircraft, without of course counting the few the Navy might be able to fly off their clapped-out carrier: leave them out of it. Ninety planes can mount a pretty serious attack if they all come at once. There will be too many targets for our three fighters to deal with. If they are prepared to accept casualties, a lot of them are going to get through, and we can expect a lot of bombs all over the place.'

'So what's your plan for *Faith*, *Hope* and *Charity*?'

The wing-commander laughed. 'Luckily they've got a lot more fire-power than their predecessors in Malta, Sir. They'll give a good account of themselves. The Argies won't make more than one mass-attack, that I promise you. My planes will knock them down in unacceptable numbers, irrespective of what the Rapiers and Oerlikons on the ground do. What we've all got to do is simply stick it out, knowing it's a once-for-all attack and that hopefully we shall also be able to stop the transport planes landing: then it'll be simply a matter of cleaning up the people who have come in the 747. I'm sorry, Sir, you asked me my plan. I think that will depend on the radar search reports: as soon as the screens start filling up with blips, I'll scramble my aircraft, and I should have plenty of time to do so.'

Colonel Makins spoke for the first time. 'What makes you think they'll make a mass-attack, Wingco? They didn't do it in 1982 – never more than seven or eight planes at a time, I gather, and sometimes only three. Why will they do it differently this time?'

'Because they've got to if they are to have any hope of success. In 1982 they were mainly attacking ships, you must remember. They did go for the shore installations in San Carlos Water once or twice, but the main action was against ships. Now they've got to try and neutralize our defensive fire here, if they're going to achieve anything: I think they'll go for one really big attack, like Pearl Harbour, and hope to damage us so much that they can fly in the reinforcements they will have to have.'

'This all makes a lot of sense,' observed Brigadier Gresham. 'Now, are we right, I wonder, in assuming it's all going to be by air? Might they not try a seaborne attack as well? Do we have any reports from the Navy?'

'Yes, Sir, we do,' spoke up the staff major who effectively comprised the 'G' or 'OPS' staff at garrison headquarters. '*Alacrity* is shadowing the aircraft-carrier and her escorts: they're steaming round the edge of the old Protection Zone. If there has been no change since *Alacrity* last reported, they should now be just over 150 miles due east of us. No reports of any other ships at all. Of course there could be some, still beyond radar range and in a different bit of sea from *Alacrity*; but frankly I don't believe in a seaborne invasion. We should know if there had been seaborne preparations: there has been nothing at all. They've not got the answer to the submarine yet, and I doubt whether they'd try it. If they did, we should know two days before they could get here.'

'Well, that simplifies things for the moment,' said the brigadier. 'Let's sum up. We don't know the scale of the incursion or its purpose, but we have to assume it's a serious attack, that they will try to reinforce by air the comparatively small numbers they have landed by a trick, and that they must make a massive air attack before they try to do that. All concerned must be prepared to endure heavy air attack from dawn onwards.'

'Now, what else? I spoke to London only three-quarters of an hour ago: they know as much as we do: I told them I wasn't going to try to do anything until daylight, but that we were treating it as a full-scale attack emergency. I have also spoken to the Governor and to the Commissioner of Police. The Governor is taking steps to warn the Defence Force for instant mobilization, and the Commissioner is warning all the details in Stanley and out in the field, the mine-clearers and so on. Maximum alertness until daylight, and then we shall see what our problem is, and deal with it accordingly. Are our chaps in good heart, Makins?'

'Rarin' to go, Sir, but I wish we were not so thin on the ground. We can't man all the posts properly, but we're doing our best.'

'Can't be helped,' said the brigadier. 'Let us all be of good heart, and let every man do his duty. Personally, I shall be glad when this night has ended.'

At the western end of the long runway, all was quiet round the darkened 747. In the wind, the long emergency chutes, and the rope ladders which had supplemented them, hung swaying in ghostly fashion in the gradually lightening gloom. The Marines had all dug themselves shallow pits in a defensive perimeter off the edges of the runway, and had been trying to catch a couple of hours' sleep. A few hundred yards to the east, strong observation patrols watched with night glasses against any movement from the direction of the British camp: none came. The three disabled British weapons-carriers lay deserted: they had not caught fire. Inside the 747, eight British and four Argentine wounded were bedded down in the aisles, tended by two Marine medical orderlies. It had been a fearful job to get them up into the aircraft: it had been necessary to strap them securely into stretchers and then to haul the stretchers up the emergency chutes, which had not been designed for such a reverse process. Still, it had been done. On the ground, under the looming tail of the huge aircraft, the fifteen British prisoners lay disconsolate, guarded by two Marines. Not too far away, the bodies of Pilot-Officer Anthony Soskin and the six men who had died with him had been laid out in a rough line. The moon, dodging between banks of cloud, lit up the scene from time to time. In the east, a lightening of the horizon heralded the coming of the day.

The immediate neighbourhood of the 747 was not the only place where there were dead, wounded and prisoners. No 3 Rapier Post of 14th Air Defence Regiment, Royal Artillery, had been totally surprised when the Argentine Marines had burst into the small perimeter: the crew of the Rapier, caught unawares and unarmed, could do nothing but give up. No 4 Post was not so lucky. Like his counterpart in command of No 3 Post, the sergeant in charge of No 4 had been informed of the 747's landing: both posts had followed it on their Blindfire radar. But the No 4 sergeant had a more enquiring intelligence, a more suspicious cast of mind: he called his men to full alert and made sure that they had their defensive small-arms ready. But he only had twenty men. Once it was clear that the shadowy figures who came at them on their hilltop out of the night were hostile attackers, they did their best to resist, but the odds were impossible against them. There was a fire-fight, which ended with the sergeant and six gunners dead, four more wounded, and the remainder prisoners. The Marines had themselves suffered casualties, three dead and seven wounded. A period of clearing-up therefore followed, the Marine lieutenant being ordered by radio to do his best for the wounded of both sides and to remain where he was until daylight: he was to fix a white bedsheet to the Rapier itself as a signal to the Air Force that this particular weapon was no danger to them.

112

A hundred and sixty miles east of the Falklands, the aircraft carrier 25 *de Mayo* turned westward into the wind, which was blowing at moderate strength.

In that more eastern longitude it was lighter than it was in the Falklands by some ten minutes. The advancing dawn revealed in ever-clearer definition the outlines of the ten A 4 Q Skyhawks, the maximum number of strike aircraft the old ship could fly off. Bells rang in the carrier: aircrew, long since breakfasted and clothed, fully ready for action, made their way to their aircraft, ready and tended by their technicians. Carlo Martinez, loaded down by his flight-suit and helmet, climbed up and was inserted into his seat: at this, the most serious moment of his life so far, the image of Alicia came with great strength into his mind: he thought, my God, how can I be doing this? I love you, I love you, he said as he successfully plugged in all the things that needed plugging in until, irresistibly, the pressures of his service duty took over and he found himself fully employed checking all the things that should be checked, until he was able to declare himself ready for take-off.

In HMS *Sceptre*, Commander Hugo Fitzherbert RN saw through his periscope the old aircraft-carrier's turn. He was at a discreet distance, keeping the two supporting destroyers in mind, if not always in view. The carrier was silhouetted against the dawning eastern sky, and he was able to follow her movements easily. Presently a seaman brought him a cup of cocoa, which he sipped reflectively.

Sceptre had been in touch with the Argentine force from the moment it had left the shelter of Puerto Belgrano harbour. Certain information had been forthcoming, and had brought the submarine to the Argentine naval base, at the precise moment when the carrier and her attendant destroyers had headed out past the moles into the wave-flecked South Atlantic ocean.

Since then she had tracked them faithfully in their long southward journey until they had turned east and had reached a point nearly due east of the Falklands, about 160 miles from them. Now a sudden turn westwards, into the wind. Commander Fitzherbert knew enough about aircraft-carriers to appreciate what such a manoeuvre might portend: he watched with avid interest the carrier's next actions.

These were not long in happening. Against the dawning sky, he saw with excitement an aircraft leaving the carrier's deck, then another and another. In all, he saw ten aircraft fly off. The carrier then appeared to reduce speed: at that moment he was aware that one of her escorts was on a course that would bring her uncomfortably close to his position. He gave the necessary order to the coxswain, and *Sceptre* slid away down and out into an area of sea not likely to be troubled by inquisitive escorts, but still within contact range of the Argentine carrier. Here, having re-established visual periscope contact, Commander Fitzherbert sent his amplified message to Northwood by radio teletype, using the 'Submarine Satellite Information Exchange System'.

He had previously reported to Fleet Headquarters twice in the past two days: a brief acknowledgement had been received on each occasion, with an order to stay in touch and report further. Now the reaction was more interested.

The return message, when it came through on *Sceptre's* teleprinter, was categorical. Stay in contact and be in a position to make an attack if so ordered. For information, there had been an incident on Mount Pleasant airfield during the night, which required action to be taken by the land and air forces at dawn. Decisions as to naval action would be taken at highest, repeat highest, level: meanwhile, stay in contact with the Argentine force and await further orders.

Sceptre's message had been at once shown to the Commander-in-Chief, Fleet: he had heard about the trouble at Mount Pleasant, and had gone into his office. He, of course, was no more able to order Commander Fitzherbert to sink 25 *de Mayo* than his duty officer would have been. Nor would the First Sea Lord be able to do so, when the C-in-C informed him, which he did at once: nor in his turn would the Chief of the Defence Staff. Only the Cabinet could order a British submarine to sink a presumed enemy in cold blood, in time of peace. When told, both the First Sea Lord and the Chief of the Defence Staff were actually on their way to Downing Street, summoned from their breakfasts by the Minister of Defence himself.

So HMS *Sceptre* slid silently through the grey South Atlantic, her periscope and its attendant aerial clear of the wave tops, her tubes loaded with torpedoes. Her captain had no way of

114

knowing whether he would in the end receive the order to fire: he found himself rather hoping that he would not.

The assault by 3rd Naval Attack Squadron came in at earliest dawn. Approaching Cape Pembroke at two thousand feet, they were picked up clearly by the big radar on Mount Kent, which flashed its warning to the defenders. One by one the three Phantoms roared off down the runway, leaving the ground well before the end where the 747 lay, and swept round eastwards to deal with these presumptuous intruders. Meanwhile the Navy Skyhawks, having faithfully carried out the initial part of their job, which was to be detected first, dived steeply to near sea-level and came in over Cape Pembroke and Port Stanley at their best speed of 550 mph. Shortly after they had swept past Mount Kent the airfield lay spread out before them in the half-light: they saw, with sufficient clarity, the sector of the hutted camp which had been allotted to them as their target area, and fingers went onto the bomb-release buttons. They bombed, but now the first Phantom, flying at three times their speed, was in Sidewinder range: the other two were not far behind, and four of the Navy Skyhawks exploded in the air. Carlo Martinez was not fired on by the Phantoms, but a second after releasing his bombs he flew into a stream of Oerlikon cannon shells coming up from one of the perimeter defence posts. There was a loud bang and his perspex canopy shattered: he felt nothing but knew he was hit, so badly hit he could no longer fly the Skyhawk, nor even reach for the ejector lever which might have saved his life. In that fraction of time while he was still conscious, he saw Alicia's face, and then he knew no more as the stricken Skyhawk hit the ground at maximum speed and disintegrated into a ball of flame.

Desperately, using all their flying skills and flying so low that the rooftops of Stanley were almost level with them, the surviving Skyhawks sought to avoid the pursuing Phantoms; but now every radar screen in the Falklands was full of blips, and there were ninety more targets for the Phantoms and the surviving Rapiers. The Air Force pilots, timing their arrival with the great exactitude demanded by the plan which they had so carefully rehearsed, came in at extremely low altitude and maximum speed, and arrived in three divisions. The Mirage III's of 2nd and 3rd Air Brigades roared in from the north, leaving Douglas and Teal Inlet on their port side: the Daggers of 4th Air Brigade came in from due west, passing at low level over the Falkland Sound and San Carlos Water, and the veteran Skyhawks of 5th and 7th Air Brigades attacked from a more southerly direction, coming in over Goose Green and the Choiseul Sound. All the aircraft pressed home their attacks with great gallantry and skill, oblivious of the mushrooming balls of flame to right and left which betokened missile hits. Their orders were to bomb, in defined sectors, the western edge of the garrisoned area, and that is what most of them did. The three Phantoms, by now almost out of missiles and relying mainly on their cannon, and the depleted Rapier force inflicted serious casualties on the attackers, destroying no fewer than twenty of them: but they were quite unable to prevent the bombing – a total of over three hundred 100 kg bombs fell on the complex of barracks and defensive emplacements. Having dropped their bombs, the surviving aircraft escaped in all directions, scattering to make the Phantoms' task more difficult, and quickly making off in a westerly direction: as in 1982, they were at the limit of their range, but this was mitigated by their relatively light bomb-loads and the short time they needed to stay over the target. Eastwards, four survivors of 3rd Naval Attack Squadron, unmolested now by the Phantoms, made their best speed back towards 25 *de Mayo*.

But now, on the ground where all the bombs were falling, a curious phenomenon was immediately apparent to the embattled defenders in their slit-trenches and emplacements. The bombs were not going off with much of a bang. A 100 kg bomb delivered at low level by an aircraft travelling at 550 mph or faster comes to ground with quite a thump, smashing holes in wooden hutments and tearing rents in tarmac roadways. These results are normally obliterated by the massive bang resulting from the explosion of the bomb. This was not happening: the bombs came noisily and painfully to rest, sometimes after a ricochet or two, and then a small explosion split the casing apart. A smell of ammonia was apparent, and then, all over the area of the camp and its defensive positions, the defenders started collapsing where they stood or crouched. They were affected by a creeping paralysis which knocked them out as fighting soldiers as surely as if they had been hit by a bullet. Unable to speak or to move very much, many men had that sensation so familiar to dreamers – of trying to run on leaden feet that will not move, of attempting to speak with words that the mouth will not utter.

The 100 kg bombs purchased in Libya had been filled with one of the latest-generation binary nerve-gases, manufactured at a Central Siberian military chemical plant. This particular gas was of violent efficacy, but the full effect on a stricken individual lasted but nine hours: after that the victim could be expected slowly to recover the powers of movement and speech, and full recovery would almost invariably (in young and fit people) be achieved on the following day. The weapon was specifically designed to stun rather than kill. Conventional military respirators were not proof against it: the sales package included respirators of a special pattern which gave the wearer complete protection, and it was those which had been contained in the packages marked 'Surgical Equipment'. The gas was heavier than air, and this could require the follow-up troops to wear respirators for longer than they wanted to: the present day was however ideal – a moderate westerly breeze wafted the gas from the western side of the camp perimeter, which had been the main target area for the Air Force planes, quickly over the whole camp complex, but it would not persist there for too long. As an insurance policy, the Navy Skyhawks had been given a target area in the centre of the complex. Between them, the attackers had achieved complete coverage.

Everywhere throughout the big camp the scene was the same – in the perimeter weapon-pits, in the Air Force hangars, in the cookhouses and messes, in the Garrison Commander's headquarters, in the airfield flying control tower; everywhere, men who were able to see but not to speak or move their limbs (except that some who had got less gas than others were able to move with agonizing slowness) lay where they had been stricken, wondering what was happening, feeling no pain but fully conscious of their total helplessness. Their respirators, which would have been useless even if they had been wearing them when the attack came in, were attached to their webbing combat equipment. Mount Pleasant was a city of the temporarily dead.

Now came the Argentine Marines, careful, steel-helmeted,

wearing the special respirators with which they had been issued. When the Air Force planes had roared a few feet over their heads they had risen from their shallow foxholes and had begun a cautious advance in extended order down both sides of the runway. They had brought a number of small mortars with them, and had used these to lay a smoke-screen in front of their leap-frogging advance. Only the comparatively few Marines who were allocated the southern side of the runway had any fighting to do, for there the effects of the gas were comparatively thin, and several of the Mercian and RAF Regiment machine-gun posts retained the ability to fight and shoot. On this side of the runway a methodical advance had to be made against a spirited defence, and it was not until later in the day, when these defenders were finally made aware under flag of truce of what had happened to their comrades in the main camp, that firing ceased and they gave themselves up.

On the northern side of the runway, smoke was used to cover the Marines' advance to the camp (in the course of which they overran a number of machine-gun and anti-aircraft posts, the occupants of which were gassed and helpless), and all precautions were taken. But no real fighting was necessary. Methodically, the Marines went through the whole camp to ensure that no pockets remained in a position to resist: they found a couple of storemen whom the gas had missed entirely, and a number of other non-fighting personnel who had been indoors when the attack came, and who had been only slightly affected. Apart from that, it was a clean sweep. Nearly a thousand British servicemen of all arms and all ranks, from brigadier to private, lay disabled and helpless.

The 5th Marine Infantry Battalion now firmly established its grip on the conquered territory. All British weapons were collected and locked away securely. The prisoners were for the moment left to lie where they had fallen: eventually, when the power of movement began to return to them, they would be slowly assisted into their own living-huts and quarters, to await transport by C-130 Hercules transport planes and the British Airways 747 to airfields in Argentina, from where they would within a few days be transported back to Britain. It is easy to imagine what their state of mind would be during this process, but in his heart every man would know that he was extraordinarily lucky to be alive.

A number of officers specially chosen for their good command of English accompanied the Marines. These took over the flying control tower and the command telephones. Medical officers and orderlies took over the small camp hospital, where they found a few paralysed and speechless patients as well as medical staff. Contact was established, after some trial and error, with the outlying Rapier air-defence posts, and the process (which was to prove quite protracted) of convincing them that the hostilities were over and that their side had lost, began: This was to be completed later in the morning when small parties went out in British Land-Rovers under flags of truce, to convince the gunner detachments and the machine-gun posts still holding out on the southern side of the runway, that the main body of defenders had been neutralized by unusual methods of warfare.

Long before this, the crews of the three Phantoms, elated by the number of kills they had made, but puzzled by a total lack of communication from the ground, had decided that they should land to refuel and to re-arm: after all, who knew when another attack wave might come? One by one they landed and taxied up to their reception area, to find respirator-wearing strangers in foreign uniforms waiting to take them into custody. By this time the gas had cleared from the runway and from other open spaces exposed to the wind, and the Marines there, encouraged by the fact that the British airmen suffered no ill-effects, were the first cautiously to remove their respirators.

Elsewhere in the camp, and especially in confined spaces, the attackers were, sensibly, more careful. Doors and windows were thrown open to let in the breeze, and two NCOs carrying special detection instruments moved through the camp carrying out tests, before the general removal of respirators was authorized.

Rear-Admiral Ricarda decided to establish his headquarters in the flying control tower: it was fairly spacious and he felt in command of events there. His staff moved into the British garrison headquarters offices next door. Some specialists in flying control and in telecommunications had accompanied the force: these latter were shortly able to establish communication with General Romera at his headquarters, which had been set up on the airfield at Comodoro Rivadavia; and when the last of the Rapier posts had signified its acceptance of the new status quo, the C-130 Hercules aircraft carrying the three hundred men of the 1st Parachute Infantry Battalion were called forward: these aircraft would be used on the following morning to start ferrying the disconsolate, dejected and still dazed officers and men of the British garrison and their personal kit back to the mainland.

Ricarda felt a bit more secure once he knew that the Army paras were on the way. There was nothing to be feared from the British prisoners for a few more hours yet, and even then they would have no weapons; but his Marines were thin on the ground. They had had a disturbed night, and an exhausting morning wearing their respirators: only the light packed rations which they had brought with them would be consumed that day: next day, with most of the prisoners gone, they could start getting the British cookhouses going and begin dipping into the British Army's no doubt extensive and first-class edible stores. Until then they would be stretched, and the Admiral would be glad when the paratroopers and the specialized back-up teams which would accompany them arrived.

He did not expect to come under any attack. He had already been informed that the number of helpless and paralysed British whom the Marines, at that moment, were starting to carry into hutments, so that they should not suffer from the coldish night that would come in a few hours' time, roughly tallied with the known numbers of the British garrison: they were all in the bag, and in the rest of the Malvinas there were no other British units of consequence – some engineers, no doubt, still looking for those stupid and inhumane 1982-vintage mines, some policemen, and even, he understood, a sort of Dad's Army (for he had followed the British television series avidly when naval attaché in London in the late 1970s) called the Falklands Local Defence Force: no problem with them, surely, and The Plan had assumed there would be none. Perhaps there were some helicopters at large, and they could be based at the old Stanley airfield which had played such a part, under constant British naval and aerial bombardment, in 1982. One of the paratroopers' first tasks would be to go in strength and look at Stanley airfield, and ensure it would be no menace: in the circumstances, it couldn't be – its runway couldn't take a big jet and, apart from possible helicopters, there were no other British aircraft in the South Atlantic area except the four modern and expensive Phantoms now immobilized on his, yes, his airfield. He had raised the question whether the British might not somehow fly in Harriers to operate from Stanley airfield: the answer to that was that the nearest Harriers, apart from those on the ground in the United Kingdom, were in a light carrier of the 'Invincible' class, at present making for Hong Kong. Anyway, the paras would check-out Stanley airfield, and if thought necessary, crater its runway to make it unusable, before returning to base, or staying there, if that seemed advisable.

Meanwhile, besides the police and Dad's Army in Stanley, there was also a Governor and a Government: it was time to try to establish contact with them. From his time in London Ricarda was familiar with British telephone procedures: he knew that the Malvinas telephone system, formerly magneto-powered and routed through manual operators, had recently been converted to a British-style STD system. As he picked up the black receiver on his desk, he wondered wryly whether he would dial a wrong number the first time he tried, as one so often did in London. The Islands' directory gave him the Governor's number, and he dialled it.

In Buenos Aires, an hour before Admiral Ricarda picked up his telephone, all radio and television programmes were interrupted and listeners were told that an important announcement would now be made. The text was then read as follows:-

'The High Commands of the Navy, Army and Air Force announce that a successful occupation has been made of the main airfield on the East Island of the Malvinas. The entire British garrison has been neutralized and has surrendered, and will shortly be transported to this country for onward routing to Great Britain.

'Casualties among Argentine ground forces, and in the British forces, have been on a light scale. However, a number of Navy and Air Force aircraft have not returned to their bases and must be presumed lost. We salute these brave young men who have died for their country.

'The High Commands consider that it is sufficient at the present time to occupy securely the main Mount Pleasant

121

airfield, and there is no need or intention at this time to extend our occupation to Port Stanley or to other inhabited areas of the islands, or to interfere with the established civil administration, pending international arbitration on the future sovereignty of the islands. In the expected event that Argentine sovereignty over the Malvinas is confirmed, the High Commands intend to suggest to the Government that the Malvinas be established as a self-governing region of our country with the right to conduct their own local affairs.

'The High Commands have taken certain measures to safeguard the security of the country, and to ensure that public order is maintained. The President of the Republic has been taken into temporary protective custody. All Government ministers and public officials are to remain at their posts and continue carrying out their normal duties. The High Commands of the Armed Services have no intention of interfering with the Constitution of the Republic or of assuming any responsibility for the internal government of the country or for the conduct of its external affairs.

'The High Commands call upon the Argentinian and British peoples, and upon all member states of the United Nations Organization, to take note of the conditions under which the present occupation of key points in the Malvinas has taken place, and to take all steps towards a speedy resolution of the question of sovereignty over the Malvinas, in the interests of world peace and of the inhabitants of the islands.

'Long Live the Republic.'

When the Argentinian public had got over the first shock of surprise at this news, which was quickly confirmed in the capital by special early editions of the evening papers, the predominant emotions were pride that their armed forces had been able to achieve such an astonishing result, and amazement that they had been able to do it with apparently few ground force casualties on either side: this particular conundrum was resolved to most people's partial satisfaction only in a television interview broadcast that evening, in which an Air Force spokesman explained that the airmen, at considerable cost to themselves, had managed to deliver a completely successful blanket attack using a chemical agent which had temporarily immobilized the garrison. He would not divulge the precise nature of the chemical agent used, but it was clear to all that it had been some form of nerve gas, and military commentators had to brush up their knowledge of this subject very quickly.

On the wider front, the civilian population seemed easily to accept the assurances given in the announcement, that the armed services did not intend to start running the country. There was suddenly a military presence in the capital, but it was not obtrusive: strong guards were posted outside the presidential palace, the parliament building, and the offices of the broadcasting and television services. But there was no disorder: in the evening a large crowd gathered outside the palace, but it was entirely peaceful and contented itself with shouting patriotic slogans linked to the Malvinas issue. After about an hour of this, the big French windows on the second floor were thrown open, and there emerged onto the balcony the three service heads accompanied by the Prime Minister, who was carrying a large laurel wreath: this he formally presented to Major-General Romera, in a gesture of public recognition of his pilots' heroism, which caught the imagination of the crowd. The leaders went inside without any speech or announcement being made, and shortly afterwards the crowd dispersed peacefully. In the following days there was speculation in the country about the position of the President, a popular figure, and about why it had been found necessary to detain him; but there was fairly early recognition that his detention might have been in his best interests, and would probably be of only a temporary nature.

The Government and Members of Parliament had not been so easy to convince. Minutes after the announcement had been first broadcast, the Prime Minister and three of his principal ministerial colleagues had presented themselves at the palace: they found the three service heads ensconced in President Menem's office; no-one was sitting in his chair. A furious conversation ensued, the ministers accusing the service heads of treason and many other crimes, and threatening them with the direst penalties of the law. The service chiefs remained calm and polite and, when the embattled politicians had had their say, Admiral Vasquez was able in a rather calmer atmosphere to explain to them, one, that it was a *fait accompli*, two, that the person who now withdrew Argentine forces from the Malvinas would win no popularity, three, that there was no intention of

123

harming the President: his detention was simply to spare him embarrassment and preserve his international integrity; and, four, they (the politicians) were on a good one-way option. If the result was recognition by the world, including Britain, that the Malvinas belonged to Argentina, immense kudos would be acquired by the Government as well as by the services: if, on the other hand, the unlikely happened and disaster or failure resulted, it would be the services' fault: a fifth point, which the Admiral did not find it necessary to stress but which dawned on his hearers fairly early in the proceedings, was that if they did not co-operate they might well find themselves under arrest. The country had been run by the military and the civil service on several occasions in everyone's memory, and could be again.

In the end, therefore, the Prime Minister and his colleagues accepted the situation and undertook to explain it in Parliament. Argentine diplomatic missions throughout the world, who had wondered when they heard the news what it meant for them and how they were to comport themselves, were soon to be told that it was business as usual, with the added ingredients that the operation should be represented as having been conducted as humanely as possible, and that an enlightened attitude towards the Malvinas population was to be taken once formal sovereignty had been conceded.

As the news of the coup-de-main flashed across the world, it made headlines everywhere. It being a Thursday morning, most world leaders were in their capitals, and their first reaction was one of disapproval. This seemed to be the second occasion within ten years when Argentina had embarked on a course of aggression. Several statesmen, however, in considering the statements drafted for them by their advisers, found that they contained the words 'unprovoked aggression', and then found themselves wondering whether the word 'unprovoked' was justifiably used. After all, had not the British Government resolutely refused, even during the past couple of years, during which they had moved so much closer towards normal relations with Argentina, even to discuss the question of sovereignty? Did not this in a way constitute provocation? Furthermore, if the announcement was to be believed, this occupation presented a number of unusual features. First, it appeared that the British garrison had been easily 'neutralized', with very few casualties: considering the well-known fighting qualities of British troops, it seemed likely that some very unusual means of attack must have been used: the near-absence of casualties, and the stated intention to repatriate the prisoners were favourable points. Finally, there was the point that the occupation seemed to be a limited one, aimed mainly at bringing the British in earnest to the negotiating table. Might it not be wise to tone down one's statement a bit?

Most world governments friendly towards Britain did in the end make statements deploring the use of force, but throughout South America the attitude seemed to be different, and most governments managed to avoid making statements at all.

All over the world, newspaper correspondents were packing their bags and trying to book tickets on all airlines (which did not at this point include British Airways) able to fly them to Buenos Aires. An avalanche of newsmen began descending on the city. Once there, quite a few of them began making determined efforts to get to the Falklands, but were frustrated by strict controls placed by the Argentine Government on air and sea transportation. The newsmen had to be content with the briefing facilities provided in the capital, and these were extensive. Every morning a press conference was given at the Ministry of Defence, which was televised not only for domestic consumption but also for the benefit of foreign networks.

At these morning conferences, chaired usually by General Gonzalez or Admiral Vasquez, the same messages were unremittingly (and ultimately monotonously) hammered home. The apparent aggression had been brought about by Britain's continued refusal to negotiate in a meaningful way: it had been carried out in a way most economical of casualties, in fact in the most humane way. Yes, a nerve gas had been used. No, it was not a killer – it just knocked you out for some hours: you get gas when you go to the dentist, don't you? This did not impress every correspondent.

The main feature emphasized by the service spokesmen was that this was a very limited form of occupation, wholly consonant with the suggestion that, once sovereignty had been conceded, the Malvinas population should be left very much to themselves to run their own lives in a devolved status within the overall framework of the Argentine state. It had been a serious mistake to try to impose a fully military occupation in 1982, but the mistake was inevitable then because of the near-certainty that the British would try to retake the islands. Those considerations did not apply now.

What if the British do try to retake the islands? was the correspondents' question. Then we should have to defend them, was the answer. We are in a position to pour in massive reinforcements at very short notice. But we do not think that will be necessary: it would be manifestly unreasonable of the British, in the new circumstances which exist today, to try to mount an expedition. In the unlikely event that they do, with the improved weapons and systems now at our disposal we would expect to be victorious: but we repeat that a far more likely result is that meaningful negotiations will quickly get under way and lead to a permanent solution to the Malvinas problem which will prove fair and satisfactory to all.

In spite of the newsmens' frustration at not being able to visit the islands (for the Government's ban was strictly enforced within Argentina, and successful efforts were also made to persuade the neighbouring countries not to allow facilities), they did on the whole sound in their despatches, during these first few critical days, a fairly understanding note. In spite of the aggression and the use of gas, the approach adopted by the Argentine authorities did seem to be a considerable advance on 1982, and to offer some prospects of producing a reasonable settlement of a difficult and intractable problem. Argentina received, on the whole, a fairly good press in the world's newspapers; but now the eyes of the world turned to Britain to see what her response would be.

12

The party which assembled in the Cabinet Room at 10
Downing Street shortly after eight-thirty am on Thursday
morning consisted of the Defence Minister, Sir Henry Jones;
the Chief of the Defence Staff, Admiral of the Fleet Sir Thomas
Higgins; and the First Sea Lord, Admiral Sir Douglas Green-
acre, whom Higgins had co-opted as soon as he received his
own early-morning summons. The party had called at the
Defence Ministry in order to take in the latest news before
going on to Downing Street. They found the Prime Minister
impatient and anxious, as they took their seats on the other side
of the Cabinet table.

The first thing to emerge was that there was, at that stage,
very little more news. The duty officer at the Ministry had
spoken, shortly before the top brass came in, to the Garrison
Commander, who had only been able to tell him that it was
still dark, but that all preparations had been made to clear up
the incursion, whatever it amounted to, at daybreak. The
Brigadier had also said that the general opinion there was that
the incursion was a serious one, but that in view of the limited
numbers which could be carried in a 747 it would require
reinforcement to be credible: in view of these suppositions, an
air attack was to be expected because without one the reinforcements had no hope of landing: the silence of the two Rapier
posts was also indicative of this theory: they were therefore
planning on that basis. The duty officer had also put through a
call to the Governor, whom he had found aware of what had so
far happened (having been kept informed by Mount Pleasant),
but unable to add any further information to what the
Garrison Commander had said. He did, however, add that he
understood the soldiers discounted a seaborne invasion: whatever was happening seemed likely to be an aerial affair.

In summer, the Falklands are four hours behind London.

However, May in London is November in Stanley: dawn does not break there until about seven am. These factors had not been in the Prime Minister's mind when he was awoken early that morning by the bedside telephone: he had called his advisers forward too soon. Nevertheless, there was quite a lot to talk about, on a hypothetical basis.

'If the Garrison Commander is right,' the Prime Minister said, 'how do you see this attack going?' Rather unexpectedly for all the others in the room, he had not dwelt unduly on the circumstances of the 747 being allowed to land. Consideration of the point over the cornflakes had led to his admitting to himself that if he had been one of the duty officers at the Ministry of Defence he would have responded exactly as they did.

'I think, Prime Minister,' Admiral Higgins said, 'we are all inclined to agree with the Garrison Commander. It can't be just a gang of loonies. They would not have been able to organize it. It has to have the full resources of the Argentine forces behind it, therefore it has to be a serious attack. Because I agree they can't be coming by sea and must be coming by air, there has to be a serious air attack to neutralize the defences, otherwise the back-up people won't be able to land. This actually ties up quite well with the information we had last year, about the increased flying activity in Patagonia: we bumped up the garrison a bit, if you recollect. Well, I think the people there are right in expecting a massive air attack.'

'And how will that go?'

'I can't say, Prime Minister. All one can say is that their aircraft that can reach the Falklands are now mostly very old. Also, last time round the course they were not very good at co-ordinating their attacks and choosing their targets. They may do better this time, because basically they've just got one very big target. But it's very well defended: the Phantoms will knock them down like skittles, one after the other.'

'Well,' said the Prime Minister, 'we clearly won't know very much until about two or three hours' time. Then we may be told it's all about nothing, or it has been contained. We're in limbo until then. Meanwhile, is there anything we can usefully do?'

'For the moment, not much that we have not already done,' said the Minister of Defence. 'As soon as you rang me this morning I had the spearhead battalion, 2nd Battalion Parachute Regiment that is, put on two hours' notice to move. When we went into the Ministry and heard what the duty officer had to say, we gave orders for immediate emplacement. They're on their way to Lyneham and Brize Norton now. With them we're sending a medical team from a field ambulance, and also some spare gunners in case the Rapiers get roughed up. They refuel at Ascension, and go on from there when ordered. Of course things might not turn out quite so serious as we anticipate, in which case they can stay at Ascension for a bit. The authorities at Wideawake airfield have been warned. We felt we had to do this at once, Prime Minister: I hope you approve.'

'I certainly do,' he said. 'Now, quite clearly we shall have no more news until it's daylight down there. You will all be better off at the Ministry for a bit, and I have to rearrange my day here. Shall we meet here again at, say, eleven-thirty?'

The Minister and the two admirals went out into Downing Street and walked over to the Ministry of Defence. They checked with the duty officer for more news (he had none) and then went into the big map room where a huge map of the South Atlantic dominated half of one of the walls. They sat down and rang for coffee. The day staff of the Ministry was beginning to come in. The night duty officer had just been relieved and came in to ask permission to go home. He was not very happy about what had happened during his tour of duty, and did not know quite what to expect. He was relieved when Admiral Higgins told him they all felt he and his superior had been bowled a horrible googly, and could not have been expected to play it in any other way. The Prime Minister, the Admiral added, seemed to be of the same opinion, because he had not said very much about it.

All three men had morning schedules to rearrange, and this took some time. That done, the Chiefs of the Army and Air Staffs, who had come quickly into the Ministry after being telephoned, had to be briefed. It was agreed that the rest of No 23 (Phantom) Squadron RAF, based at Scampton in Lincolnshire, should proceed immediately to Ascension en route for the Falklands. The other two battalions of 5th Airborne Brigade were put on two hours' notice to move, as were their transport aircraft.

There remained the Navy. All were agreed that, while the problem at present appeared unlikely to be primarily a naval one, certain preparations had to be made. While it was still uncertain what the naval requirements might be, it was agreed that a squadron of two aircraft-carriers and four destroyers, with a sufficient 'fleet train' to nourish it at sea for several months, should be assembled and sent to the South Atlantic. Of the Navy's carriers, *Ark Royal* was in the Persian Gulf. *Illustrious* had just entered the Mediterranean on her way to Hong Kong: she was ordered to turn round, take on some extra stores at Gibraltar, and rendezvous there with *Invincible*, which would sail from Portsmouth next day. The destroyers would come from various directions, as would the ships of the fleet train.

Both aircraft-carriers had on board their normal complement of five Sea Harriers and nine Sea King 5 Helicopters. A second Fleet submarine, the *Spartan*, would sail from Faslane to reinforce *Sceptre*.

No more could reasonably be done for the moment, but by the time it had all been done the clock had advanced quite a long way towards eleven-thirty.

Shortly before they were due to go over to Downing Street, HMS *Sceptre*'s message was received, and the reply sent. It was not possible, in the circumstances, to send any other. As they walked over from the Ministry, Sir Henry Jones and the service heads agreed that this was a sinister development, but that at least it did appear to diminish still further the likelihood of any seaborne invasion: if almost the whole Argentine navy was so engaged, they could not also be convoying troop-carrying ships.

☆   ☆   ☆

The telephone call made by Rear-Admiral of Marine Infantry Ricarda to Government House in Port Stanley was answered by the Governor's secretary. 'Yes, His Excellency is here: who is calling?' The Admiral, in his excellent but by no means unaccented English, announced himself. The Governor came to the telephone.

Sir Hereward Gurney was an unusual diplomat. Nearing the end of his career, he had surprised the Permanent Under

130

Secretary by hinting that he would actually like to be sent to the Falklands if that post fell vacant, as it shortly did. He was a widower, and now the ruling passions of his lonely life were birds and animals, particularly penguins and seals, and the wild and beautiful, sometimes inhospitable, places where these creatures lived. He was very happy in the Falklands, as he had known he would be. He enjoyed the informal society of hard-working farmers and fishermen. Also, there was now actually quite a lot of work to be done, with the large visiting foreign fishing fleets and the new contacts with Argentinian agencies and companies which required careful handling.

He had been woken in the middle of the night by the Brigadier at Mount Pleasant, who had told him the story of the British Airways 747's landing, its non-appearance at the head-quarters tarmac, the dispatch of the duty platoon to investigate, the non-return (after audible shooting) of that platoon, and the lack of contact with two of the Rapier posts. The Brigadier had told him how he proposed to deal with what clearly seemed to be some sort of hostile incursion, and of his fears that further air-landings might be preceded by heavy air-attacks: any seaborne attack appeared to be most unlikely. The Governor had gone back to bed, which seemed the most sensible thing to do; but he had then been awoken again by a call from the Ministry of Defence duty officer in London, to whom he had told all he knew. After that he had failed to go back to sleep and had been lying awake when, shortly after seven o'clock, a number of aircraft coming from the east had nearly taken the roof off Government House. After that, the sky had been full of aircraft coming from all directions: he had watched from his bedroom window the big Phantoms swooping on the attackers, the explosions and balls of flame which the missile hits caused, and the columns of black smoke which indicated that another attacker had hit the ground. He had also observed a large volume of anti-aircraft fire from the airfield and its surrounding eminences, both missile and cannon-fire. It had been clear that the attackers were subjecting Mount Pleasant to a heavy bombing attack, although curiously enough he heard few bomb explosions. It had all been over in five minutes, and then he had been unable to raise anyone at Mount Pleasant on the telephone, although he had tried repeatedly. He had contacted the Commissioner of Police and the Harbour Master, but neither of them could tell him anything he did not already know. He had had another call from the Ministry of Defence, and had been able to tell them that there had been a heavy air attack, and that he was unable to get through to anyone at Mount Pleasant. He had been on the point of getting into his official Range Rover and going over to the airfield when the call came through.

When his surprised secretary told him that a Rear-Admiral of Marine Infantry Ricarda was on the telephone, Sir Hereward had a nasty feeling at the pit of his stomach. Surely not? It couldn't be. He took the instrument.

'Señor Governor,' said the voice on the other end, 'I am an Argentinian admiral and a force of Marines under my command has just occupied the British base at Mount Pleasant. I am speaking from the garrison headquarters. We are in full control and the entire British garrison are our prisoners.'

Sir Hereward Gurney had the sensation that he was not really there: he was somewhere else, in a bad dream. 'I suppose you came in the 747?' was all he found to say.

'We did indeed, Señor Governor. We then put in a successful attack after, ah, preparation by our air forces.'

'So I understand you to say that the whole British garrison are your prisoners? Are there large numbers of casualties?'

'Fortunately not, Señor Governor. The air forces attacked with a paralysing gas which neutralized the garrison so that not much fighting was necessary. The main body of prisoners are temporarily incapacitated, but I assure you they will suffer no permanent damage. They are to be repatriated to London, via Argentina, very shortly. I do however have just over twenty British wounded and about half a dozen of my own men. Some of the British are quite bad, and I would like to ask you for your help. May I send the bad cases, about twelve actually, to your hospital in Stanley?'

'You amaze me, Admiral,' said Sir Hereward. 'As for the wounded men, of course we can help. How shall we arrange this?'

'There are, Señor Governor, a number of matters which I should like to discuss with you in person. May I suggest that you assemble as many ambulances as you can, and bring them to the eastern perimeter gate of this camp? No doubt you would like to bring a police escort, but they must please be

132

unarmed. What sort of car will you come in? A black Range Rover, flying your official pennant? Good. Shall we say in forty minutes' time? I will meet you at the gate, and I suggest we can talk in your car about a number of things we have to discuss. I ought to tell you briefly that we do not intend to occupy Stanley or, in fact, anywhere outside the two airfields. We intend to leave you to carry on the administration of the rest of the islands in your own way. So we have to talk about such things as food supplies. I will explain all this fully when we meet. Thank you, Señor Governor: in forty minutes then.'

Sir Hereward Gurney put down the telephone in a daze. His secretary, who had been listening on an extension earphone, looked at him like an owl. For both of them, it was unbelievable, but it had to be believed.

'Right,' said the Governor at last. 'Get hold of the Commissioner of Police and tell him I want him and one of his trucks, no arms, to escort me. Find the Chief Medical Officer and tell him we have to take in a dozen or so badly wounded men in the hospital; and we need ambulances to set off from here with me, as soon as they can get together. Me, I'm going to call London.'

☆   ☆   ☆

At the appointed hour the Ministry of Defence party, now augmented by a General and an Air Chief Marshal, assembled once more at 10 Downing Street. It was a fine May morning. At the back of the old house, the Queen's Guard was being mounted from Horse Guards Parade, in early rehearsal for the Queen's Birthday Parade which was to take place early in the following month. What Harold Macmillan had once rather petulantly referred to as 'the constant repetition of the *March from Figaro*, was, all too audibly, in full swing.

As well as the Prime Minister, the Cabinet Secretary, Sir Humphrey Williams, was in the Cabinet Room. The ministerial party sat down, and Sir Henry at once told the Prime Minister of *Sceptre's* message and the inferences which the chiefs of staff drew from it. He finished by saying '*Sceptre* is of course in a position to sink the aircraft-carrier. However, that may be a rather difficult question.'

'Difficult indeed,' said the Cabinet Secretary, 'What if it was

133

only a training exercise? Murder on the high seas, in time of peace? Prime Minister, you can't do it. Think of all those questions from the member for Linlithgow for the next five years!'

This relieved the tension, and was so obviously right that there could be no argument about it. 'Poor Tam, he doesn't know what a chance we're not giving him,' said the Prime Minister.

It was agreed that circumstances could change if the incident was to develop as it seemed likely to. *Sceptre* was to stay in touch and await orders. Similar instructions were to be given to the frigate *Alacrity* which had also been shadowing the Argentine force.

Apart from that, there was little fresh news as yet, and what there was was not good. For the past half-hour it had become impossible to raise an answer from Mount Pleasant. However, the Governor had been reached, and he had said that a very heavy air attack had just taken place with many attacking planes shot down, but that he also could not get any answer from Mount Pleasant. He undertook to go on trying, and if necessary to go and see for himself, and to put a call through as soon as he had found out anything. There, for the moment, things had to rest. It was not much good ringing up anyone else in Port Stanley, because they would know no more than the Governor.

'This is obviously good for the character,' observed the Prime Minister. 'I can't recollect being so frustrated or anxious. Charles, are you sure all the telephone hook-ups are in place?'

His Private Secretary, who was about to leave the room, paused. 'Yes, Prime Minister,' he said patiently. 'The Ministry of Defence and Foreign Office switchboards have absolutely categorical instructions to transfer any call through here. Our own girls know all about it, but I'll just go and encourage them.'

'Thank you, Charles. I'm sorry. I'm sure all is arranged.'

So for another thirty minutes or so they all had to fill in time: well, not exactly. The arrangements so far made by the Minister and the Chiefs of Staff were explained to the Prime Minister. He indicated his approval, and then the telephone at his elbow rang. 'Governor, Falklands, on the line,' said the No

10 operator.

Although curiously disembodied, as all satellite transmissions seem to be, the voice from Port Stanley was audible and clear.

'Hereward Gurney here, who am I speaking to?'

'The Prime Minister, Sir Hereward. I have all the Chiefs of Staff here, and the Minister of Defence. They are all listening, so please go ahead.' The Prime Minister had switched on the general receiver set, so all in the room heard the governor's words.

'Prime Minister, I have very bad news indeed for you. I am sure you know what I told the MOD earlier: that there was a very heavy air attack early this morning. Since then I have had no contact with Mount Pleasant. I have just been telephoned from there by a man who says he is an Argentine Marine Admiral, and he says the air attackers used some sort of paralysing gas which knocked out the entire garrison. What was that? Yes, the entire garrison. Knocked out, he said, not killed; apparently they will recover and the intention is to fly them all back to England via Argentina within the next day or so. Meanwhile, I'm afraid the Argentines have taken over the whole airfield camp, and they are in complete control.'

'Does that mean that our planes cannot land?'

'Yes, Prime Minister, I suppose it does. I think, it can't mean anything else. I am due to go and talk to this Admiral in a few minutes' time. There are a few British wounded, only about a dozen I understand, whom we are going to take into hospital here. This Admiral says he is in no way going to disturb me or my administration here, and he wants to talk about whether we have enough food supplies for the islands. It is all very strange: he says he and his men are going to stay on the airfield, and they won't occupy Port Stanley, or in fact anywhere except the two airfields.'

'I find that hard to believe,' the Prime Minister said, 'but we shall see. I don't understand about this paralysing gas; and how can people recover so fast if they've been gassed as badly as that?'

'I don't understand either, Prime Minister, but I am due to meet the Admiral at the airfield perimeter in a short while, and I'll get as much information out of him as I can. He seems a reasonable sort of man and speaks good English: he was Naval

Attaché in London I believe – name of Ricarda: the admirals will probably remember him. May I suggest, Prime Minister, that I go to this appointment now, because I've told you all I know. Then I will call you back as soon as I can and fill in some gaps. Shall I ask for you, or what?'

'Call the Foreign Office as you normally do, Sir Hereward, and for today at least the call will automatically be put through to me. As you know, Parliament is not sitting. We have cleared our desks and schedules for today, and will be in continuous session here. So go on calling your usual contact, and we will organize at this end who actually speaks to you. I am relieved that you are unharmed. Obviously you will find out what he means about only occupying the airfield, and whether it really means you are going to be left to run the islands as usual. The other thing is – will you find out for sure whether the soldiers are really all right, and what the arrangements for their repatriation are? I think that's all for the moment. Yes, thank you, Sir Hereward. Goodbye.'

There was quite a long silence in the Cabinet Room. The muted roar of the traffic in Whitehall could be clearly heard. On the other side, *Figaro* was finished, and the diminishing sound of the massed bands indicated that the Guards had left the Horse Guards Parade.

'Well, gentlemen,' the Prime Minister finally said, 'this is just about as bad as it could be. We're stymied. The spearhead battalion won't be able to land: obviously they'd better stay at Ascension for the time being. We've been humbugged, by God, humbugged. Goodness knows where this is going to lead.'

Nobody disagreed with him, and nobody could think of anything intelligent to say: there were still too many unresolved questions. But at that moment the private secretary came in with a telex sheet, saying

'Prime Minister, this is just in from our Embassy in Buenos Aires. As you will see, it is the text of an announcement made on radio and television a short time ago. Your Press Secretary has a copy and he is already dealing with calls from the media.'

'Read it out, will you, Charles, as there's only one copy.' The private secretary did so. When he had finished the Minister of Defence exclaimed,

'Well, that fills in a few gaps. It seems to be a naval and military thing, behind the backs of the politicians. They've arrested the President, presumably because they knew they wouldn't get any change out of him. I bet that right now they're putting the screws on all the other politicians to make them toe the line.'

The Cabinet Secretary spoke up. 'The interesting bit, Prime Minister, is that these military people seem to have an entirely new political line. Softly, softly, we won't do anything except what is necessary to stop the British sending reinforcements, and it will all be settled peacefully by international arbitration, and then we'll give the islanders total freedom in practice, with just nominal Argentine sovereignty. Whoever thought this up is a subtle operator: it's a very good sales pitch.'

'Well, I'm not a buyer, Sir Humphrey,' the Prime Minister remarked. 'I'm not a buyer at all. It's barefaced, unprovoked aggression, just as it was in 1982, and I'm not standing for it, not for one minute. What a laughing-stock we are going to be in the world: a whole battalion caught unawares, the defence system overwhelmed by a lot of twenty-year-old aircraft, and then that crazy story about the 747.

'Obviously we must try and solve the problem through the United Nations, but in my judgement we have to consider the military option as well. I suppose we can assemble another Task Force? Sir Thomas, what's your answer to that?'

The Chief of the Defence Staff looked at his colleagues before replying. 'My first reaction is that, as in 1982, it will be first and foremost a Navy show. The General has confirmed to me that he can find the troops on that scale, including the Marine Commandos of course, and I also gather the RAF could do once more all the things they did last time. The Navy position is a little more complicated: may I ask the First Sea Lord to explain?'

The mantle of Sir Henry Leach thus fell gently on the shoulders of Admiral Greenacre. He did not seem to wear it too comfortably, but he spoke up.

'Yes, Prime Minister,' he said slowly. 'I agree with Sir Thomas. We can do it, and it goes without saying that we will do it if we are ordered to. I must be honest – and I trust you will not misunderstand me – and say that I hope it will not prove to be necessary. I say that for two reasons: one, although we are in some respects better off for warships than we were in 1982, and they are better armed, on the other hand we are going to find it very much more difficult to get the merchant ships we need from the trade sector. There just are not enough ships now flying the Red Duster to enable us to make a proper choice for what we need. We shall be forced to charter in some foreign-owned ships, and of course we can't use requisitioning powers there, and there are all sorts of problems. A further difficulty is dockyard capacity for converting merchant ships to our specifications: the run-down of the dockyards has now gone so far that it will not be easy to get all the necessary work done. Those are the principal snags: I suppose we can get over them, and we will, but it is not going to be very easy. Finally, may I venture to say that we all realize that we were extraordinarily lucky last time round. Very nearly every small warship in the Task Force was hit by a bomb which did not explode. None of the big ships was hit and neither of the big troop transporters; and it would have been difficult if any of them had been. I don't know whether we shall have as much good luck second time round: we might easily have very heavy casualties, on a scale that might not only necessitate the abandonment of the expedition but might also seriously affect our capacity to play our part in the global integrated arrangements with our allies.'

'Well, thank you, Sir Douglas,' the Prime Minister said, 'we shall have to think about those points of difficulty you mention; but I am relieved to hear you say that it can be done. As to possible casualties, that is a risk one always runs in war. We were certainly lucky in 1982, but we deserved our luck. Our cause was a just one, and it is a just one now. If we cannot get this put right in New York, we shall have to consider sending a task force. That means we have to start preparing for it now, on a contingency basis.

Sir Humphrey Williams, who had been studying his blotter with some intensity, now coughed and said,

'Prime Minister, may I be forgiven for reminding you that this is not just a naval and military problem: it is also a political problem – both domestic and international. In meeting force with force, you have to carry with you not only your own Cabinet colleagues (and I assume you will succeed in doing that) but also Parliament, and that could be more difficult. Your overall majority is only twenty, and a few abstentions could make things tricky. It is really going to be a question of what public opinion in the country thinks, what comes up to the members of parliament from the grass roots: pray God it will not be another Suez sort of climate. Finally, we have got to pull it off internationally as we did in 1982, with our allies, with the EC and at the United Nations. That bothers me a bit: I am not sure this new line the Argentines are taking may not make the international going a bit more difficult.'

'I can vouch for the Cabinet, I think,' the Prime Minister said. 'What do you think, Sir Henry?'

The Defence Minister paused before replying. 'Yes, I think so,' he finally said. 'I can think of one or two who won't like it too well, but I believe they will go along with it. I think you must realize, we must all realize, that this is going to cause an enormous sensation in the country. I agree with Sir Humphrey that we should not take public opinion for granted: surely we shall have to recall Parliament?'

'Not recall, Sir Henry: call. Parliament was dissolved before the Election.' This was the Cabinet Secretary speaking again. 'I am not sure, but I don't think there is any precedent for actually calling a new Parliament early, as opposed to recalling a sitting Parliament. I shall have to consult the Speaker and the clerks of the House of Commons: but in fact my belief is that, precedent or not, somehow it has to be done, on Saturday too: in my view this is too important to wait till next week: the regular opening by the Queen is on Thursday, so with any luck all the emergency debates will be over by then, and the Queen's speech can happen normally. Do you agree, Prime Minister?'

'Yes,' he said, 'let's try and do that. I certainly don't think we can wait until the opening, and we also don't want this to be mixed up with the Queen's speech business. Do what you can, would you, Sir Humphrey?'

'Now,' he went on, 'we have to organize ourselves for today. I think we should remain together here: by this evening we ought to know for sure what the position is: the Governor will have rung back, and hopefully he will know whether they are going to let him stay: then we can settle communications procedure. I believe we are going to have to have a "war cabinet" like we had in 1982: that means the Foreign Secretary and the Chairman of the Party must join us: Sir Henry and Sir Thomas will present Service matters, bringing the Chiefs of

Staff with them as they think desirable. I suggest we have some lunch here. But first we must find out what my Press Secretary has been doing – I should think all hell has broken out on his front.'

So the wheels of war began to turn, while a shocked and amazed country, alerted by the BBC's hourly radio news bulletins and then by the one o'clock television news, began to ask ten thousand and one angry and bewildered questions.

The Governor's call came through to No 10 just after half-past three in the afternoon. Lunch had been an affair of sandwiches and Perrier water. The First Sea Lord and the two other Chiefs of Staff had gone to the ministry to attend to various pressing matters, and had returned: they reported that a throng of newspapermen and television reporters and cameramen had assembled in Downing Street and were avid for news: they were being kept in play by the indefatigable Press Secretary, but there was no doubt who they wanted to talk to.

'Later,' said the Prime Minister.

The Foreign Secretary had come in to join them. A call had been received from the Queen's private secretary: it had been explained that a lot more information was likely to be available by the end of the afternoon, and the Prime Minister had undertaken to go to the Palace at six o'clock in order to brief Her Majesty as fully as possible on the situation and on the Government's intentions.

The Governor gave a full account of his meeting with Rear-Admiral Ricarda. As arranged, he had been accompanied by the Commissioner of Police and a few of his men, and by the requested ambulances. The twelve badly-wounded RAF Regiment and Gunner soldiers, who were accompanied to the gate by an Argentine medical officer and orderlies, had been transferred to the ambulances: two journeys had to be made to take them all. Admiral Ricarda, immaculately dressed in combat fatigues, was also there: a Marine guard was positioned some distance behind the gate. Ricarda had saluted and then they had both got into the back seat of the Governor's Range Rover, and had talked.

The Admiral first showed Sir Hereward Gurney the text of

the announcement which was at that moment being released in Buenos Aires. He explained at length that this was a completely new approach, not only to the immediate military problem but also long-term. With the taking of the airfield, and the consequent inability of the British to reinforce, there was no necessity for him to occupy anywhere else, and that fitted in perfectly with the political objectives described in the announcement. There had to be one exception – he did not know what condition the old Stanley airfield was in, and airborne troops under his command would shortly land there to investigate: it was likely that they would stay there in order to ensure that the facilities could not be used with hostile intent against his own forces on the new airfield: he asked that there be no resistance to his airborne forces, as that would be pointless and futile, and would only serve still further to stretch the medical facilities available on the island. Sir Hereward said he had felt it advisable to accede to this suggestion, but he had asked whether a few light aircraft and helicopters, which were usually employed on business connected with the large visiting foreign fishing fleets, might be allowed to continue to use the strip. Ricarda had reserved his position on that one, but had said he would try to oblige.

Of course, Ricarda had gone on to say, the non-occupation policy was dependent on the British not sending any Task Force to retake the islands as they had done in 1982. His masters in Buenos Aires well appreciated that London, in the first shock of the coup, might initiate some preparations, as it were by reflex action; but if that developed into a regular expedition with serious intent, then of course Argentina would have to pour thousands of troops, and many aircraft, into the islands in order to be able to defend them. He personally thought this was very unlikely to happen, but that was the position.

They had gone on to discuss the Governor's position. Eventually, the Admiral had said, on a political solution being reached, it would be inappropriate to have an actual British Governor. The senior person in the islands would have to be Argentinian, but the long-term idea was for locals to take over the top administrative posts, and until that happened (and it was appreciated that it might not happen for some years) there would be no objection to expatriate British officials continuing to do all the things they did now. Meanwhile, carry on as before: my Brigade-Major and the Marine battalion Commander speak good English, you (I understand) speak excellent Spanish, and the telephones lines are open. A free exchange should take place.

Supply was then discussed. The Admiral said that the comparatively small Argentine force would be supplied by air from the mainland: but what about the civilian needs? Agreements in principle were reached that the normal visiting supply ships could dock: this was a sector which would need working out in more detail when the Governor had found out the minutiae of the supply situation, but basically all supplies necessary for the needs of the civil population and the residual military details would be allowed in, if necessary from Argentina with the co-operation of the British Navy, subject to there being no abuse in the way of infiltrating military elements.

Finally, the Governor said, the Admiral had requested that he give an undertaking that no hostile actions would be made against his garrison, which was forbearing to act as a normal invasion force.

The Governor had replied that he was certainly prepared, as he had said, to undertake that there would be no resistance to the landing of the airborne forces at the old Stanley airfield. Further than that, he formally could not go. As the admiral perfectly well knew, the forces at his disposal were now minimal – a very few police, a local Defence Force, which was frankly a joke, and various military details – a few naval people in the harbour, and the Royal Engineer detachments still clearing the mines: half of them were of Ukrainian descent, sons of Ukrainians who had come to Britain from the Polish forces in Italy in 1945, and had thereafter served in special units under British army control, clearing over many years the thousands of unexploded projectiles littered over the field-firing ranges throughout Britain: their grandsons were now in East Falkland, doing the same thing. It was unlikely in the highest degree, as the Admiral must well know, that any offensive actions could be mounted against his strong garrison of professional regular troops by these minimal forces.

Having said that, the Governor insisted he could go no further. He was the Queen's loyal servant, and could enter into no formal undertakings without authorization from London:

the Admiral had seemed well content.

That was about it, the Governor said. The Admiral had been very correct, very sensible, and very friendly. It seemed to him that they really meant what they said: they did not need for the moment to occupy the whole of the islands, and did not intend to do so. He was going to be left to organize the islanders' life until there was an ultimate political settlement.

'Or military settlement, Sir Hereward,' observed the Prime Minister.

'Well, of course, yes. But then, in that event, the whole thing would change: we'd be right back in 1982. I expect if that happened, they would ship me out, but that would not be of too much significance.'

'That could happen. We have, of course, already made certain preparations. Whether they will develop into a full-blown Task Force expedition remains to be seen. We will keep you posted. Thank you, Sir Hereward: you have done all the right things. We shall of course be in consent telephone contact with you. Now, is there anything else for the moment?'

'Yes, Prime Minister, there is. I need a secure line. I presume that our conversation is monitored and overheard: that may not be the case, but one has to presume that it is so. I must, I simply must, have a secure way of talking to you, to everyone in London, without risk of being overheard. You will understand why, in due course.'

'Yes, I see, Sir Hereward, but there are no scramblers at your end. It looks difficult.'

'Prime Minister, my Commissioner of Police here was an Army officer until five years ago. Will you or someone please note these details? Martin, Major Peter John Martin, service number 468502. He was a regular officer, he'll be in the MOD records, and so will his qualifications. When you look at the records you will see what he is good at, and then it will be easy for you to find someone who is good at the same thing, and put him on the end of my telephone contact. Do you understand me? I must insist that this is of the highest importance.'

'I understand, Sir Hereward. It will be looked up, and you will be told over the open line when we have done so. Meanwhile, many thanks. Keep the flag flying.'

☆　　☆　　☆

143

When the Army Records Office in York produced on demand of maximum urgency the records of Major Peter John Martin, service number 468502, late 2nd/2nd Duke of Edinburgh's Own Gurkha Rifles, it was seen that he had passed, during his service with the regiment, every examination in the Gurkhali language (for which, most properly, he had received an extra pay increment) and was considered to be ninety-eight percent proficient.

It was then a fairly simple matter to find a suitable officer from the Gurkha battalion stationed at Aldershot to act as telephone link.

13

A British public already almost sated with politics after a four-week-long election campaign was now plunged into further convulsions. The news from the Falklands, which had begun to be known throughout the country just before lunch on that fateful Thursday, was by evening practically the only subject of conversation everywhere. The media were crazy for news: every Minister who might be thought to have any knowledge of, or responsibility for what had happened was pressed to give a television interview that evening. All refused, the Prime Minister having let it be known that only the briefest of statements would be made until Parliament assembled on Saturday. A huge crowd of journalists and television crews was assembled in Downing Street, and every caller had to run the gauntlet as he arrived. Microphones were thrust at Ministers: none responded.

At ten minutes to six in the evening the door of No 10 opened, and the Prime Minister came out with the Secretary for Defence, Sir Henry Jones, and his press secretary. The Prime Minister's car was waiting at the kerb. The press secretary had a microphone which he set up beside the car: the Prime Minister took it and the throng fell silent under the glare of the great television arc lights.

'I am going to ask the Secretary of State for Defence to make a brief statement on the very serious events which have taken place in the South Atlantic,' was all he said: he then handed the microphone to Sir Henry, the car door was opened by a policeman, he got in, and the car sped away towards Buckingham Palace and his audience with the Queen. It was all done in a few seconds. A great groan went up from the crowd of reporters, but there was nothing they could do about it. The Defence Secretary stood waiting with the microphone, and soon they quietened.

'In the early hours of this morning,' the Minister began, 'the Ministry of Defence was informed on behalf of the Garrison Commander, Falklands, that a British Airways 747 airliner was requesting emergency permission to land at Mount Pleasant military airfield: the aircraft was stated to be short of fuel: at that stage it was assumed that a normal complement of passengers was being carried, and the explanation of the emergency given by the captain of the aircraft appeared to be a credible one. The Ministry of Defence therefore gave permission for the aircraft to be allowed to land, but emphasized that security precautions should be taken to cover the eventuality that some trick or deception was being practiced.

'When the aircraft landed it quickly became clear that this was the case. It remained at the far end of the runway, and the duty platoon when it went to investigate was fired on by greatly superior numbers of armed men: all members of the platoon became casualties or were taken prisoner. These events took place in darkness, it being just before midnight, local time.

'These developments were quickly reported to the Ministry of Defence by the Garrison Commander, who stated that he was treating the incursion as a full-scale emergency, with which he proposed to deal with his full strength as soon as daylight came: he did not consider it practicable to take offensive action against the intruders during the hours of darkness.

'The Ministry of Defence has been informed of what followed by the Governor of the Falkland Islands, who has been, and still is in telephone communication with us. He tells us that, at earliest dawn today, very heavy air attacks were delivered by a large number of hostile aircraft at very low level using bombs; the attacks were pressed home in spite of heavy casualties caused to the attackers by our own fighter aircraft and anti-aircraft defences. Subsequent to these attacks the Governor was unable to make any contact with the garrison for several hours: he was eventually telephoned by a person who described himself as an Argentine Admiral, who stated that chemical bombs had been used containing a paralysing nerve-gas which had incapacitated the entire British garrison, who were thereupon made prisoners by an Argentine force which had landed in the British Airways aircraft.

'The Governor has since told us that he has met with the

Argentine Admiral in order, first, to arrange to take over a number of wounded British personnel and, secondly, to discuss the administration of the islands in the situation which now exists. He was given to understand that the effect of the nerve-gas used is temporary, and that it is the intention to repatriate all the unwounded British personnel to the United Kingdom as soon as possible: the Government is already in touch with the International Red Cross on this aspect.

'The Governor was further given to understand that the Argentine forces intend merely to occupy the airfield and perhaps also the old airfield at Port Stanley, and do not intend to interfere for the time being with the Governor or his administration. Further information on these aspects is keenly awaited, but attention is drawn to the statement issued in Buenos Aires earlier today by the Argentine armed forces, which appears in some degree to confirm what the Governor has been told.

'Action is being taken to call a meeting of the United Nations Security Council as soon as possible: the Government intends to press for the adoption of a resolution condemning this act of barefaced and unprovoked aggression, deploring the use of chemical weapons, and calling upon Argentina to remove her forces. We are also in touch with the United States Government and with our other NATO allies and our partners in the European Community and the Commonwealth.

'Steps are being taken to summon Parliament early, so that an emergency statement on these events may be made on Saturday. Her Majesty the Queen will then open Parliament formally, as arranged, next Thursday for normal business.

'A further statement will be made tomorrow if any fresh information, particularly on the repatriation of the British garrison and their state of health, and also about British casualties, becomes available. Our present information is that British casualties, apart from the incapacitation by gas, amount to fourteen killed and twenty wounded, of whom twelve are serious cases and have been transferred to the hospital in Port Stanley. No names are yet available.'

As Sir Henry finished a babel of questions arose. He merely shook his head, turned round and went back into No 10. The press secretary held up his hands for silence, and when he had obtained it, said:

'I'm sorry, no questions can be answered until the matter is discussed in the House of Commons on Saturday. Copies of the statement the Defence Secretary has just made will be available in the normal way. That is all: you will be informed through the usual channels if a further statement is to be made tomorrow. Meanwhile you won't see the Defence Secretary here as he won't be coming out this way. Goodnight.' And he too turned, carrying the microphone and its lead with him, and re-entered No 10. The door was shut, and after a while the media crowd began to disperse. Not for the first time, Sir Henry Jones was thankful that the private tunnel under Whitehall was there for him to use.

During the next twenty-four hours intense debate ensued on all the television channels and in the newspapers. There was naturally great anxiety about the condition of the British garrison. The public in Britain is not well informed about the latest binary nerve-gases, and no-one felt too sure about accepting at face value the statement that the effect of this one was only to cause temporary paralysis. The very word 'paralysis' induced anxiety: paralysis, as so many unfortunates know, has a way of proving to be permanent, and the spectre of nearly a thousand men of the Mercian Regiment, Royal Artillery, Royal Air Force and others being permanent sufferers from some degree of disability was a most disquieting one, which would not be laid to rest until the airliners chartered by the Argentine Government under Red Cross supervision began to arrive at Brize Norton at the weekend. There were no military bands to meet these men, only anxious doctors and a few relatives who had got to know of the impending arrivals. The men who came down the aircraft steps were very pale and very quiet: none of them had any physical disability, and none of them seemed to want to talk very much. It would not be right to say that they seemed to feel humiliated: their actual feelings were much more complex – they had nothing to be proud of, but on the other hand it had in no way been their fault. But the stuffing had been knocked out of them: they had had a shattering experience, one which had simply left them all glad to be alive. None of them had any complaints about the conduct of their Marine captors, or of those who had received and processed them on their arrival on the Patagonian mainland. All they wanted to do was to go home and try to forget about it. This was not vouchsafed to the Brigadier and the other senior officers, who had first to undergo very prolonged questioning from those who simply had to find out how it had happened, and why. The results of this questioning were, of course, extremely meagre.

The newly elected members of the House of Commons had all been looking forward to a leisurely period of relaxation from the rigours of the election campaign, before those of the new session, for many of them their first, began. A good proportion of them were still in their constituencies, either because they lived there or because they were involved in post-election celebrations with the faithful party workers. They were thus exposed to the feelings and views of their constituents. A sensation of bafflement came through first – what the hell has happened? How could it have happened? We were told the base was secure and could be reinforced in a flash: didn't they have any gas-masks? On this last point, there was an orgy of reminiscence from old-age pensioners who remembered how in 1939 the little square cardboard box on its carrying-string had had to be taken everywhere – 'Even to the loo, I do remember' – but there was a contrary vein of reminiscence which recalled how, in the services, the gas-mask haversack had quickly become something in which you kept your spare socks. There was great anxiety about the gas and whether its effect would really only be temporary, and also great indignation that such unfair methods could have been used against British troops; and there was a lot of feeling against 'the bloody Argies' who had once more stirred things up; and much sympathy, at least among the faithful party workers in Conservative constituencies, for the Prime Minister who had to face a challenge to Britain's prestige and authority in the world. Among Labour party workers, who had seen their efforts so nearly crowned with overall electoral success, the mood was of course rather different. On the whole, the people seemed frustrated and indignant: they wanted to know more, and when they did know more they would make up their minds about what they thought should be done about it. But it was not quite like 1982, when to most people of all parties the issues had seemed so clear-cut and the attitude of the government, once relieved of the honourable Foreign Secretary who had obviously had to carry the can, so clearly supportable. This time it was difficult:

not enough was known: in due course the people would decide. But already, 'Oh God, not again' was a discernible theme in their approach.

The Foreign Secretary, once apprised of what had happened, acted with speed and decisiveness. He spoke first to the British Representative at the United Nations, then to the British Ambassador in Washington. Then he continued with the Secretary-General to NATO and the Secretary-General of the Commonwealth, in that order. In every country of the European Community, startled foreign ministers received urgent visits from British ambassadors, calling on them to give support to Britain in her hour of need. The Foreign Secretary was in fact due to visit Brussels on the following Monday for a meeting of foreign ministers; he would reinforce the message then. The High Commissioners in London of Australia, Canada, and New Zealand were spoken to specially. Above all, the aid and influence of the United States Ambassador was solicited: he was a staunch friend of Britain and could be expected to exert his influence in her favour with his government, whose position was, as in 1982, of very great importance. All over the world, British representatives were pointing out to the foreign ministers of the countries to which they were accredited that here again was naked, unprovoked aggression, carried out by a trick which played on British humanitarian instincts, compounded by the use of chemical weapons, repugnant to all: and Britain was a major ally, a major community member, the mother country – in short deserving of support.

But Argentine diplomacy was not idle either. As soon as the surprised representatives all over the world had realized that their Government at home had aligned itself behind the action taken by the military, they too went into action. Tirelessly they stressed the favourable points of the new Argentine position – the adamant refusal of the British to discuss sovereignty: the almost bloodless character of the takeover, the method adopted being by no means inhumane but, on the contrary, deeply considerate of human life: above all, the totally new situation created by Argentina's declared intention that, once the principles were conceded, a most enlightened regime, a regime without parallel in such circumstances, would be applied to the islands and their inhabitants: surely now an international consensus, if not an actual commission, must adjudicate upon the situation and produce a solution, a cure for this festering sore. And it was not only the diplomats of Argentina who pressed this persuasive point of view. Brazil, Uruguay (fed up with emergency British demands to land at Montevideo) and Peru all tended to support the Argentine position: only Chile, for many years past embroiled with Argentina over the insignificant islands at the end of the Straits of Magellan and inclined therefore to favour the British point of view, held back from fairly clear support of the Argentine viewpoint.

These efforts of Argentina bore little fruit in Europe, except in Spain and Italy. It was in the United Nations in New York that they promised to be most successful. There, the Secretary General had agreed to call a meeting of the Security Council on Monday. Intense lobbying of all the members was now undertaken by both protagonists.

There are fifteen members of the Security Council, of whom five (the United States, the Soviet Union, China, Great Britain and France) are permanent members: the other ten vary from year to year. Resolutions are passed if a minimum of ten votes are cast in favour, always provided of course none of the permanent members uses its power of veto. Between them, the members invariably cover a wide political spectrum as well as being geographically scattered throughout the world. In 1982 the British Government, thanks largely to the heroic efforts of its representative Sir Anthony Parsons, had secured the passing of Resolution 502, which called for a cessation of hostilities, the withdrawal of Argentine forces from the islands, and for both Argentina and Britain to seek a diplomatic solution and to respect the purposes and principles of the United Nations Charter. The resolution, once passed, was seen as providing basic moral support for Britain, particularly in view of the reference to the UN charter, because that document recognizes a right for all members to act in self-defence, and it seemed permissible for that right to be stretched to cover defence against attacks on any territory under the complainant country's administration. Sir Montague Hesketh was now heavily engaged in exactly the same type of exercise as that in which Sir Anthony Parsons had triumphed in 1982, and found himself staunchly opposed by Señor Sanchez de Mayora, the Argentine ambassador to the United Nations Organization.

As on the previous occasion, the United States found herself in the difficult position of having to choose between supporting her staunchest and most valuable ally, and pursuing her aim of keeping as many Central and South American countries as possible on her side, in order to prevent 'the creation of more Cubas' in the hemisphere. The underlying factors were however rather different this time. The very marked progress in United States-Soviet relations in the past few years; the several arms reduction agreements which had come into effect; the dramatic collapse of the Communist system in all the Eastern European countries which had hitherto been classed as Soviet satellites; the increasing unlikeliness that war between the superpowers would ever occur or even be seriously threatened – all these factors tended to reduce the United States' need to support and propitiate her allies. Meanwhile, Central American troubles continued for the Bush administration, and the fact, so obvious to most of the rest of the world, that Communism was now a busted flush, did not seem to have got through to the revolutionaries in the western hemisphere. Once more the United States had to choose: in 1982 it had taken her a long time to come down decisively on Britain's side, and it was not until Alexander Haig's shuttle diplomacy was seen to have failed that she finally did so. During that period American public opinion had been confused; and the final decision in Britain's favour had been much eased, first by the passing of Resolution 502, and secondly by the adamant attitude of the Galtieri regime in Argentina. This time the Argentine position was markedly different. From the start, they had professed to be asking for international arbitration to solve a problem which had really become a nuisance: many Senators and Congressmen thought that that was exactly what should now happen.

On Friday, Captain Edward Symons, a company commander in the 2nd/2nd Duke of Edinburgh's Own Ghurka Rifles, stationed at Aldershot, was brought up to London and installed in the Ministry of Defence. He would eat there and sleep there for the next few days, on permanent standby in case a call from the Governor of the Falklands should come through which demanded the exercise of his special skill. That special skill was an almost perfect fluency in Gurkhali. On Friday evening the Governor came on the line, originally to his usual Falklands Desk contact in the Foreign Office, but then, under switching arrangements which had been set up, the call was transferred to the ad hoc operations room which had been established in the Ministry of Defence. After preliminaries, the Governor said,

'I am putting my Commissioner on the line: I trust he will have somebody to talk to?' The answer was in the affirmative.

On that Friday 13th May 1992, every officer and man in C and D Companies, 1st Battalion The Royal Mercian Regiment, was fast asleep. They slept, each wrapped in one blanket and a groundsheet, in a big sheep-shearing shed on the outskirts of the settlement at Fox Bay East, West Falkland. Alongside them slumbered the members of the ten-men strong Special Air Services Regiment detachment who had acted as their 'enemy' in a ten-day-long exercise in the remote interior of that almost uninhabited major island. A very large area had been set aside there, in which field-firing exercises could take place with live ammunition. It had been a wholly exhausting exercise, in which the emphasis had been placed on survival under active service conditions in the unfriendly environment of the West Falkland island. At the end, both the two companies and their 'enemy' had been completely tired out. Cold and hungry, their final endurance test had been the 'yomp' back to Fox Bay. There, a hot meal awaited them all, and a spartan roof over their heads for the night: in the morning, the big Chinook helicopters would come to begin shuttle-ferrying them back to Mount Pleasant, and a resumption of more mundane garrison duties. Since the start of their exercise, they had had little contact with Mount Pleasant, and none in the last thirty-six hours.

Now in the early morning, the postmaster-cum-shopkeeper of the small settlement came into the sheep-shearing shed where all the soldiers lay wrapped in sleep. He knew who he was looking for, but not how to find him in this throng of slumbering forms. Finally he saw a man with his eyes open, watching him.

'Which is Major Wilkins?' the postmaster asked. The wakeful soldier rose on one elbow, to economize on the amount of cold air which might infiltrate his meagre bed-clothes, and said,

'Right over there by the door, next to it. With the red hair.' The postmaster found the sleeping form so indicated, and shook it.

'Major Wilkins, Sir, wake up: wake up, you are urgently wanted on the telephone.'

'Who wants me?' the recumbent figure, now doubtfully awake, demanded. A head of reddish hair appeared above the blanket, and two bleary eyes blinked in the light.

'The Governor, Major. He says it is of the very greatest urgency and importance that he speaks to you. And we have heard, we have just heard, that things have been happening on the East Island. I think you must come, Sir.'

'OK, I will,' said the figure, now roused. 'I'll come chop-chop but it'll take me a minute. Here I come.' And Julian Wilkins hauled himself up, did up a button or two, found his boots, put them on, and followed the postmaster out of the shed.

Everyone else slumbered on.

In the small store, Wilkins finally reached the telephone.

'Major Wilkins, Mercians, here. Who is it? I'm sorry to have kept you.'

'Major Wilkins, this is the Governor here, in Port Stanley. Do you know what has happened in the last twenty-four hours at Mount Pleasant?'

'No, Sir, I don't. We have been out in the camp, no wireless contact, nothing. We got in here last night, completely finished after our exercise. We had a meal and went to bed. May I ask you what has happened?'

The Governor told him. Julian Wilkins listened with amazement and horror. He finally asked,

'Do you mean, Sir, that the Argies are in control of the airfield, and that's all?'

'That's all,' replied the Governor, 'but it's quite a big all. They are in control, your battalion and the rest of the forces are already on their way to Argentina, and no British plane can land. No helicopters will come to fetch you tomorrow: they're under Argentine control. They are in charge. Except for you.'

'Sir,' said Major Wilkins, 'you are telling me that we are here, two hundred of us give or take a few either way, and the Argies are sitting at Mount Pleasant. Do you know how many of them there are?'

'They came in a British Airways 747 which carries three hundred-plus. Since then they have been reinforced, but not by many we think, and most of the reinforcements have gone on to the old airfield to occupy it, I don't quite know why because there's not much there. I should think five hundred at Mount Pleasant. By the way, I understand you've been on a field-firing exercise. How much ammunition have you got left?'

'Practically all of it. We didn't do very much firing. What do you want us to do, Sir?'

'I want you to come back here as soon as we can get you back, and then I want you to retake that bloody airfield before anyone gives the whole shooting-match away to the bloody Argies.'

'Too right, Sir, if I may say so. We shall try to oblige. But how do we get back to you?'

'I am sending a ship for you. Not the *Canberra*, you will understand. But a ship will bring you back here, and then we'll work it all out. Meanwhile, maximum security, please. My boat won't get to you until tomorrow evening. Get yourselves in fighting trim. Rest as much as you can because it won't be restful when you get back here. And tell that postmaster chappie that you don't exist: everyone in the Fox Bay settlement must know that you don't exist. Meanwhile I'm rounding up all the stray Sappers and so on, to back you up. We shall win a famous victory, and gentlemen in England now abed – now, shut up, Hereward, and let's get on with it. Are you completely with me?'

'Completely, Sir. We shall be ready for your ship. Let's hope the Argies don't change their minds before we can do something about it. By the way, Sir, I've got ten SAS men here too: I think they might come in useful.'

'Yes,' said the Governor, 'I think they will. Well, the ship will come for you, and we'll take it from there. By the way, my understanding is that the rest of your battalion, and the others, are perfectly OK. It seems to have been a temporary knock-out drop which paralysed them for so many hours: the Argentinos walked all over them – they had gas-masks and our chaps didn't, or at least weren't wearing them. Right, we have work to do: I just thought you'd like to know your brothers-in-arms have apparently suffered no permanent damage.'

'Thank you, Sir, I am glad to know that. We'll be ready for the ship sometime tomorrow. No doubt you will give the captain his orders, Sir, but may I suggest that we reach Port Stanley after dark? That way, we can go to whatever billets have been prepared for us without danger of being seen from the air: they may put up some air patrols.'

'I agree,' said the Governor. 'All those arrangements will be made. When you get here we'll have a council of war. I am still in telephone touch with London, and I have discovered a way of talking to them in complete security. So hopefully we'll be able to co-ordinate our action here with preparations at their end. Now I think we'd better ring off. I've taken a risk talking to you on this line, but I had to do it. I have no helicopter here – they're all on Mount Pleasant and the Argentinos have got the lot. Goodbye, Wilkins. See you tomorrow night, I trust.'

Julian Wilkins put the telephone down. There were a great many preparations to be made, but there was plenty of time in which to make them. His men could sleep a bit longer – it would help them: there was little prospect of much comfort on the Governor's ship, he guessed. Meanwhile, here was the postmaster regarding him anxiously.

Major Wilkins told the man most of what the Governor had told him. He impressed upon him most anxiously the need for security. The Governor had indeed spoken on an open line, and the risks he had taken in doing so were obvious. That could not be helped, but now there must be telephone silence about the existence of his small force. The postmaster quickly understood this, and undertook to explain the position to everyone in the settlement, and to arrange for a similar briefing to be given to as many as possible of the outlying farms.

Julian Wilkins went back to the sheep-shearing shed. Practically everyone was still asleep, but both Company Sergeant-Majors were stirring and were quickly awoken, as were Captain Alan Jenkins who commanded D Company, and the Sergeant in command of the SAS detachment. All these went

156

into a huddle with Wilkins in a quiet corner of the shed, and made their plans for the day, night, and next day. After they had had breakfast, the men would have to be fully briefed and would then have a quiet day devoted to getting themselves, their kit and weapons in perfect order. Tomorrow, hopefully, they would be able to put in some rehearsal of the plans which were already tentatively forming in Major Wilkins' mind.

☆   ☆   ☆

In the small room at the Ministry of Defence, all the Chiefs of Staff and several of their senior advisers had gathered silently round the table on which the telephone stood. Captain Symons had been talking in Gurkhali now, and alternately listening, for more than five minutes. Now he laid the receiver down.

'Sir,' he said to Admiral Higgins as the most senior of the formidable array of top brass with which he was confronted, 'there's a lot to tell you. May I tell him we'll call back later tonight – say, eight o'clock their time?'

'What if the Argentinos are alarmed by all these foreign languages, and cut off communication? That would be a pity: if they did that we wouldn't be able to talk to the Governor any more.'

'I did think of that, Sir, and the Commissioner said he didn't think they could do that at all quickly: all the telephone works are in Stanley itself.'

'Very well, say your goodbyes: we'll call him at eight, local time.'

With a final few words of Gurkhali, Symons replaced the receiver, and now had his tale to tell. He was not disconcerted by having to do so to so many senior officers, all impatient for news.

'First of all, Sir,' he started, still addressing Admiral Higgins, 'the Commissioner confirms our previous information. The Argentines are on the Mount Pleasant airfield and are very quiet. But they have been reinforced by, he thinks, about three hundred airborne troops: most of those reinforcements have occupied the old Stanley airfield which only houses, as you know, a few light civil planes and helicopters, mostly in connection with the foreign visiting fishing fleets. You will remember, Sir, the Governor agreed that that would not be

157

opposed in any way. I think he wants to persuade them to allow those aircraft to go on operating, as it would be inconvenient for the fishermen if they did not do so; but the Argentines have not agreed to that yet. Early days, perhaps.'

Symons paused to marshal his thoughts, and looked at the notes he had made while talking. The Admirals and Generals waited with some impatience.

'More important, Sir,' he went on, 'is that there were two companies of the Mercians and a few SAS men who were not at Mount Pleasant when the attack went in. They were out in the sticks, or the camp as they call it, on West Falkland – a training exercise with live ammunition. The Governor has found them at Fox Bay East, where they finished their exercise. He is sending a ship to fetch them – apparently it's an old coaster which toddles round the islands with food and drink, and sheep and so on. He is going to get them back to Stanley. His opinion is that the Argentines are quite unaware of their existence: there have been a few helicopter patrols from Mount Pleasant today, but nothing systematic; and he says his conversations with the Admiral of Marines give him the impression that they think they captured our entire force yesterday morning. He wants to use the two companies, plus the SAS and whatever he can scrape up in the way of Sappers and other details, to retake the airfield.'

It is given to few officers of the rank of captain to cause such a sensation among a group of very senior officers, as that which now occurred. But it was short-lived: discipline reasserted itself almost at once. The rest of Symons' tale was quickly told. After every question which he could answer had been asked, the top brass went back in some excitement to the map-room: now there were plans to be made, and a Minister to be informed. Soon, the Prime Minster himself would have to be told of this extraordinary new development.

Rear-Admiral Carlos Ricarda, at about the same time as these events were taking place in far-away London, was surveying the state of his command. He found it good. The previous day, Thursday, had been a long day in every respect: today had been better, and real progress had been made towards establishing a settled routine and towards bringing about a state of order in the sprawling British base.

The prisoners, thank goodness, had all gone, in the C-130 Hercules transport planes which had brought in the 1st Parachute Infantry Battalion, and in the British Airways 747 which, it was found, had plenty of fuel on board for the journey to Comodoro Rivadavia. He had seldom been so sorry for anyone as he had been for those senior officers, the Brigadier, the Colonel of the Mercians, and the Air Force Wing-Commander. They were beaten men, and they looked it: they had been beaten by a weapon which had not been in their contemplation, just as the Japanese had been beaten in 1945 by the unheralded advent of the atomic bomb. He had tried to comfort them a little, but it was no good: they were still in deep shock, and suffering from an undeserved feeling of shame. They were not looking forward to the long journey back to England, and they were uncertain how they would be received by their superiors and by public opinion when they got there. The rank and file were also stunned, but seemed more fatalistic. What had happened had been an act of God: it had not been their fault: they were glad to be alive; and they were going back to England. Things could have been a lot worse. From Comodoro Rivadavia they would fly to Buenos Aires and then on to London and, no doubt, some disembarkation leave.

The three hundred men of the parachute battalion had been a welcome reinforcement for the exhausted but elated Marines. Two companies of them went straight on to Stanley airfield, where they landed without let or hindrance. They found there only a few helicopters and light aircraft, all of which were placed under guard, the servicing personnel and the few office staff being sent with their belongings into Stanley. Contact had been established with a Spanish-speaking local police officer whom the Governor had designated as liaison officer, to iron out any difficulties which might arise. The small occupying force made itself as comfortable as possible: its role was a purely negative one – to ensure that the British could not use the old field for any hostile purpose while the international negotiations were going on.

Back in the base, the Marines and the remaining paratroopers had now completed their tidying-up and organizing work. The British food stores had been found to be up to

159

expectations: there were enough provisions of all kinds to feed a brigade for a year, and it was also clear that no-one was going to go short of alcoholic refreshments. There were quite a number of Land-Rovers available, and seven helicopters, including three of the big twin-rotored Chinook type. Two or three pilots who knew how to fly these models had come in with the paratroopers, and several helicopter patrol flights had been made; not that they were looking for anything in particular, but Ricarda had thought it as well that the Governor and his officials should be aware that he had a reconnaissance capability.

In the field of communications, a direct radio link had been early established with General Romera's Air Force head-quarters at Comodoro Rivadavia: in fact, it would be perfectly possible to ring up Buenos Aires or anywhere in the world by simply asking the Stanley operator to get the number; but at this stage there was no telling how such a request would be received. The communications expert had also managed to establish a 'tap' on external calls: he could by no means spend the whole of his time listening in to the traffic between Stanley and London, but he had reported today that there were conversations taking place in an entirely unknown language which seemed to be Asiatic in character. Perhaps, he thought, a Chinese restaurateur was talking to his relations in Wardour Street.

The British base was found to be very large, with lines of empty barrack-huts and big stores containing furniture and blankets, besides the occupied portions of the camp in which the garrison had been living. These were now clear of the British servicemen's belongings: the Argentine personnel simply moved into the already warm and lived-in buildings. To his surprise, however, the Marine Quartermaster found that there were two hut-complexes which were only semi-empty: there were suitcases under the beds, and dress-uniforms hanging in the wardrobes. Busy man that he was, with a hundred and one things to sort out, he stored this fact away in his mind and decided that he must inform Admiral Ricarda about it next day. Meanwhile his cookhouses were in full blast, and the officers' and sergeants' messes were in business with their new clientele. Only in the garrison cinema was a check experienced: the investigating Marine, who had been a projectionist before he joined up, reported that there was not one Spanish-soundtrack film among the large stock that he found.

Yes, Ricarda thought to himself as he sipped a whisky-and-soda in his control-tower office before going over to the mess for dinner, it was all going well. The Governor had been reasonable: he was clearly a sensible man who, once he had given his word, could surely be relied on not to break it: it was a pity that it had proved impossible to persuade him to give a general undertaking of non-belligerence, but that was quite understandable. Perhaps in a few days' time he would prove more amenable over that; but as he had absolutely nothing to be belligerent with against six hundred or so heavily-armed professional soldiers, the point was really of very little importance.

Tomorrow General Romera, accompanied by Captain Varela of the Navy, would come on a visit of inspection. He knew that Romera was anxious to make a start on finding the twenty-six or so wrecks of the shot-down Air Force and Navy aircraft, and bringing in the remains of the pilots if they could be found. This would no doubt be grisly work, but it would give his men something to do: exhausted yesterday, they would soon lose their edge with enforced inactivity. Meanwhile there were guard-posts to be manned, and a start must be made tomorrow on clearing-up and repairing the rather superficial damage caused by the bombs.

14

'Order!' said the Speaker. 'Statements to the House. There will be two statements on the situation in the Falkland Islands. The Secretary of State for Defence.'

The House of Commons was crowded on this Saturday afternoon. Practically all the Members, nearly a third of them new ones, who had been elected in the preceding Tuesday's General Election, were present: they were squatting in the aisles and on the steps of the Speaker's Chair: a throng of them stood behind the Chair.

In the morning they had assembled for the process of 'signing-on' and settling-in: it had been a lengthy process, and the bars and the Members' dining-room had done good business at the appropriate hour.

In the afternoon the first business, this being a new Parliament, had been to elect a Speaker. This was a formality. Mr Speaker Weatherill had previously signified his willingness to continue in office, and this was welcomed by all parties: there were no other nominations. Although the old beneficent custom of not opposing a sitting Speaker in his constituency had not been followed, his previous majority had been large, and he was duly re-elected with a somewhat smaller one. He had come into the House and, in accordance with precedent, had stood hesitantly near the Chair while his election was proposed: the proposition was approved with a thunderous roar, and the Speaker was, again in accordance with ancient precedent, ceremoniously 'dragged' against mock resistance on his part, to the Chair: now the real business of the day could begin.

Sir Henry Jones rose and went to the dispatch box.

'Mr Speaker, with your permission and that of the House, I should like to make a statement on the events which took place in the Falklands two days ago, and on the situation which now exists there.'

162

The first part of the statement consisted of a repetition of that which he had made to the media in Downing Street on the Thursday evening: the hushed House listened to this with ill-concealed impatience. However, as he got well into the statement, variations began to appear: for instance he made no reference to diplomatic or United Nations proceedings, these being the province of his right honourable friend the Secretary of State for Foreign Affairs, whose statement would follow. He completed his statement by saying:-

'The whole House will, I am sure, be glad to know that our garrison who have been overcome in such an underhand way seem, apart from those killed and injured by gunshot wounds, to have suffered no lasting ill-effects. We have been informed by the International Red Cross, whose officials at our request went immediately to Argentina, that arrangements for their repatriation are proceeding smoothly. It appears that, as stated in the announcement made by the Argentine Service Commands, the effects of the nerve-gas used were purely temporary. All the officers and men were flown out of Mount Pleasant to Comodoro Rivadavia in Patagonia yesterday: the Red Cross officials were present when they deplaned, and report that all were in good condition. I am informed that they are being flown up to Buenos Aires today, and will then be transferred to a number of civil aircraft chartered in by the Argentine Government, for their onward flight to this country. They are expected to arrive at Brize Norton some time tomorrow afternoon. The whole process has been overseen by the International Red Cross, working with the Argentine authorities. On arrival, our officers and men will undergo medical examination and, on the assumption that they are adjudged fit, will then be given disembarkation leave. I am sure the House will give its sympathy to these servants of the Crown who, in the course of their duties, have undergone an extremely unpleasant and no doubt frightening experience.

'As to those actually wounded,' Sir Henry went on, 'as stated, twelve relatively serious cases have been transferred to the civilian hospital at Port Stanley where adequate facilities exist for their care. We are in touch with the Governor, who remains for the moment undisturbed in his office; and he tells us that in his opinion none of these cases is in a dangerous situation, and that all should eventually recover their health:

there have, however, been three necessary amputations. The remaining wounded have, I am informed, been transferred, along with a number of Argentine wounded, to military hospitals in Argentina for treatment until they are well enough to be returned to this country.

'Names of all these casualties, as well as of those killed, have been notified to the Red Cross by the Argentine authorities, and the next-of-kin have now been informed.

'Finally, Mr Speaker, I would like to inform the House that, for the present, no further military action of any sort is taking place in the Falklands. The occupying forces are in control of the new Mount Pleasant airfield and also of the old airfield at Stanley: their occupation of the latter seems to be of a protective character, and was unopposed as the result of a local agreement between the Governor and the commander of the occupying forces, in the interests of avoiding further bloodshed. There are in fact no forces now available to the Governor with which he could have opposed this extension of the occupation. Apart from the small police force and the Local Defence Force which is of an auxiliary character, there are only comparatively small numbers of Royal Engineers personnel in Stanley: most of these are engaged in clearing the mines still remaining from the conflict of 1982. The local Argentine commander has informed the Governor that he has no intention of extending his sphere of occupation beyond the two airfields, or of interfering in any way with his continued administration of the islands. The Governor informs us that he is receiving co-operation on the matter of necessary supplies, and that the local commander has assured him that, subject to safeguards from the Argentine point of view, such co-operation will continue in order to ensure a continuance of supply. We remain in telephone contact, daily, with the Governor.'

'Mr Speaker, that completes my formal statement to the House on these singularly unfortunate matters.'

And the Minister of Defence sat down, uncomfortably aware that his statement had not gone down very well, and that he was now due for a roasting, accompanied no doubt by calls for his resignation at least, if not that of the whole Government: how could it be otherwise, he thought ruefully as he resumed his seat on the Government front bench.

The Leader of the Opposition rose: he had the air of an

opening batsman put in to bat on an easy wicket, who is bowled a nice medium-paced half-volley. He started slowly.

'Mr Speaker,' he said, 'I would like to assure the Right Honourable Gentleman that this side of the House does indeed extend its sympathy to our former Falklands garrison members who have clearly been subjected to a humiliating and frightening experience, and we sincerely hope his confidence that they have suffered no lasting ill-effects proves to be justified. But we have far more sympathy for them, Mr Speaker, and for those who were wounded and for the relatives of those who so unfortunately lost their lives, for the reason that these things happened to them purely through the incompetence of the Right Honourable Gentleman.'

The Speaker opened his mouth to remind Mr Kinnock that he was making a speech, something not strictly in order on this particular occasion. He was forestalled by a roar of cheering from the whole opposition side of the House: order papers were waved, and cries of 'Resign' were heard.

It took a little time for order to be restored: the Government benches mostly sat glum and silent, uncertain how to respond. The Front Bench displayed studious indifference.

'Mr Speaker,' Mr Kinnock continued when the hubbub had subsided, 'I would just like to ask the Right Honourable Gentleman how, when our troops in the Falklands have been surprised and overcome without hardly firing a shot, he can possibly deny a charge of massive incompetence?'

This time the reaction from the Labour benches was more restrained, a strong chorus of 'Hear-hears'. The Defence Minister rose to reply.

'The Right Honourable Gentleman will be aware from the statement I have just made that our troops defended themselves to the best of their ability, and in particular that very heavy casualties were inflicted on the attacking aircraft. Our forces were overcome by unexpected methods of warfare. I totally reject the charge of incompetence.'

A brief interlude of tumult was stilled by the Speaker, who called Mr Paddy Ashdown. His handsome presence and his background as a Royal Marine invested him with an importance which transcended his party's meagre representation in the new House. Leaning forward over the dispatch box, he asked whether, in view of what had happened, the Minister could really maintain to the House that the arrangements for the defence of the Falklands had been adequate in all respects; and, if not, did he not feel that his resignation was a necessity? To which the hapless Minister, in an increasingly unruly and confused House, could only reply to the effect that if you played cricket against people who bent the rules whenever they wanted to, you might be excused if you lost: as to the second half of the question, that would be a matter for the House to decide in due course.

It was left to the Deputy Leader of the Opposition to ask the sixty-four thousand dollar question. Would the Minister kindly tell the House whether the Government had any plans to restore the situation in the Falklands; and, if so, what those plans were?

The House fell silent as Sir Henry rose to make his reply.

'My Right Honourable friend the Foreign Secretary is to make a statement later,' he said, 'about the diplomatic processes which, both at the United Nations and, is to be hoped, by negotiations through intermediaries, will shortly be in train under his auspices. It is very much to be hoped that by means of these initiatives the Argentine Government will be persuaded to overrule the pretensions of its military men, and agree to remove its forces pending a peaceful negotiated solution. Meanwhile, the Chiefs of Staff committee is in session, and detailed plans are being drawn up for consideration by the Cabinet in case of need.'

It was the word 'detailed' which did it. Mr Hattersley put his supplementary question: 'Does the Right Honourable Gentleman indicate by his reply that the Government are prepared to consider sending a Task Force to the South Atlantic to recover the Falklands by force of arms?'

'Yes, Sir.' answered the Minister.

Nobody on the Government front bench was fully prepared for what happened next. As one man and woman, the Opposition benches rose, booing: quickly, the booing changed into a chant, 'No Task Force', which was reinforced by rhythmic thumping on bench-backs, and which seemed to be taken up to some extent almost all over the House: shocked Ministers, looking round at their own back benches, saw at least two dozen of their own members on their feet and chanting. Some of them were undergoing restraint attempts by their neigh-

166

bours, and a number of furious altercations were taking place. The Speaker rose and finally managed to quell the tumult. Mr Kinnock, scarlet with emotion, sprang to the dispatch box.

'Does the Right Honourable Gentleman realize,' he cried, Welsh ebullience at last in full flow, 'that mothers all over the country will react in utter dismay to the answer which he has just given? Does he realize that the country simply will not stand for a repetition of the tragic events of 1982? Does he realize that any further attempt to meet force by force would be utterly unjustifiable in 1992?'

There were reserves of toughness in Sir Henry Jones' character which, over the years, had enabled him to climb the parliamentary ladder to the high rung which he now occupied. He stood unflinching at the dispatch box and replied.

'The answer to the first part of the three-decker question is No. As to the second, the country will expect its Government to do its duty, and will react accordingly. As to the third and final part of the question, it is very much hoped and anticipated that it will not be necessary to proceed to extremes, as the Right Honourable Gentleman will understand better when he has heard the statement that my Right Honourable friend the Foreign Secretary will make.'

There were a great many more questions on this theme during the next half-hour from all sides of the House, giving evidence of opposition to further armed action: to all of them Sir Henry returned the same unwavering reply, to the effect that the Government very much hoped and expected that the problem would be solved by negotiation; but that, if not, they were in the last resort prepared to consider a resort to arms to defend Britain's interests. A noted stodgy opening bat in his youth, he was afterwards to say that it was the most difficult stonewalling innings he had ever had to play.

Finally the Speaker, with his eye on the clock (for it had never been intended that this initial day should be a very long one) called the Secretary of State for Foreign Affairs.

'Mr Speaker, with your permission and that of the House, I also would like to make a statement on recent events in the Falklands,' the Foreign Secretary began. 'I am sure the House has listened with interest and with respect to the statement made by my Right Honourable friend and the answers which he has given to questions put to him. I associate myself with all that he has said, and I have this to add.

'The attack on the Falklands about which my Right Honourable friend has told the House, seems to have been entirely unpremeditated by the Government of Argentina. It seems indeed to have been the work of dissatisfied elements in the highest echelons of the Armed Forces, acting behind their Government's back. It appears to us today that the civilian Government, which with the exception of the President has been left in place, has been persuaded by the military to give its provisional endorsement to what has taken place. The statements made on behalf of the military reveal, in my opinion, a fundamental weakness in their position: they were only in a position to conduct a strictly limited operation: it was not an outright occupation of the whole of the islands – it was simply the obtaining, by deceit and the use of unauthorized weapons, of a bargaining position from which they hope to negotiate from a position of so-called strength.

'We propose to meet this challenge head-on. Our representative at the United Nations in New York has been instructed to seek an immediate meeting of the Security Council, with a view to securing the passage of a resolution which will embody the disapproval felt by the Organization of what can only be described as an act of irresponsible aggression. I am informed that the Security Council will meet on Monday to begin its discussions. We are also in touch with all our friends and allies in the European Community, the Commonwealth, and the North American Treaty Organization, with a view to securing their unqualified support over this issue. We have already received valuable assurances of understanding from the government of the United States. Finally, the Soviet Union has assured me through its Ambassador in London that it condemns the Argentine action and is anxious to see a peaceful outcome. Therefore, I am very hopeful that before long the Argentine Government will see sense, overrule the military, and agree to withdraw its forces. We shall then be in a position to resume the discussion process in which, the House will be aware, we have been engaged with Argentina over the past few years, and in which, until the unhappy and unjustifiable events of the last few days, such promising progress had been made in resolving the two countries' differences.'

The House could not find very much in this bland statement

to be angry about. They had had their fun, and now it was getting late in the afternoon: soon, there would not be much weekend left, and they all had much constituency work still to do. After a further twenty minutes of questions, answered with quiet skill by the Foreign Secretary, it was apparent that the proceedings were drawing to a close – but what came next?

That question was solved by the Speaker, who announced that he had received a request from the Leader of the Opposition for an emergency debate under standing order number ten. He said that he was minded to grant the request but that, in view of the discussion which had taken place that day, he did not consider that a sitting on Monday was warranted. The Government's business managers had agreed to the debate starting at two-thirty on Tuesday afternoon.

This announcement was greeted with vociferous approval on the Opposition benches, and with rather less enthusiasm on the Government side: it was clear to all that this debate was likely to lead to a full-blown motion of no-confidence in the Government.

Members of all parties departed belatedly to their constituencies, there to take the voters' temperature. Meanwhile, the Prime Minister and his colleagues retired to No 10 Downing Street to consider how to play their hand, an important card in which had not been revealed to the House of Commons that afternoon. For the first time, they were joined in their deliberations by the Chief Whip.

The coaster *Marianne* was quite a big ship as Falklands ships went. Of 1932 vintage, she at least burnt oil instead of coal. For many years she had been in the ownership of the Falklands Islands Company, to which most of the commercial enterprises in the islands belonged. She operated a sort of very irregular cargo-bus service, carrying cargo of all sorts where it was wanted. There was also accommodation for passengers: the difficulty there was that the ship's movements were entirely dictated by her cargo commitments: if a big flock of sheep needed to be moved, the sailing schedule went to blazes. It was just something which intending passengers had to put up with: nobody ever seemed to mind very much when told that their journey to Port Howard would take six days instead of two.

The *Marianne* was 682 tons deadweight, surprisingly large by Falklands standards. At most times her carrying capacity was largely unused: this made her an expensive vessel to run,but it would have been a great deal more expensive to replace her, and the Falklands Company was in a monopoly position in the islands: the only restraint on their freight structure was their customers' ability to pay: so the *Marianne* lingered on in service, passing by a miracle her periodical surveys by Lloyds of London. Luckily she had been well and sturdily built in one of the Clyde yards, and her owners had always been sensible enough to employ first-class engineers to look after her old-fashioned reciprocating engines.

By good fortune on Thursday afternoon, the day on which so much had happened, the *Marianne* was tied up in Port Stanley harbour: she was due to load cargo in a few hours' time, and to depart two days later for a run round the north coast of the East Island. Mounds of fence posts, pig-netting and other more perishable goods were already being assembled on the quay-side. Captain Jones was having a quiet cup of tea in his cabin with his chief engineer Mr Maconachie, when a seaman announced a visitor: he turned out to be the Governor's secretary, a youngish man slightly known to the Captain.

The visitor lost no time in coming to the point.

'Captain,' he said, 'I take it you observed and heard the aeroplanes this morning?'

The Captain had indeed heard and observed, as had everyone else in Port Stanley; but precise news as to what had actually happened had been slow in getting around; everyone was agog for hard news, and rumours (mostly accurate, as it happened) were rife. The secretary enlightened him.

'Those planes were dropping gas, Captain. They knocked out the whole garrison at Mount Pleasant, and then some Argentinos who had sneaked in in a hijacked British Airways airliner took over the whole place. The Argentinos are in control of the airfield, so no British planes can land. They've told the Governor they will not advance beyond the airfield, and he is being left alone to continue running things.'

'Do you mean to say they've got the whole British garrison dead or knocked out, as you put it?' enquired the Captain.

'Knocked out, I think: it seems to have been some sort of

nerve gas with temporary effect. And no, that's the point, they haven't got the whole British garrison. There are two companies of the Mercians at Fox Bay East, which they don't know about. The Governor wants you to go and pick them up and bring them back here.'

'So that they can fight the bluidy Argies for the bluidy airfield, no doubt?' Mr Maconachie, normally a man of few words, exclaimed. 'Och, the puir laddies, they'll have a hard fight of it.'

'I expect they will,' said the secretary, 'but it's got to be done. The Governor wants you to leave for Fox Bay as soon as possible after nightfall, Captain.'

'And what if I say my ship is booked to do other things, young man?' enquired Captain Jones.

'Then the Governor will serve a requisition order on your owners. I have it here in my pocket. In fact, I'll serve it anyway, to protect you. But you won't say that, Captain Jones: we're at war, like in 1982. Your country needs the *Marianne*.'

'Right,' said the Captain. 'Right, of course. No argument about it. How soon can we raise steam, Maconachie?'

The secretary stayed for a few more minutes to give detailed instructions. It was recognized that the invaders might mount aerial patrols, and that although on the face of it an old coaster about her apparent normal business might not excite curiosity, the need for security was paramount. There was no knowing for certain whether the Argies knew that there were two spare infantry companies which had escaped their net, but the Governor had a hunch that they did not know. He therefore was imposing maximum security on everyone, not an easy thing to do in a place like Port Stanley. Even if it turned out that the Argies did know, it would not alter his basic plan. But, so far as possible, important movements – in particular, the embarkation at Fox Bay and the disembarkation at Port Stanley – should be carried out in the hours of darkness.

At six o'clock the *Marianne* disengaged herself from her berth and steamed out of the harbour, setting her course for West Falkland. At three o'clock the following afternoon she arrived off Fox Bay East settlement. There was no question of tying-up there at any tide, owing to insufficient depth of water. The old ship anchored off the settlement, as close in as she dared come: loading would take place via an ancient, underpowered, lighter owned by the Falklands Company, and kept at Fox Bay. Luckily the sea was fairly calm.

Major Julian Wilkins and the postmaster were standing together on the little quay when the ship appeared on the horizon. The two companies and the SAS men, who had spent a day of rest and equipment maintenance while maintaining a high degree of aircraft watch, were awaiting the ship that might or might not come.

When the *Marianne* let down her anchor chain, a light winked from her bridge. The postmaster (now, as on all such occasions, also a harbourmaster) was good at Morse, and he translated 'Hello Soldier'. They both laughed, and Wilkins spoke into his radio set: 'She's here, Company Sergeant-Major. Tell the Captain I think it's safe to start coming down to the quay now, in open order, artillery formation I mean. C Company first, remainder when called forward.'

The process of loading two hundred fully-equipped soldiers into the old lighter was a laborious one: nor was the embarkation on the *Marianne* free from complications: she was not designed to take on troops, and all had to climb up one rickety companion-ladder. Once on board, however, the soldiers found that their accommodation in the cargo-holds, although primitive in the extreme, was sufficiently capacious for everyone to stretch out in fair comfort. Luckily they had eaten an early meal, and Wilkins had had the foresight to tell his cooks to prepare sandwiches for breakfast.

Julian Wilkins went in the first lighter. Before he left he shook the postmaster by the hand. He had come to know the man quite well during the course of the long day. A small knot of local inhabitants, silent and concerned, had gathered behind the postmaster.

'Good luck, Major,' said the postmaster, reluctantly relinquishing Wilkins' hand. 'I reckon you may need some luck, and God send you get it.'

'Of course we'll get it,' said Wilkins, 'the luck of the Mercians is proverbial. Goodbye, and thank you for all your care. Remember the security angle for the next few days, won't you?'

So saying, Wilkins stepped down into the waiting lighter. When the embarkation had been finally completed, and all the soldiers had been established in their sleeping-holds, the

Marianne pulled up her anchor and moved slowly out into the bay on the start of her long coast-hugging voyage to Port Stanley. As she left, the Morse lamp winked again from her bridge. 'Nothing ventured, nothing gained', and after a few moments the answer 'God speed' came from the shore. Smoke streaming from her tall funnel, the *Marianne* increased her speed and was quickly lost to view in the gathering darkness.

At eight o'clock on the evening of the following day, Saturday, the old ship came quietly to her berth in Port Stanley harbour. The quayside was deserted, save for a lone figure waiting at the spot where the gangway would be put up to the ship. As soon as that was done, Sir Hereward Gurney came on board and spoke with Major Wilkins and his officers in the ship's little saloon. He had a lot to tell them.

While he was so doing, a number of guides from the Local Defence Force arrived at the quayside to take the soldiers to the billets which had been prepared for them in several large buildings – one was a school and another the community centre – not far from the dock area. Here they would be given a hot meal prepared by the Local Defence Force, before settling down to sleep.

The Mercian men, some of whom had been very seasick at moments on the voyage, were delighted to have arrived, and were in high spirits as they humped their packs and weapons down the gangway and filed off after their guides. They were accompanied by their platoon commanders. Major Wilkins, Captain Alan Jenkins and the second-in-command of C Company, Captain John Jerman (D Company boasted no such luxury at the moment), stayed behind in the saloon for a preliminary talk with the Governor. As they talked, the Captain's steward produced one more meal of chop-and-chips for all of them.

The chief imponderable, said the Governor, was whether the Argentines really were ignorant of the two companies' existence. It seemed, on the face of it, extraordinary that they should be, because the Governor knew very well that, when the garrison strength had been restored a few months before, the step (as well as the reasons for it) had been confidentially intimated to the Argentine Government. They should therefore have realized that the numbers they took at Mount Pleasant did not amount to a full battalion, plus, of course, the numerous other-arms personnel.

Nevertheless the Governor believed that the discrepancy had somehow not been noticed. The complete confidence displayed by Admiral Ricarda at their meeting: his lack of reaction when the Governor remarked that he had no forces with which to oppose him; and the almost complete lack of any co-ordinated aerial reconnaissance efforts from either the new or the old airfield – all these things led him to believe that Ricarda was living in a fool's paradise.

It was vital, said Sir Hereward, that this happy state of affairs should not be disturbed, lest the Argentines reinforce their small garrison (about a third of which was effectively isolated on the old airfield) and adopt a very much higher state of alertness than otherwise might be the case. The problem was how to achieve this. The present situation was a very peculiar one from the security point of view. The telephone system was still operating, both for calls to and from abroad, and for internal calls between all destinations – both categories including the Mount Pleasant camp. It was now an automatic STD system, so it was not simply a matter of telling the operators not to accept calls: the only way of preventing calls was to shut down the whole system, which was almost unthinkable and could actually alarm the Argentines. External calls could be controlled by pulling out the satellite link in the central exchange, but that would restrict London's ability to call him, and might also alarm the Argentines. He saw no alternative to living with the situation as it was – for as short a time as possible.

Here was the rub. When should the envisaged operation be carried out? Clearly it was desirable that it should take place as soon as a plan of assault could be formulated. This was not only in the security interest. The Mercian infantrymen, basically at a high pitch of training and fitness, and also of morale, had already been living in cramped conditions for two days: the prospect of a further spell confined to improvised billets by day and night was not attractive. The officers debated with the Governor the extent to which this seclusion must be enforced: after all, it was unrealistic to suppose that the population of Port Stanley was not already well aware of their presence and, no doubt, of what it might portend. Were the troops to be kept absolutely incommunicado, and if so why? In the end a compromise was agreed upon: the men would be allowed out for exercise in platoon-strength, but no general 'walking-out' would be permitted in the evening. Even this, it was recognized, must lead to a loss of edge and morale within a very few days.

'Luckily, Sir,' Julian Wilkins remarked, 'the platoon officers are all very good. This is the moment when that mythical paragon in the officer recruiting advertisements really comes into his own!'

'Yes,' said Sir Hereward, whose own youthful adult days had been spent as a National Service subaltern. 'It's man-management that counts. Now I'd better tell you about the other forces I've managed to scratch up to help you. First, the police: as you probably know, there are only fifteen of them in Stanley, including special constables: I don't think much can be done with them, although they'll have their part to play in the background. Sappers are more important – I've managed to assemble just over seventy of them, under two officers: a Major Revington is the senior one. They've all been mine-clearing in various places and they're tickled pink at the idea of something more violent. Nearly a quarter of them, by the way, are not strictly speaking Sappers at all – they are second-generation Ukrainians in the Volunteer Corps; but they're good lads, brought up in England, and they'll serve. Revington swears by them.'

'Finally,' went on the Governor, 'there are seventy-five men of the Local Defence Force who are available for duty. As you may know, the training and equipment of these men has improved a lot in recent years, thanks to the big military presence here. They've got light machine-guns, rifles and grenades – nothing bigger. By the way, what have you got?'

'Three General Purpose Machine Guns per company, three LMGs per platoon,' replied Wilkins, 'but I wonder how much we shall use them in the actual assault?'

'Well, that brings me to the next question,' said the Governor. 'Do you have a plan in your mind, Major?'

'If I'm the General, Sir, I'd better have a plan. Yes, up to a point I do. Shall I sketch it out, Sir?'

The Governor nodded, and Wilkins continued, 'I think it has to be a dawn attack, Sir, and as you say it will be so much easier if it can come as a complete surprise. The perimeter fence itself presents no problem – it's for sheep, really. What we don't know is the extent to which it is sentried and patrolled by the Argies: that can be the SAS's job – to recce this end of the perimeter and to organize our entry in the morning.

'As you know, Sir, Mount Pleasant is a very big camp indeed, almost a small town. Our first problem is to find out which bits of it the Argies are occupying: it may well be that they're in the Mercian lines, because the huts would be warmer and more organized; but conceivably they might have opened up one of the unused sections. I think the SAS had better find out that one too.

'Basically the plan must be to rush them in their huts while they are still asleep. Then, supposing we surprise a hut and take its surrender, we shall not be able to leave any men behind to guard the prisoners: we simply haven't got enough men. That's where your Sappers and LDF men will come in: I see them as a second wave following us through the camp, taking over custody of huts as we subdue them. Of course, there is bound to be a lot of fighting, especially as we get further into the camp: the people there will hear the firing in the first huts we reach, and they will wake up quicker. And that brings me to the next thing, Sir: how about medics? We have only got one medical orderly per company, and of course we've got no doctor. I'm afraid there are going to be an awful lot of casualties, on the most favourable assumptions.'

'I've thought of that,' said the Governor, 'there's an LDF section which has medical training, and one of the hospital doctors is a member. A number of the Police are trained in first aid and they will make up another small unit to follow you in.

'Next, I've warned the hospital director that he'll have to make some people available. None of this adds up to very much, I'm afraid. I gather the facilities in the camp are very good and presumably the Argies have their own MO there. It's not a very good aspect, I'm afraid.'

'Can't be helped, Sir, we'll just have to make the best of it. We'll do some refresher first-aid work with the men tomorrow. Now, Sir, I've been thinking about the chaps on the old airfield. With our limited numbers, there's no question of attacking them too, and frankly we don't need to. The question is, what will they do when they learn Mount Pleasant is being attacked? Personally my bet is that, being Argies, they'll sit on their backsides and do nothing, but one can't be sure. Presumably they have vehicles there, and they just might try to break out and take us in rear. Luckily the airfield is practically on an island: the road runs through that narrow isthumus of land. I suggest the Major of Sappers, with some of his own men, some LDF, and two of our GPMG's, constitute a blocking force. Come to think of it, the Sappers can lay some mines in the road, Argentine mines, poetic justice. But my bet is all we'll have to do with that lot is go over and take their surrender next day. That's my basic plan, Sir. But may I ask one thing? How long do we have to hold the place after we've taken it? How long will it be before people start arriving from UK to help us? How much does London know about this idea?'

The Governor told him of the conversations which he had had, via the Gurkhali language, with London.

'They tell me the spearhead battalion, plus half a field-ambulance, plus some air-defence gunners, plus the rest of 23 Phantom Squadron RAF, plus some spare pilots, are all at Ascension. They were sent there early on Thursday: luckily I was able to telephone and they stopped them coming on. What we've got to do is telephone just as soon as we are sure the runway is usable, and hope they're quick off the mark. We'll get the Gurkha experts to tee it up the night before. You may have to expect some air attack in the interval before they arrive. One thing you must do once you've won, and that is dish out all the Argies' gas-masks to your men: we don't know for certain if yours are proof against that stuff. Now, do you think that's enough for tonight? I suggest I send my barouche for you tomorrow at nine, and we'll have a full-scale conference at Government House. We can ring up London and get the latest.'

'Thank you, Sir,' said Major Wilkins, rising from the table round which they had all sat in the *Marianne's* saloon. The other officers, whose part had been to listen, rose also. 'Just one more thing, Sir – timing. We can't go tomorrow, obviously. Depending on how the SAS get on with their recces, we might be able to go on Monday. Most likely, I feel, is Tuesday, and I certainly don't want to keep my men confined to billets any longer than that.'

'Agreed,' said the Governor, also rising, 'we'll put it to London tomorrow. Now it's bed-time. See you in the morning, gentlemen.'

The whole party said their goodbyes and thank-yous to Captain Jones and his steward, and left the ship. On the quayside, besides the Governor's car, there was a solitary soldier. Company Sergeant-Major Mineur, thoughtful as ever, had sent him to guide his officers to their billets.

There was to be no sleep that night for the SAS section. Donning their operational gear, and borrowing a Land-Rover from the Police Station, they set out on their clandestine tasks.

☆   ☆   ☆

On Saturday morning, Major-General Romera and Captain Varela flew in from Comodoro Rivadavia. Accompanying them were a number of Argentine journalists and photographers, and a television crew. To his ill-disguised annoyance, Admiral Ricarda found himself obliged to spend a large part of the day with the media people: he did his best to head them off the more absurd statements and claims which they wished to make: they were inclined to take an unduly nationalistic and jingoistic attitude to the operation. Ricarda, by the end of the day, thought he had achieved a degree of success in heading them off this tack, and in encouraging them to stress the statesmanlike nature of the situation which his force had created. Over and over again he emphasized that the object was simply to bring Britain to the negotiating table, in a frame of mind where she was prepared to discuss sovereignty and to make concessions to international opinion which, Ricarda like all the other conspirators was convinced, was bound to come down on Argentina's side in view of the circumstances.

There also came with Romera in the big Hercules transport a large detail of war-graves specialists with their equipment: it would be their task to spearhead the search for the fallen Argentine warplanes and their dead pilots.

Admiral Ricarda had spoken to the Governor on this subject on the telephone, the evening before. The Governor had conceded that he was in no position to object to such a search if the Argentines wished to make it, but stressed that he had few personnel available to escort the search-parties: he did not think it advisable for the parties to roam about unescorted, in case of hostility from the local population. In the end it was agreed that there should be only three search-parties, that they should be unarmed except for side-arms, and that each should be accompanied by a police officer and a Sapper, the latter to indicate known mine-dangerous areas. The Governor was also able to stipulate that the search-parties should start nearest the airfield and work outwards to areas further away. From his point of view, the request added some dangers and complications to his immediate plans. On the other hand, the escorts might be able to pick up some useful information, and would at least be able to tell him where the respective parties were. It was arranged that the searches would begin on Sunday morning.

In the intervals of Admiral Ricarda's involvement with the media, his two visitors brought him thoroughly up-to-date on developments on the international scene. It was too early yet to be able to predict accurately what might happen in the United Nations Security Council, which was due to begin its emergency debate on Monday morning; but the general tone was one of optimism. The Foreign Minster had taken up temporary residence in New York, shuttling back and forth between that city, seat of the United Nations Organization, and Washington, seat of the US Government. He had spoken to innumerable Congressmen as well as to State Department officials, and had reported a considerable groundswell of opinion, if not in outright favour of Argentina, at least in favour of not encouraging Britain to attempt a military solution: the general view seemed to be that the clock could not be put back, and that this time the Malvinas problem, absurd when judged in comparison with other major problems, simply must be solved in a permanent way. The redoubtable Mrs Jeane Kirkpatrick, who as US Ambassador to the United Nations in 1982 had been forced to cast her country's vote in the Security Council in a way far removed from her personal inclinations, had written an article, all the more persuasive for its moderation and thoughtfulness, recommending that the US administration should take the lead in setting up an arbitration commission, and that the United Nations should back the idea with its full authority. President Bush had not yet declared his position, but people close to him thought that he was likely to be favourable to the idea: since he had incurred a lot of international opprobrium over the bloodshed and violence occasioned by the

179

US operations in Panama and the Gulf, the President had been known to be actively seeking opportunities for showing himself in a different posture – that of the leader of the world's most powerful nation, taking the lead in promoting an international peaceful solution to a problem instead of a violent one. Also, throughout Administration and Congressional circles, the views of those who followed Mrs Kirkpatrick in thinking that US interests in Latin America were too important to be overridden by loyalty to an ally which was anyway bound indissolubly to the US, seemed to be in the ascendant.

Captain Varela had also taken the opportunity to make a thorough inspection of the British base. He was impressed by what he saw, and by the efficient way in which the Marines and paratroopers had repaired the damage done and made themselves comfortable. He had made his rounds in the company of the Marine Quartermaster, who had been appointed camp commandant. This worthy showed Varela the two hut-complexes in which he had found suitcases and occupied wardrobes, a thing which had puzzled him. They discussed the matter but could come to no likely conclusion.

Varela continued thinking about this sporadically throughout the afternoon, and finally mentioned it to General Romera in the plane on their way back to Argentina. It was a long flight because, freed of the burial parties, they were routed back to Buenos Aires rather than to Comodoro Rivadavia. The General said at once,

'Do you think there were some we didn't get? Could they be off training somewhere?'

Captain Varela said he understood that the numbers taken corresponded pretty well with the known numbers of the British Garrison: it seemed an unlikely eventuality. Nevertheless the two officers agreed that, in view of the absence of any other likely explanation, the matter must be explored and they would do it at the first opportunity: next day was Sunday, and they agreed that they would attack the question first thing on Monday morning.

15

In Britain that Sunday, the papers were full of the Falklands. Never had there been such a two-day scurrying of investigative journalists, or so much midnight oil burnt in a desperate effort to make bricks with clearly insufficient straw, to get something into the Sunday papers which at least looked as if it contained some exclusive and even interesting information. It was not too easy to do this, once the writers had exhausted all the available knowledge about modern binary nerve-gases, which was not much, and as a certain proportion of the papers' contents clearly had to be devoted to the debacle in the South Atlantic, there had to be a good deal of comment as well. On the whole this comment was markedly unfavourable to the Government.

The criticism was made under a number of headings. Most general was the accusation that the Falklands garrison had been allowed to fall too low: there should have been more men and more aeroplanes. This was strictly speaking unfair, especially as the Army was known to be experiencing recruiting difficulties caused by the 'demographic trough': this is not however the sort of scruple that normally deters newspaper editors. A more telling, and fairer, criticism was that not all the eggs should have been in the one basket. It was also freely said that respirators should have been worn at all times, certainly when hostilities were seen to be imminent. The Government had been lulled into a state of insensibility by the seeming success of the campaign of rapprochement with Argentina. There had been a fatal flaw in the Government's whole scheme for defending the Falklands by rapid reinforcement. You name it, the Government had done it wrong.

At the foot of all this criticism, of course, lay the fact that all the people, the readers of the newspapers as well as their writers, felt unbearably shocked and humiliated. The ghosts of 1982 rose up, pointing the finger of accusation: the drowned sailors, the guardsmen burnt at Bluff Cove, the crashed SAS men, the Marines and paratroopers who had died at Mount Longdon and Goose Green – all seemed to be saying 'We did it for you, and then what did you do? You say you did your best, but what sort of a best was it? All that effort, all that money, all that suffering, all those lives (ours!) lost, and you still lost the game. Why did we bother?'

So the Members of Parliament, many of them newly-elected, found in their constituencies that week-end a mood that few of them had ever expected to encounter among the voters – a sort of shocked indifference. The voters did not seem willing to believe that the country was up against a real problem: still less did they wish to believe that the problem was one which needed to be dealt with by urgent military measures. The Argentines said they wanted to negotiate about sovereignty: well, why not negotiate about it? They said they wanted the problem sorted out by an international consensus: well, was that not quite a good idea? From uncounted small sources the innumerable trickles fed into the flood of feeling which washed over the Members as they laboured in their constituency surgeries that Sunday, or celebrated among the so-recently embattled party workers. In Labour or Conservative circles, even in Tunbridge Wells where 'Disgusted' held sway, the message carried on the flood was the same – 'Enough. Make an end.'

Against this unpromising background the First Sea Lord threw all the levers which lay at his hand to throw, in order to get the Navy into a posture where it could carry out the Cabinet's presumed intention – the sending of a Task Force to the South Atlantic. With well-oiled precision, the Navy Department went into action just as it had done in 1982. Storing of the ships due to sail in the first wave was proceeding apace at Portsmouth and Devonport and Gibraltar: the two carriers were already at sea and approaching their rendezvous at the Rock, on which their escorting destroyers were also converging. Behind this first wave, the whole huge organization was swinging once more into action. 42 Commando was in process of hurried extraction from a NATO exercise in Northern Norway, and 40 Commando was on its way from the western isles of Scotland to join 45 Commando, the Commando Logistics Regiment RM and No 29 (Commando) Regiment,

Royal Artillery, all of which units were either already at Plymouth or converging upon it. At Aldershot, 1st Battalion The Parachute Regiment was at maximum readiness to join 2 Para at Ascension. In ports all over the country, but especially in the surviving naval dockyards, work was already going on throughout every night to ready the armada for its duty in as short a time as possible.

None of this activity had, as yet, any real underlying authority except the expressed determination of the Prime Minister and Minister of Defence. No Cabinet meeting had been held to consider the project, though one was scheduled for Monday. Not until Tuesday would the House of Commons formally debate the way in which the Government had discharged its Falklands responsibilities, and the way in which it should discharge them in future. But Admiral Greenacre could not wait for these niceties – he had to make his preparations, as Admiral Leach had had to do in 1982, on assumptions: assumptions that the Cabinet and the House would do their duty as they had done ten years earlier, and order the Navy, backed up by the other Services, into action to restore order.

The more the Admiral thought privately about these assumptions which he was obliged at this stage to make, the more unlikely he found them. Isolated in some degree though he was by his exalted position and by the all-consuming responsibilities which dominated his waking hours (which included many hours when he ought to have been asleep), he was nevertheless still recognizable as a normal human being: he read newspapers, and he had a wife to whom he returned at odd hours for comfort and rest. He even watched the evening news on television. He was therefore not immune from the sentiment which rapidly throughout that weekend began to prevail throughout the country. The greater the exposure that he had to this national sentiment, the more he began to see a degree of unreality in what he was doing by day and half the night at the Ministry of Defence. Still, he had to go on doing it – it was his job.

In another part of his mind, the Admiral knew that there were other urgent possibilities. He had been present when the young officer of Gurkhas had dropped his bombshell, and privy to the instant but fairly temporary euphoria which had followed it. In their subsequent discussions, all the Chiefs of

Staff had agreed that the situation was one of great and unexpected promise; but would it work? Could two hundred determined and gallant British soldiers really put the clock back by successfully storming a big location, held by twice their number of well-armed professional regular troops? Would the position of surprise, which seemed to obtain at the moment, hold? How could it, when every telephone line in the islands remained open, and when the Argentines, with plenty of British helicopters at their disposal, to say nothing of their own, were in a position to mount a blanket reconnaissance effort at will? How long could the projected assault remain a secret? When, indeed, could it take place? And, when it did take place, and if by the grace of God it was successful, how long could they hold? Would this tiny force, presumably attenuated by casualties, be able to hold against possible counter-attack, long enough for the Phantoms and TriStars from Ascension to come to their rescue? In these hours of danger, there would be no fighter aircraft, no Rapier batteries, no radar surveillance, to help the exhausted men on the ground. Soberly, the Chiefs of Staff had realized, almost at once, that the sturdy Governor's plan was not without problems.

Still, it was a potential lifeline, and even before they told the Prime Minister about it the Chiefs of Staff busied themselves about giving it the maximum chance of success.

There was not in fact very much to do. The spearhead battalion with its important ancillary troops and the main part of the RAF Phantom Squadron had been at Wideawake Airport, Ascension for over twenty-four hours already. They were, and would remain, in a maximum state of readiness. Their aircraft, and the numerous tanker aircraft necessary to sustain them in their long flight, were also at Wideawake. There was fuel in abundance. All that was needed was the word – the electric word over the telephone link, that the airfield was won and the runway was usable without danger: once that word was given, Wideawake would reverberate to the thunder of departing jets – Phantoms, tankers, TriStars, more tankers, tankers to top up tankers which would in turn top up other tankers – the whole panoply of Falklands reinforcement which had been worked out in such meticulous detail and rehearsed so often. And what would *Invincible* and *Illustrious* and their attendant destroyers and oilers be doing? They would be pounding south at full speed, but it would be many days before they could reach the South Atlantic: perhaps in three days' time, with benefit of air refuelling, some of their Harriers could be flown off to join the air defence of Mount Pleasant. And yes, there was another ship coming along behind at her best speed, with some replacement Harriers.

One thing the Army Chief of Staff could do was to appoint a Force Commander to fly from Ascension with the paras and their supporting arms. There were many officers who might have been chosen, but the one the General chose was particularly well fitted by experience and ability, as well as by the rules of poetic justice, for the post. Brigadier Tony Leatham had commanded a company in 1st Battalion Welsh Guards in the Falklands in 1982, when nearly one-half of the divided battalion had been knocked out in the air attack on the *Sir Galahad* – a cruel stroke of fate for a fine unit. For the second time in his life (and, he fervently hoped, the last) Leatham found himself, with his faithful orderly Guardsman 27 Davies, heading towards the South Atlantic.

There was a further task to be performed by the General and his staff at the Ministry of Defence. Immediately after that fateful telephone conversation with the Falklands Commissioner of Police had taken place, the question of security began to loom large in everyone's mind. How could the Argentines be prevented from realizing that there were still two hundred British soldiers at large in the Falklands? It was a difficult enough problem at local level, with open telephone lines and the ever-present possibility of detection by aerial reconnaissance; but how about the situation here in Britain, where eight hundred men of the Mercian battalion should have returned in a shell-shocked condition, but only six hundred had in fact done so? Luckily the problem surfaced well before they actually landed, late on Sunday night: the whole force had in any case to stay at Brize Norton one night for medical examination and debriefing before proceeding on disembarkation leave: the debriefing therefore contained the most stringent admonitions, communicated to every man individually, against speaking to any representative of the media during the following days. But this was not all: officers visited the next-of-kin of every single man in C and D Companies, to explain why their menfolk had not come home with the others, and to impress the absolute need for discretion. In most cases the initial reaction of relief turned quickly into one of apprehension, but all the next-of-kin understood at once that their men could be imperilled by loose talk. After some debate the Chiefs of Staff decided not to take any direct steps with the media, such as an appeal to editors or the issue of a 'D'-notice: the operation had to take place in the next two days, and it was decided to watch and pray.

The question who should be told in political circles was a more difficult problem, and one which the Chiefs of Staff were glad to leave to the Prime Minister. It did not take him many minutes' thought to decide that the House of Commons could not be told – at least on the day of statements on Saturday: if there was then to be a debate on the following Tuesday (as it swiftly turned out there was), then a decision could be taken at that time: in the best possible scenario, good news would come through before the debate was finished, and that would enable him to triumph. He must simply wait and see.

The Cabinet was another matter. The traditions of Cabinet government in Great Britain are fixed and certain. The Cabinet has collective responsibility for the government of the country. This being so, it seemed to the Prime Minister that there was no way in which he could avoid telling all twenty-five members of the full Cabinet which was to meet in Downing Street on Monday morning, the full facts of the situation. If this meant twenty-five people, instead of two, dissembling to the House of Commons in what might well prove to be an exceedingly difficult debate – so be it.

In Argentina that week-end the general mood was one of sober optimism. The Generals and Admirals had pulled it off: Britain was for the moment impotent: international reaction to the limited nature of the occupation, and to its consonance with the announced aims of the Armed Services chiefs and the Government, had been on the whole favourable. In the United States the speeches of Congressmen, and the remarks of Administration officials, seemed to be disposed towards the adoption of an international solution to the Malvinas question: the continuance of a warlike stance over these quite unimportant islands was seen to be an absurdity, and as a fait accompli had been achieved and seemingly constructive ideas put forward to turn it to good account, was this not an opportunity to be grasped?

Above all, the countries of South and Central America, with the sole exception of Chile, seemed to be rallying to Argentina's cause. In Mexico, Brazil, Venezuela, Peru, and Uruguay the press comment was favourable, and statesmen both in the capital cities and in the corridors of the United Nations building in New York gave solid assurances of support to their Argentine counterparts. The Security Council was due to debate the matter at British request, starting on Monday afternoon. Señor Sanchez de Mayora, going his patient rounds, more and more got the impression that he would carry the day – at least in a negative sense. To be sure, the Security Council would probably pass a resolution condemning the Argentine action in some sense, but it would not be like Resolution 502, of that he was certain. At worst, it would be an anodyne type of resolution with no real teeth, no foundation on which Britain could go forth and rattle her ships and aeroplanes with tacit approval from the international community.

On Sunday in Buenos Aires a solemn Requiem Mass was held in the Cathedral for the glorious dead – the Air Force and Navy pilots, and the handful of Marines who had died in the brief struggle for the airfield. The service had been well publicized, and the great square outside the Cathedral was filled with a vast crowd of respectful people, to whom the proceedings were relayed by loudspeakers.

Alicia Martinez was accorded a place of honour inside the Cathedral, along with other widows and sorrowing, bereaved parents. Carlo's death had been notified to her on Friday evening. She was in her small apartment: the door-bell rang, and when she opened the door she found a young officer in naval uniform who looked so woebegone and apprehensive that she instantly divined why he was there. She asked him in and gave him a cup of coffee while he stammered through his sad story. The story itself came as no particular surprise to her: she had known the details of the plan all too well, and it had been clear to her that Carlo and the other pilots of the 3rd Naval Attack Squadron had been selected for a sacrificial role – that of attacking first from a different direction, and so drawing off the first fury of the British fighter defence. The last two days had been unmitigated hell for Alicia, with no definite news, only the knowledge, which quickly spread through the armed forces, that the Navy pilots had suffered heavy casualties. Now that the feared confirmation had come, she felt stunned and grief-stricken, but also curiously at peace. She had known it was likely to happen: it had happened, and she had to accept it. They had married with their eyes open, in full knowledge that their marriage might be a short one. God had seen fit to claim Carlo's life, and the only thing that she could think of now was that he was a hero, someone to whom she would look back in honour and love for all the rest of her life: someone who as well as having been her adored lover and husband had, she was now becoming virtually certain, also given her his child. He would be a boy, and she would bring him up in his father's image. Meanwhile she was going to have to make her way through a desert of grief and loneliness.

These first thoughts came back to her that Sunday afternoon in the packed Cathedral, with the thunder of the great organ rolling over her head in waves of sound. Veiled in black, she sat proudly with the other bereaved women as the Archbishop of Buenos Aires praised the courage of the dead men. The Virgin of Lujan and the Virgin of Rosario would watch over their souls in perpetuity, he said. Behind her the young officer who had broken the news to her, and who had come again in a Navy car to escort her to the Cathedral, sat ready to take her home at the end of the service. Then she would have to start picking up the bits in earnest.

In Puerto Belgrano, some nine hours earlier, the carrier 25 *de Mayo* had been eased by tugs into her accustomed berth. It was at the same time a triumphant and a tragic homecoming. A naval band was playing on the quayside, but they were solemn airs that it played. An immaculate Marine guard of honour presented arms, and the strains of the national anthem rolled out. At the top of the gangplank the carrier's Captain stood at the salute, his officers and ship's company lining the flight deck at attention. Behind them, clearly visible to all, the twisted remnants of a Skyhawk were crushed up against the ship's 'island': the body of her pilot, coffined under the blue-and-white Argentine flag, would shortly be carried with honour down the gangplank. Admiral Vasquez, as soon as the national anthem died away, ascended the gangplank. He and the Captain exchanged formal salutes, and then the Admiral seized the Captain's hand and shook it warmly: a microphone was brought forward for him: the ship's company, and the guard of honour on the quayside, were stood at ease, and the Admiral spoke.

'Captain Sanchez, officers and men of 25 *de Mayo* and of the 3rd Naval Attack Squadron. I honour you and I thank you today.'

It was an emotional occasion. The old carrier had at last made a place for herself in the history of Argentina. Her fliers had carved for themselves their own niche in their country's hall of valour.

No-one present paused to think what might have happened to the carrier and her ship's company, had her constant underwater companion during the last three days flown the flag of a more ruthless foe. Indeed, no-one knew for certain that there had been an underwater companion. *Sceptre* had slipped away unseen, to await whatever further duties might come her way. She had, on the fateful Thursday, duly reported that of ten Skyhawks which had left the carrier's flight-deck at dawn, only four had later returned; and that one of those, trailing a wing and gushing black smoke, had made a heavy crash-landing on the carrier's deck.

This message had been swiftly reported to Admiral Green-acre. At that stage on Thursday, there was no other news except that Mount Pleasant was off the air. It was nevertheless fairly clear to the Admiral, given the reports of the previous night, that an attack on the Falklands was in progress and that 25 *de Mayo*'s aircraft had taken part in it. The Admiral chewed his pencil reflectively.

'Shall we sink her, Sir?' asked the Director of Naval Operations, who was also present in the Ministry's operations room. 'There doesn't seem much doubt about it.'

'I don't actually see much point in sinking her,' said the Admiral. 'She's done her stuff: she won't be able to do it again, because she's lost almost all her aircraft. She threatens nobody now: it seems to me,' he continued, warming to his theme, a lifeline that had suddenly come to him from his dim past as a law student at Cambridge, before he had joined the Navy, 'it seems to me rather like a burglar.'

'A burglar, Sir?' enquired the astonished DNO.

'Yes, a burglar. If a burglar comes into your house and puts you in fear, you can kill him or maim him with whatever weapon you have to hand, including a gun. And you'll get clean away with it. But if you wait until he's getting over the garden fence and shoot him in the bottom, you'll be done for GBH, or murder if you kill him. It's rather like that. It's no good, DNO, I can't do it. Actually, I couldn't do it anyway, I'd have to refer to the PM. I'm going to spare him that decision. We'll not sink her.'

'What orders shall I give *Sceptre*, Sir?' asked the DNO, rather austerely.

'Follow her back to port, make sure she's going there, then resume patrol and await further orders. We particularly want to know whether any volume of seaborne traffic is headed towards the Falklands. Keep me in touch, will you?'

☆   ☆   ☆

On Monday morning, the Cabinet assembled in No 10 Downing Street. Of these ministers, about a quarter were new ones. The Prime Minister's consideration of his appointments list had, to be sure, been considerably disrupted by the bursting upon him of the bad news from the Falklands: nearly a third of the more junior appointments remained undecided. But the Cabinet was complete: the Prime Minister, amid the alarms and excursions of the past few days, had managed to complete his first eleven, or rather twenty-five. Of these, seven were new Cabinet appointments: of the former ministers, five had lost their seats in the General Election, and the other two had agreed to return to the back benches, against promises of uplifting to the House of Lords as soon as the political situation made by-elections a practical possibility: for the moment, it was a case of battening down the hatches, and seeing how the Government's business was going to go in the House of Commons with a very small overall majority. Soon, it was assumed, by-elections could be held.

In this Cabinet, as it assembled, one factor dominated everyone's thoughts – the Falklands. The minsters were also Members of Parliament, with constituents: they had been made aware during the weekend of the way their constituents

190

were feeling about things: they were therefore deeply uneasy as they took their seats round the long green baize table.

The Prime Minister appeared relaxed and confident. He welcomed his new Cabinet members, thanked everyone for their efforts during the election, and allowed himself a few moments during which he dwelt on the Party's astonishing success in winning four elections in a row. He then turned to the matter which was uppermost in everyone's mind. The Cabinet listened with fascinated attention as he told them about the two companies of infantry who had escaped the Argentine net and whose presence was still apparently unsuspected. He finished by saying:

'So, you see, we are going to have to go into tomorrow's debate without news of their intended attack, and there is no way in which we can mention it in the House until we get firm news one way or the other – whether it has succeeded or failed. Of course we all very much hope that it will succeed, and that we shall get good news before the debate is finished. We do have to envisage, I am afraid, the possibility that we shall be told the attack has not succeeded: in that event, I or the Minister of Defence will have the difficult task of telling the House what has happened, or rather failed to happen. From my experience of the House I should expect that to go down extremely badly, and we might get a very close vote. I ought to tell the Cabinet that the Secretary of State for Defence has placed his resignation in my hands. He is the very last person I would wish to lose from this Cabinet, but we have to face facts. Henry himself is adamant that he must be prepared to take the full responsibility for what has happened: I have persuaded him to hold his hand until tomorrow's debate is over, but I think we must all realize that if the vote goes badly, and especially if we have to announce further bad news, and probably the added bad news of more British casualties during the debate, then we are likely to be in trouble, and in that situation it may be inevitable that the Secretary of State should resign, as he is himself honourably determined to do.'

Heads nodded all round the table, and there was a sympathetic murmur of approval directed at Sir Henry Jones, who was sitting impassively, doodling on his blotter.

'May I ask, Prime Minister,' one member asked, 'at what stage do we expect to know the results of the proceedings in the

UN Security Council, and also what are the prospects of our getting a satisfactory resolution?'

'I think the Foreign Secretary had better speak to that,' said the PM. 'Douglas, will you tell us?'

'They are starting their meeting today,' said the Foreign Secretary. 'As I expect most people know, a good deal of time can be taken up at meetings of the Security Council in agreeing the terms of a resolution, and only when they manage to get something which they think has a chance of getting a clear-cut vote does the debate proper start. I would expect this one to take nearly two full days, that is to say the actual vote might be held some time on Tuesday. Of course there is the time difference, and if the vote drags on late into their evening it could be we won't get the result before the end of our debate. If we do get it, and assuming it's a good strong resolution passed by a decent majority, that can only of course help us enormously, both in the actual debate and in the way in which we can act to restore the situation, in the event that the Governor's counter-attack fails to restore it.

'But I must introduce a note of caution, Prime Minister, about these proceedings in the Security Council. Our representative there, Sir Montague Hesketh, is working his heart out putting our case to all the Council members, and he's getting plenty of help from our Ambassador in Washington: they are working as a team. However, Sir Montague does tell us that it's not entirely plain sailing. A number of the Council members are proving very hard to convince that this is just another case of smash-and-grab which has to be dealt with very firmly. There does seem to be a strong current of opinion, especially among the South American and African countries, to the effect that this is an occasion for the UN to come down firmly in favour of an imposed negotiated settlement. I don't want to be pessimistic, but I can't help wondering if we're going to get the firm backing we want.'

'What about our allies and the European Community? Are they being helpful?' another member asked.

'Yes, I think so. I am actually due in Brussels this afternoon for a routine meeting of Foreign Ministers; in fact with your permission, Prime Minster, I shall have to leave this meeting in a few minutes' time to catch the plane. Our European ambassadors report a lot of sympathy in all countries of the Commun-

192

ity. Needless to say I shall put our case very strongly, and frankly I expect to get a lot of support. That leaves the United States, the most important ally of the lot, and while there have been plenty of sympathetic noises, as yet there has been no firm declaration in our favour. We're working on it, and I hope the President will come out strongly on our side in time to influence the UN debate. I think that's all I can tell Cabinet at this moment, Prime Minister. May I dash for that plane?' He gathered up his papers and made his exit.

A short silence followed the Foreign Secretary's departure, and then one of the Ministers spoke up.

'Prime Minster,' he said, 'obviously we all hope this counter-attack with the two companies will prove successful; but if it does not, may I ask what your suggested policy will then be?'

To most of his listeners, not excluding the Prime Minister, the word 'suggested' seemed plucky, especially as he was not a particularly senior Minister. The Prime Minister, however, showed no annoyance. He said 'Well, as you know I would very much prefer to see a diplomatic solution where the Argentines were persuaded to withdraw. They have a very much more plausible case than they had in 1982: their approach is much more moderate, and it seems to me that a compromise solution might be possible. Now that we have been re-elected, it might be possible to consider some sort of joint-sovereignty situation, provided always that we could achieve that without undue humiliation. The trouble would come if the Argentines proved obdurate, and unwilling to budge at all from their present position. In that event I really think we should have to consider a measured military response.'

The Cabinet digested this. Then the last speaker said 'Prime Minister, do I understand you to say that if our immediate counter-attack does not succeed, you would consider assembling a 1982-style task force and sending it to the South Atlantic?'

'Yes,' replied the Prime Minister, 'I am afraid we should have to consider that most seriously. We have already been humiliated once: if the two companies fail, we shall be humbled again. There is a limit to the amount of that sort of stick a government with a majority of twenty can take. I am afraid we might very well have to take up arms in earnest.'

'Would you do that, irrespective of the way the vote went in the Security Council?'

'Depending on the exact wording of the resolution, yes, I think we might have to.'

The Cabinet dispersed in a thoughtful mood.

☆   ☆   ☆

On Monday morning, General Romera and Captain Varela met at the Defence Ministry to investigate the problem they had encountered at Mount Pleasant. It was difficult to know where to start, but they set enquiries on foot all over the building. By lunchtime nothing concrete had emerged at all. The records were clear that the British garrison had been reduced both as to men and as to fighter planes in 1990. These reduced numbers tallied almost exactly with the numbers of men captured at Mount Pleasant: the fighter numbers also tallied. There was no record in any of the files searched of any subsequent adjustment.

It was not until just before lunchtime that Varela suggested they consult the Minister of Defence himself. The elderly General had already gone out to lunch and was not expected back until four o'clock, as he had an engagement in the city. An appointment was therefore made to see him then.

When Romera and Varela explained their problem to the Minister, he at once said yes, he remembered very well that the British had made a modest increase in their Malvinas garrison, an increase which practically restored their numbers (of men, but not, he understood of fighters) to the former pre-reduction levels. He recollected the circumstances quite well. The British had apparently become alarmed by a sudden and sustained increase in flying activity in Patagonia, and evidently considered it politic to show Argentina that they were not asleep. They had been quite gentlemanly about it: they had not wished to make a public fuss or to embarrass the Argentine Government – they simply wanted to make their point, and the way they chose to go about it was to have their Foreign Secretary tell the Argentine ambassador in London that they suspected something was afoot and were therefore making up their garrison to its former strength. The matter had reached him via the Foreign Minister: at the time, they had both been mystified by the circumstances: he had tried to contact Gen-

194

eral Romera, but he was away, and he had therefore made his enquiry of one of his senior air staff officers, who had confirmed that there had indeed been a temporary upsurge in flying training in the southern provinces, but that it was all over now, and no further offence would be caused to the British.

'Minister, may I ask who was the officer you saw?' asked Romera.

'Your Director of Flying Training, Colonel Alfonso Jones. His explanation satisfied me completely, and he undertook to inform you fully. I fail to understand why you do not know all about it, because he was concerned, rather exceptionally concerned I thought, and he said he would brief you fully. Has he not done so?'

'Unfortunately, Minister, Colonel Jones was knocked down by a car, probably immediately after you saw him, and he has been lying in a coma in hospital ever since. Thank you for what you have told us, Minister. It will enable us to take appropriate action.'

It was no use involving that old fool any more, they said to each other as they returned to Romera's office. When they got there a call was put through to General Gonzalez, and the tale was told to him. A meeting was quickly convened in his office to discuss the implications of what had emerged.

At that meeting, two decisions were taken. One, that next morning Admiral Ricarda must be informed that there was a possibility that a substantial British force was still at large: he must mount a sustained reconnaissance effort, using all his available helicopters, in an attempt to verify or disprove these suspicions. Two, two hundred men of the 4th Marine Infantry Battalion would be flown in Hercules transports to Mount Pleasant. The C-130s would then go on to the old Stanley airfield and pick up half the paratroopers who were there at present, and bring them back as further reinforcements for the main Mount Pleasant position. By the time this had all been agreed and the necessary instructions given to the 4th Battalion (who were at a fairly high state of readiness) and to the transport aircraft, it was already eight o'clock in the evening. The senior officers' initial reaction of alarm had been tempered by common sense: the measures taken were obviously sufficient, and more than sufficient, to deal with a threat which had still not been proved to be a real one; and the reinforcements would be on their way by mid-morning next day. It was arranged that General Romera would telephone Admiral Ricarda early next morning to brief him and tell him what had been decided.

A sharp look-out was kept that Monday night, as it had been on the preceding nights, by the night guard at Mount Pleasant. The perimeter fence was patrolled at regular intervals, especially on the runway's eastern end nearest to Stanley town. The runway itself was also continually swept by the revolving searchlight on the control tower. Sentries in pairs patrolled the streets of the huge hutted camp. Nothing untoward was reported. The black-clad figures who flitted like ghosts between the sleeping-huts and the warehouse buildings, and who lay immobile out near the fence, were not observed as they went about their stealthy business.

In Port Stanley, early to bed was the rule for all the soldiers. Reveille was to be at four-thirty, and breakfast would be eaten before the men boarded the buses, only three buses because only three were available, which would shuttle them down the road to Mount Pleasant, for three-quarters of the distance, after which they would proceed on foot to the area near the airfield fence where they would meet their SAS guides. After taking the Mercian men, the buses would return and pick up about half the Local Defence Force, stiffened by forty Royal Engineers and other regular soldier details who had surfaced in Port Stanley in the past two days: this was the follow-on wave which would go in after the Mercians with the idea of performing guard duties over surrendered Argentine personnel.

Julian Wilkins with his officers and sergeants had spent the day at Government House, poring over the detailed drawings of the Mount Pleasant base, which fortunately were available, and concerting the plans. Also present was Major Harold Revington RE, a cheerful Sapper officer who embraced with gusto his new role as the commander of an independent fighting force. He was to have under his command the remaining thirty Royal Engineers, including seventeen Ukrainians, and forty men of the Local Defence Force, plus two GPMG sections from the Mercians. He even had artillery. A grinning LDF man had appeared with a World War Two-vintage two-inch mortar, complete with several dozen high-explosive bombs, which had been sitting in his cellar since 1945. In normal times this discovery might have led to his being asked some questions, but not now: in any case, it was his father who had hidden it, and his father was dead. This was a much-prized addition to Major Revington's resources.

The indefatigable buses, after ferrying the follow-up wave, would return and transport the scratch medical teams from the hospital: they would then assist the transport of Revington Force to their blocking defensive position on the isthmus between a recess of Stanley Harbour and the open ocean at Hooker's Point.

The Ukrainians in particular were in high fettle. They had been brought up on their elderly relations' stories of the fierce anti-partisan warfare which the Galician Division, under SS command, had conducted in the snow-covered forests of Byelorussia. Never in their most optimistic dreams had these men, born into families whose menfolk had found integration into post-war British society so difficult that they had joined the Volunteer Corps, engaged for many years in clearing unexploded bombs and shells from the ranges of Britain, never had they imagined that they would be allowed to fight as real British soldiers: well, they would show those steak-eating bully-boys of the pampas what stuff real men were made of. Unfortunately Major Revington, their much-respected chief, seemed to have hidden all the vodka tonight: there was nothing to do except give the rifle one more squirt of oil, and go to bed.

☆   ☆   ☆

Also on that Monday night, the Prime Minister saw the Chief Whip at No 10 Downing Street.

'How do you think it is going to go tomorrow?' he enquired when he had taken his seat.

'Frankly, I am not quite sure, Prime Minster,' the Chief Whip replied. 'I see you have the text of the motion put down in the Leader of the Opposition's name. I am afraid it is a rather clever one.' He read it out:

'That this honourable House censures Her Majesty's Government for its failure to make adequate provision for the defence of the Falkland Islands, and calls upon the Government to co-operate fully with the United Nations Organization in bringing about, without the use of force, a permanent and just solution to the Falklands Islands question.'

'It amounts, of course, to a motion of no confidence. What is perhaps more serious is that it obviously seeks to tie the Government's hands: it seeks to restrain the Government from a 1982-type solution; and it seeks to put the Government at the mercy of whatever the UN Security Council may resolve tomorrow; and that, I understand, is dicey.'

'Yes,' said the Prime Minster, 'it is dicey. I have just had a message from our UN representative: it's not going too well. The resolution that seems likely to be put forward may be a very wishy-washy one, not much good to us.'

'I suppose you do not have any idea when the result in the UN may become available tomorrow?' enquired the Chief Whip. 'I ask, because it could materially affect the way the Members vote, or fail to do so. This is a new Parliament, Prime Minster: a lot of them are new Members. You might think it would be very easy to whip such people into line, but I'm afraid it isn't. They are confused, they are getting a marked lack of enthusiasm and approval from the grass-roots, and they are inclined to be starry-eyed about the United Nations. The new ones, I mean, not the old hands. We simply have not got the new ones in hand yet, Prime Minister. There's no telling what they might do.'

'So how would you sum it up?'

'I would sum it up like this, Prime Minister. If you can announce, during the debate, a good strong UN resolution result, then I think it's plain sailing. If you can't, if the result doesn't come through at all, or if it's a bad result, then I think there could be a significant volume of abstentions. I don't think anyone will actually vote against the Government: but they could abstain.'

'And if we are able to announce good news from the Governor?'

The Chief Whip attended Cabinet meetings: he knew.

'That might have a very marked effect in our favour: in fact, I think it certainly would.'

'Thank you, Hector,' said the Prime Minister. 'I know that you will all do your very best.'

He rose. The Chief Whip smiled and shook his head reflectively, and departed.

The Prime Minister picked up the telephone receiver. 'I want to speak to President Bush,' he said to the operator. 'He ought to be at the White House at this time.'

In a few moments' time the call came through. 'President Bush on the line, Prime Minister.'

'George! How are you? I hope I don't grab you at an inopportune moment?'

'Not in the least, John. I have a full afternoon ahead of me, but I have got some time for you.'

'Frankly, I am worried about this UN vote. We have been hoping, and our representative is pressing, for a good strong resolution deploring the use of force, telling the Argentines they've gone over the top, and telling us both to respect the UN charter. I should like to be assured that you will stand behind us in our effort to get such a resolution.'

'To be honest, I am not at all sure that we can. That's just the sort of resolution that enabled you to go to war in 1982, with my predecessor's blessing, I may say. I am not sure we have quite the same situation. May I ask you, do you really intend to have recourse to arms this time – is that why you want such a resolution?

'I would very much rather not have recourse to arms, as you put it. I just want the ability to do so, if we have to. A weak resolution will simply encourage the Argentines to dig their toes in. A strong one, giving us in effect the military option, will tend to make them more ready to agree the sort of solution we might be willing to agree.'

'I see what you mean, but you also have to understand that American opinion, and that means South American opinion, as well as North American, is now simply not prepared to encourage you to use the military option. If you were to do what you did in 1982, opinion on this side of the pond would just not accept that that was the right solution to the problem. Putting it another way, things are not the same as they were in 1982: people just are not prepared to allow Mickey Mouse wars, that's how they see it to be brutally frank, in the South Atlantic when there are so many more real problems in the world.'

'Mr. President, may we leave Mickey Mouse out of it? This is a serious case of unprovoked aggression, which has to be dealt with firmly, like Saddam Hussein. The military option is one of last resort, but unless one is in a position to use it one is unlikely to get a negotiated solution. That's why I ask for your help. I remember, the day I was re-elected you called me and said, anything you could do for me, just ask. Well, I do ask you to give us the backing we need over this.'

'I'll do what I can, I really will, but I must warn you that it does not look good in the Security Council. I know they've only just started their debate, but the Secretary of State tells me that, already, there seems little hope of the Council passing the sort of resolution you want. Our representative has instructions that, if that indeed proves to be the case, he is to jump in with our own substitute resolution. It won't be what you want, but we feel we have to be pragmatic at this point.'

'I am very disturbed by what you are saying. I simply can't understand how the Security Council can stomach this sort of behaviour from the Argentines, and using gas too. It really is becoming a very difficult world to live in.'

'I agree. That's one thing we can agree on. But, forgive me for saying this, you have to look at this thing in the wider context of world affairs, the incredible things that are going on in Eastern Europe, in the Middle East, and in the Soviet Union itself, and probably soon in China. With all this happening it's just not real, in many people's minds, to go to war over small islands. I'm truly sorry, but that's the way it is. We will do our best to salvage something for you at the UN, that's all I can promise right now.'

'Well, thank you for that, anyway. And now you must be busy and wanting to see all those people. Goodbye, Mr President.'

'Goodbye for the moment, John. We'll keep in touch.' And the receiver was replaced in the White House.

16

Six o'clock on Tuesday morning. It was still dark, but the faintest lightening could be seen in the east as the Mercian companies marched quietly forward on the grassy verges of the road from Stanley. Steel-helmeted, their faces camouflaged, they were in 'fighting-order' – their packs had been left behind. Now they were near the airfield perimeter fence, and figures rose up at them out of the gloom, to guide them through the gaps which they had cut in the fence. Nearby, under close guard, the members of the Argentine perimeter patrol were lying or sitting propped up against their Land-Rover.

Quickly and quietly the Mercians moved up the north side of the runway: they met two more SAS guides on the way. Now they could see the street-lights of the big hutted camp, and the outlines of the hut-complexes. They shook out into extended order, each company two platoons up with one in reserve. C Company was to assault parallel with the runway: D Company moved over to the right to come in at an angle: behind each platoon the allotted Sapper and LDF members of the back-up wave followed closely: two general-purpose machine-guns were left with their crews on the edge of the runway. Now it was getting perceptibly lighter: they paused for a few moments to await the assault signal. Julian Wilkins went quickly down the line of the leading platoons until he met Captain Alan Jenkins; they conferred: this was it, the moment for which they had waited, and for which they had planned so carefully.

The storm burst upon the still sleeping Argentine Marines without warning. In the first hut-complexes which the Mercians reached, in which they knew from reconnaissance by the SAS that men were quartered, surprise was complete. Doors were flung open, lights switched on, commands shouted by the sections as they fanned out through their allotted huts. In these first huts, the sleepy and surprised Marines had no chance to resist: they froze in their sleeping-wear beside their beds, under the gun-barrels of the attackers. In each hut, two men, assisted by the back-up personnel, went swiftly round collecting weapons, which were then dumped outside the door of the hut: when this job was completed the Mercian infantrymen went on to the next hut-complex, leaving the Sappers and LDF men to continue holding the Argentines at gun-point. So far, so good.

But it was too good to last. In one hut several Argentine paratroopers snatched up their weapons in time to fire them before being themselves cut down. This alerted their fellows, and now Marines and paras were tumbling out of huts with their automatic rifles, and taking up improvised firing positions. It was getting light, and attackers and defenders could nearly see enough to fire at one another with precision. A confused mêlée followed, and a number of the attackers fell dead or wounded.

Now it was a regular battle between two bodies of well-armed professional soldiers. The attackers held the advantage because they had planned their attack, and they were in full fighting trim, while the defenders had been surprised and had to improvise their defence with whatever clothes and weapons they had been able to snatch up. Nevertheless they too had an advantage: they were defending and they were able to take cover of a sort, while the attackers were forced to advance in the open street-ways between the buildings of the base: nor could they afford to leave unsubdued huts or buildings in their flank or rear. As the German Sixth Army had discovered nearly fifty years previously at Stalingrad, fighting in built-up areas mops up infantry; and the Mercians were few in numbers for such a job. In these circumstances a confused and bloody 'soldiers' battle' developed, which was to last for some hours.

Admiral Ricarda, in his quarters in the control tower, was awoken by the sound of gunfire. He was out of bed in a flash, threw on his combat uniform and grabbed his personal sub-machine-gun. The Adjutant of the Marine battalion burst in.

'We are being attacked, Sir,' he said urgently. 'A number of huts on the eastern side of the camp appear to have been surprised and overrun. The rest of my battalion, and the paras, are up and fighting. It's a question of just fighting them to a standstill, step by step, but they're coming on like devils. At the

moment the front line is about four blocks away from here, Sir. I'll send some men in to defend you.'

At this moment the direct radio link with Comodoro Rivadavia signalled it wanted to talk. Ricarda put on the headset and spoke:

'Hello, Mount Pleasant here, Admiral Ricarda speaking. Over.'

'Good morning, Mount Pleasant. General Romera here. I have to inform you there is a possibility that some British troops, perhaps two hundred, may have been absent from the base on Thursday and could be elsewhere on the island. We are therefore sending you two hundred men of the 4th Marine Infantry Battalion. They have already left here in C-130s. When they arrive, the planes should go on to Stanley airfield and bring back half the paratroop garrison there. Please warn the commander this will happen. That should give you ample reinforcements to cope with any surprise attack. Meanwhile you should mount maximum reconnaissance effort with all available helicopters, and tell the Stanley commander to do likewise. If these British troops are really around, it is essential that they are located and closely watched. Please acknowledge these instructions. Over.'

'General, the 4th Battalion men will be highly welcome, but we are already under attack. A surprise infantry attack at dawn. They got into the camp and took several huts by surprise. The rest of our men are up and fighting hard. We still hold the greater part of the camp and I hope we can stabilize the situation, but it's too early to tell yet. I only hope the C-130s will be able to land. Over.'

'I hope so too. You should still outnumber these attacking people, and I trust you will be able to fight them off. The honour of Argentina, and the whole success of our enterprise, is in your hands. You will wish to get on with your battle. Please confirm you will call me as soon as you have news to report, and I hope it will be favourable. Over and out.'

'Thank you, General. I should indeed like to get on with the battle. We shall fight our hardest, and I will report to you in one hour's time. Out.'

The Admiral took off the headset. 'A fine time to tell me I might be attacked,' he remarked to the Marine Adjutant who had been listening-kin on the spare headset. Outside, the din of small-arms fire and exploding grenades seemed to be getting closer. 'Right,' the Admiral continued, 'let's be taking a look at what is happening out there. You get those men in here as fast as possible. At all costs, we mustn't lose this place.' So saying, the Admiral made for the door, but stopped before he got to it.

'You heard that they intend the C-130s to go on to Stanley and bring back half the paratroopers. That's not going to be practicable. Get onto Major Roatta at Stanley, tell him what's happening, and tell him my orders are he must load his whole force onto all available transport and bring it here. He will probably have to fight, but with luck he'll take the attacking force in rear and we'll bag the lot. Do that now.' And the Admiral went through the door and down the stairs.

On the isthmus to the east of Port Stanley, through which the road ran to the old airfield, Major Revington's force was moving into position. Although narrow on the map, the isthmus was too wide to be fully covered by the small force at his disposal. He therefore concentrated it on a front of about a third of a mile, on either side of the road, at a point where reasonably good defensive positions seemed to exist among the rocks which were to be found in the rough and soggy terrain. He had also reconnoitered a fall-back position in case it proved necessary to retire from the first one. The two Mercian GPMGs were carefully sited on the flanks, to fire in cross-enfilade across the open ground in front of the position: the two-inch mortar was sited in a hollow in the centre, where he himself remained. The rest of the Sappers and LDF men with their LMGs and rifles were spread out in points of vantage behind rocks: they were busy bringing up more stones to make these improvised positions into sangars.

In this posture Revington Force, which had moved into position half-an-hour after H-hour at Mount Pleasant, awaited developments. Just before eight o'clock things started to happen. A column of Land-Rovers, small trucks and commandeered civilian cars (in fact everything on wheels which the paratroopers had found at Stanley airfield) was seen moving up the road. The two Mercian GPMGs waited until a good portion of this column was in view, but its head was still a comfortable distance from the British positions: then they both opened fire. The three leading Land-Rovers burst into flames. Behind them all the other visible vehicles veered off the road and men in combat gear could be seen dismounting from them and fanning out to take up positions in extended order on either side of the road. Conserving their ammunition, the GPMGs ceased fire.

Now was the moment for which the two-inch mortar had been waiting for so many years. On a word from Major Revington, the crew of the little weapon fired eight high-explosive bombs at the enemy's presumed positions on the left of the road, and then another eight on the right-hand side. The small bombs, clearly visible as they climbed into the sky, exploded with a series of satisfying crumps in what appeared to be approximately the right places.

It was not possible to see what was happening on the enemy's side of the fence, except that the three Land-Rovers were write-offs, and all their occupants dead or wounded. It seemed to Revington, however, that the loss of these vehicles, and the subsequent mortar bombardment, might have upset and demoralized the enemy. In fact, nothing happened for nearly twenty minutes, and then a Red Cross flag was seen being waved on top of a stick: the flag was followed by a number of Argentine soldiers carrying stretchers and medical satchels, who rose somewhat nervously from their recumbent positions. When they found they were not shot at they came rather hesitantly forward to the burning Land-Rovers where, evidently, wounded men lay. It took about fifteen minutes for this operation of mercy to be completed, the laden stretchers being carried down the road and out of sight: finally, the Red Cross flag, after a last vigorous wave, was also withdrawn from view. Perhaps now hostilities would recommence.

The resumption of hostilities took the form of a sustained shower of small mortar-bombs. There were several mortars firing, and some seventy or eighty bombs arrived, distributed fairly evenly over the British front. The range was however largely a matter of guesswork for the firers, and most of the bombs fell behind the British weapon-pits. The sangars and hastily-dug shallow pits which the force was occupying af-forded adequate cover, and there were only two casualties, LDF men killed when a mortar-bomb fell directly into their sangar.

The next development was the switching of the mortar bombardment to a shorter range, the points of aim being some hundred yards in front of the British positions on the left of the road: smoke bombs were fired. The wind, which was blowing rather more briskly than was ideal, caught the smoke and distributed it, but by no means uniformly densely, over the front. Picking their moment, the corporals in charge of the two GPMGs began to fire on their enfilade lines into the smoke. The riflemen clutched their weapons and prepared to use them.

Now came the Argentine paratroopers, ghostly figures emerging from the smoke, firing their automatic rifles from the hip. The GPMGs, through whose fire they had run, continued to fire into the smoke in order to catch the second wave. A ripple of fire ran along the whole front of the left-hand half of the British position. The paras were out of the smoke now, and were falling everywhere. At no point did they succeed in getting nearer than fifty yards from the British positions, although they pressed home their attack with commendable courage. It was evident to Major Revington that they had suffered serious casualties: they began to fall back through the thinning smoke, into which the British machine-guns continued to fire steadily. A few, however, went to ground in front of the British positions: they were to keep up a tiresome harassing fire throughout the next few hours. To assist the withdrawal of the remainder, Revington allowed his mortar crew to fire ten of their now dwindling stock of bombs into the presumed area of withdrawal. From the Argentine side, a further shower of smoke bombs arrived to revive the screen and cover the attackers' retirement. Finally the GPMGs ceased fire, and the battlefield fell silent. When the last vestiges of smoke finally dispersed, at least forty khaki-clad figures could be seen on the ground over which the attack had come. Most lay still, but a number were moving, and one was limping towards the rear: nobody on the British side shot at him. After about a quarter of an hour, the procedure with the Red Cross flag was repeated: on this occasion, the process of removing the wounded took much longer.

Although sporadic sniping was to continue from those few Argentines who had gone to ground in front of the British positions, there was to be no further organized Argentine attack for several hours. Their losses had been severe: summoned in a hurry to relieve Mount Pleasant, their reconnaissance had been non-existent, and they had been brutally surprised by the storm of fire into which they had run: the Major in command had been wounded by the first salvo of British mortar-bombs; and they had no means of knowing how slender were the forces at Major Revington's disposal. Throughout the hours that followed, irresolution prevailed. Later, one more determined offensive effort was to be made.

☆   ☆   ☆

At Mount Pleasant, the savage and bloody hand-to-hand fighting continued. Crouched behind the corners of the huts, emerging every so often to fire down the streets, the Argentine Marines and paras fought fiercely. The Mercian men crept up to the hut corners, lobbing grenades as close as they could get to the defenders crouched behind, and then rushing them. In one or two instances, fire came from the huts themselves; however they were of timber construction, and quickly became death-traps for the attackers' light machine-guns.

Slowly but surely the defenders were being forced back. D Company was coming in at an angle from the defenders' left flank, and now on the Company's right the section of SAS men were in the line, and were able to assume an outflanking role. In a camp laid out on a square grid pattern, this was deadly. Finding themselves enfiladed from their left flank, and unable to use the wooden huts as fortresses, the defenders had no option but to withdraw, fighting doggedly all the way.

They took a terrible toll. Two of the three platoon-commanders in D Company, and one in C Company, were killed charging at the head of their men. Major Wilkins was killed, caught by a burst of machine-gun fire as he ran across one of the camp streets. Captain Jerman, who was second-in-command of C Company, took over its direction, overall command passing to Captain Jenkins of D Company. In the ranks of the companies, there were many dead and also many wounded: the company medical orderlies did their best to help these unfortunates, applying first field dressings and, with the aid of a number of LDF men who had been detailed to act as stretcher-bearers, getting the worst cases away to the aid-post which had been set up by a medical team from the Stanley hospital in an empty hut. A number of other LDF men, and some Sappers who were not required for the job of guarding the Argentine prisoners, came up into the line to fill the gaps in the Mercian ranks. Company Sergeant-Majors Hillier and Mineur, as is the way of their kind, were everywhere, encouraging the young soldiers, taking temporary command of officer-less platoons, and generally animating the assault. The Colour-Sergeants, aided by their clerks, concentrated on bringing up and distributing ammunition: the supply of this was by no means unlimited, as there had been no appreciable reserves found in Stanley, and the companies were dependent on what they had taken with them to West Falkland and had not expended in their field-firing exercises. The CSMs were in their peregrinations constantly exhorting the soldiers to conserve ammunition, and to fire short bursts and aimed shots only.

In fact, the Argentine defenders had the same problem. Initially they only had what they had been able to snatch up when they hurriedly left their huts. A certain amount of replacement ammunition was distributed successfully by the quartermasters and their staffs; but now the lieutenant-quartermaster of the Marines was shot down as he was lugging a box of ammunition up to his forward positions: this disrupted the process. Modern automatic rifles use huge amounts of ammunition, especially in the hands of men with Latin temperaments. Both sides were to feel increasingly constrained by this factor as the morning, in all its dust and din, wore on.

On the runway quite early on, two helicopters had attempted to get airborne, and were promptly riddled with bullets by the GPMGs. That was the end of that idea, and thenceforth one of the guns was able to assist C Company's advance by ensuring that nothing moved on the runway's edge. Now it was approaching midday, and suddenly Lance-Sergeant Smith on that gun saw a very large aircraft approaching: some way behind it flew another, and behind that a third could be dimly seen in the distance. Smith signalled to the commander of the other gun-team, some way behind him: he had seen them too. The three Hercules C-130 transports roared over from west to east and then described a wide circle in the air, evidently preparatory to landing into the wind. They had got no joy out of ground-control as the tower radio was actually unmanned at the time, and the pilots had to make up their own minds whether to risk a landing. Finally the leading aircraft shaped up to land: the other two continued to circle for the time being.

The rearmost GPMG was moved round to face at the left limit of its traverse the landing C-130. The sergeant in charge started to fire just before it touched down: the bullets could be seen striking all over the nose of the huge aircraft, and the windscreen was shattered into a thousand fragments: still the Hercules came on, lumbering down the runway like some great beast in torment. The sergeant traversed his gun to fire straight across the runway: he simply held it steady and fired as the nose came level with him, stitching a long line of bullet-holes down the side of the transport. Now it was the turn of the leading GPMG to do the same, and the second gun started to fire forwards as the Hercules advanced down the runway, into the wing-roots and the backs of the engines. Suddenly the Hercules veered sharply to the left, careering at speed off the runway onto the rough grass at its southern edge: a fireball appeared on the starboard wing-root and instantaneously mushroomed: the whole aircraft was engulfed in a shattering explosion, a huge cloud of oily black smoke towering up into the sky as the plane lurched to a halt and disintegrated. Elated but appalled, the two GPMG crews watched in disbelief. Then they turned their attention to the second and the third aircraft: these had ceased to circle and were on a westerly course, making height as quickly as they could. Shortly they disappeared from view, evidently on their way back to Patagonia.

This startling tragedy was not unobserved by the Argentine defenders, or at least by those who were not so closely engaged that they had no time to see what was going on elsewhere. It was clear to all the defenders who did see what happened, that there was now no hope of airborne reinforcement. Brave and stubborn men though the Marines and paras were, this was a profoundly discouraging realization. In front, the battle was unremitting as the British troops continued to press home their attack. On the Argentine left flank, the outflanking process was continuing slowly but inexorably: the defenders found themselves constantly looking over their left shoulders, and wondering whether a long burst of fire would come from that direction and force them to fall back to the next hut-corner. Seeing the success of the outflanking tactic, Captain Jenkins now reinforced it by switching the left hand platoon of D Company over to the right flank: seeing it coming, the SAS section took off and doubled still further to the right hand flank: here they found themselves in an almost undefended area, with cooks and storemen running about in confusion: and now they were inside the main Argentine ammunition-store, shooting down two· men, each of whom was on his way out of the store carrying a metal ammunition-box. In this area, for the first time Argentine soldiers began to surrender individually and in small groups of three or four. Elated, the SAS and the Mercian platoons pressed on. The defenders in front of C Company, increasingly under pressure from their left flank and rear, began reluctantly to accelerate their step-by-step withdrawal. More and more, they were being compressed into the area round the control-tower, with their backs to the runway, which was swept by the lethal Mercian machine-guns.

Over on the isthmus at Hooker's Point, things had been quiet for over three hours, apart from the intermittent sniping on the left half of the British position, and occasional mortar-bomb showers which, fortunately, had caused no further casualties. The British force had been able to relax a little in its positions: there had even been a delivery of sandwiches, brought up from Stanley by the LDF administrative staff. The enemy in front had been ominously quiet. Now, suddenly, they moved.

Sighing through the air, the mortar smoke-bombs fell in a tight pattern all over the right-hand half of the British front and a bare seventy yards short of it. The wind had fallen, and a dense smoke-cloud was achieved. The GPMGs began to fire steadily into it on their cross-enfilade lines. Cheering and shouting was heard from inside the smoke, officers and sergeants urging their men forward. Combat-clad figures appeared at the front of the smoke-cloud, and there they were, nearly sixty Argentine paratroopers, pressing resolutely forward, twinkling points of fire indicating, as did the accompanying noise, that they were firing their automatic rifles from the hip. The right-hand GPMG was masked by the smoke, and could do no more than continue to fire on its accustomed line into it; but the left-hand one, at very much longer range, was able to fire visually, and figures began to fall in the charging Argentine lines. Still, there were a lot of them, and they were very close now.

By chance, the Ukrainian element of the Sappers was concentrated on this right-hand sector. They had insisted on fighting together as a sub-unit: Major Revington had accepted this, and had put them under control of an experienced Sapper sergeant whom they seemed to admire and respect. Now they were to bear the brunt of this menacing Argentine assault.

John Sofiesku had been born in Bradford. Most of his young life had however been spent in the various hutted camps of the Volunteer Corps – Felixstowe, Skegness, Hull, all the other places near the ranges of wartime Britain where the men of the Volunteer Corps lived with their families while they pursued their hazardous daily life of clearing unexploded shells and bombs. It had been almost a regimental life: in the British Army, so to speak, but not exactly of it. John had been to school in various places up and down the English east coast. When he grew up, he joined the Volunteer Corps in his grandfather's footsteps. He had his heroes, and foremost among them was Lance-Corporal J.P. Kenneally of the Irish Guards, whose exploits at the terrible battle of the Djebel Bou Ahkouaz in Tunisia in 1943 had won him the Victoria Cross and imperishable fame.

Now, seeing the Argentine paratroopers advancing on him out of the smoke, John Sofiesku remembered Kenneally, and he suddenly resolved to do or die. Rising out of his weapon-pit, firing his rifle from the hip he dashed forward, shouting an Ukrainian fighting-cry. The surprised paras made way for him: he continued, firing and shouting, through their midst: then he veered off right-handed, turned round, and charged back through them, firing as he went. The bemused paras fired at him and then at each other: at that moment the other Ukrainians as one man rose to their feet: shouting a terrible Galician yell, with the pale southern sunlight glinting on their levelled bayonets and the muzzles of their rifles spitting fire, they hurled themselves upon the Argentines. After some confused moments of mêlée in which men fell on both sides, the

211

Argentine paratroopers began to fall back through the now thinning smoke. The startled Sapper sergeant, who had been jolted into joining the assault, was rounding up his charges with cries of 'Come back, you fucking Balkan idiots!' Come back they did, reluctantly, with several of their bayonets scarlet-stained. But John Sofiesku was lying still on the grass among a number of other khaki-clad figures. He was to be awarded, posthumously, a very important decoration indeed.

When the Ukrainians, minus several of their number, had with difficulty been persuaded to resume their defensive posture, and when the smoke had finally cleared from the battle-field, the same palaver involving the Red Cross flag followed after a short interval; but this time the Argentines were joined by British stretcher-bearers. The battlefield had fallen quiet: even the snipers on the left-hand side of the road had ceased their sniping. There was a feeling that it was all over.

The control-tower was now under attack. Next to it was the big aircraft-hangar where the four British Phantoms stood, together with several helicopters. This was otherwise empty, not being a suitable place for defence. Adjoining the hangar was the RAF workshop, a cluttered place full of workbenches, lathes and other machinery. There was cover for defenders in there, and a savage struggle raged for nearly an hour before the Mercian men could call it their own. Now they were working out how to attack the administrative block next to the control tower and the tower itself, which was a circular structure with wide windows facing onto the runway: from those windows there was a comprehensive view of the runway in both directions.

Admiral Ricarda had found to his dismay, when he had left his headquarters in such a hurry, that he could exercise very little control over the battle. The Marine and parachute battalion commanders had their men in hand and were doing all that was necessary to keep them in the line and firing: ammunition supply was being organized, as was the evacuation of casualties to the regimental aid post in the western part of the defended area. At that early stage of the battle, the outflanking movement which was to prove of such importance was not yet perceived to be a threat. The Admiral therefore made his rounds, showing himself to the soldiers and conferring hurriedly with both Colonels. Then he remembered his undertaking to radio General Romera on the hour, and made his way back to the control tower in order to do so. He did not have very encouraging news to give the Air Force General, but at least was able to say that his men were fighting strongly, that in the main the defence was holding, and that serious casualties were being inflicted on the attackers. In return he was told that the C-130 aircraft carrying the reinforcing men of the 4th Marine Infantry Battalion should be arriving in the near future.

Buoyed up by those hopes, Ricarda then telephoned the paratroop detachment at Stanley airfield to find out how that relieving effort was progressing. The only person he found to speak to was a company clerk who had been left behind to man the telephone, but that man was well-informed. He told the Admiral that virtually the whole contingent had moved out as ordered, but he understood they had encountered serious resistance from strong British forces after only a couple of miles on the road. Several vehicles had come back into camp loaded with wounded men who were being cared for by the medical detail, which had also been left behind. The sergeant in charge of the stretcher-bearers had told him that there were a great many British, well-equipped with mortars and machine-guns, in concealed positions astride the Stanley road. The first attempt to dislodge them had narrowly failed, and the Major in command had been wounded by a mortar-bomb. They would be making further efforts to get through, no doubt about that: that was all he could tell the Admiral for the time being.

This was not very encouraging. The Admiral remained in the control-tower with his orderly and his staff-officer: periodically, reports came in from one or other of the commanding officers. Ricarda was just preparing to leave the tower for a further spell on the battlefield when he observed the three Hercules aircraft making their approach from the west. What then followed was even less encouraging. Gazing grimly out of the big picture-window at the blazing wreck of the first C-130, from which not one figure had the slightest chance of emerging, Ricarda felt for the first time that the battle might be lost. Leaving the staff-officer to hold the fort, he once more put on his steel helmet and sallied out with his attendant orderly to see if he could do anything to influence the battle.

Now, after another hour-and-a-half in the thick of the fighting, he was back in the control-tower, nearer to which the firing was steadily approaching; and he was wounded. A small British bullet, one of a burst fired from a SA 80 automatic rifle, had taken him in the left shoulder, narrowly missing his collar-bone. The shock had nearly knocked him over: there had been a lot of blood, but for the moment he felt very little actual pain. His Marine orderly had hauled him behind a hut, and had there ripped open his combat jacket, done all the right things to staunch the flow of blood, and applied a first field-dressing with entire competence. He had then managed to persuade the Admiral to leave the battlefield and return to the control-tower.

Before being wounded, Ricarda had made a fairly full tour of his whole front line. What disturbed him most was that a lot of his men, Marines and paras alike, seemed to be getting very short of ammunition. It was just not getting through to them. They, of course, were getting through it at an enormous rate: give a South American a modern automatic rifle with a high rate of fire, and he will fire it in unnecessarily long bursts. Everyone had now been in action for several hours: at the start, the ammunition supply had been efficiently organized by the quartermasters and their staffs: now it seemed to have dried up. Ricarda knew where the main magazine was located, in the northern sector of the occupied portion of the camp in which the fighting was taking place: he set out to see what was happening there, dodging across the long streets swept sporadically by British fire. Passing numerous improvized Argentine positions, the occupants of which confirmed to him that bullets were in short supply, he finally reached a point where the defenders were looking and firing northwards: the magazine was two blocks further on, but the embattled paras told him he could go no further: this was now the front line. With a sinking heart he realized that the magazine was in enemy hands. He began retracing his steps back to the control tower, and he was half-way there when the British bullet spun him round and knocked him flat.

Now he was sitting in his headquarters, wondering what was going to happen next. He tried another call to Stanley airfield, but the clerk there told him he understood the British position astride the road had still not been forced: more wounded paras had been brought back to the camp.

Up the stairs came the Marine Colonel. Outside, the din of battle had fallen strangely silent. The Colonel was dirty, exhausted, and distraught.

'Admiral, we have no more ammunition. The men are down to their last clips. The shots you hear out there are all British shots. Our chaps can't fire back – they're clean out. Our Quartermaster was coping well, the ammo was getting through, and then he was killed: that didn't help, and then those devils of British got round our left flank and captured the magazine. We can't go on, Admiral: if we try to, it'll just be murder, and nearly half my men are dead or wounded already. The paras are in the same state – heavy casualties, and no more bullets. I've just been with Colonel Artuso, and he is in agreement with what I am suggesting to you.'

'You suggest we have no alternative but to surrender?'

'Unless you know some relief is on the way, either from Stanley airfield or the mainland – yes, that is what I suggest.'

'There is no relief. You saw what happened to the Hercules? I have just spoken to Stanley and I understand they are stuck: held up on the road by well-entrenched British positions. Quite a few casualties, and they can't get through.'

Both men looked at each other. The Marine Colonel shrugged his shoulders. 'We did our best, Sir. If only we'd had some warning they might come this morning.'

'Yes,' said Ricarda, 'if only you had. If only they'd warned me last night, instead of waiting until this morning. But there it is. We must surrender before all our men are shot down defenceless: we can't fight without ammunition. Go down now, and get some white sheets and put them on bayonets, and wave them round the corners. Do it now, before more men get killed.'

The Marine Colonel saluted and turned on his heel. It took another fifteen minutes for the firing to die away altogether. All round the small defended perimeter, men laid down their arms and waved doubtfully-white things round corners. With great caution, still doubting that it was really all over, the British soldiers came forward to collect weapons and marshal their prisoners into places where they could be overseen.

Ricarda sat on in the control tower: there seemed nothing else to do for the moment. His wound was beginning to hurt him a bit, with a sort of painful stiffness rather than real pain. He thought about radioing Comodoro Rivadavia, but it then occurred to him that the British might misunderstand such an action. Now there came a step on the stair, and a British officer came into the room, followed by another soldier, an upright man with a rather fierce moustache: a Sergeant-Major, the Admiral thought to himself. He rose to meet his visitors.

Captain Alan Jenkins saluted with his left hand. He did this because he too was wounded in almost exactly the same way as the Admiral, but in the right shoulder: his right arm was in a sling, and the shoulder of his combat jacket was stained darkly with blood.

'Admiral Ricarda?' he enquired. Ricarda nodded, and Jenkins continued: 'Your men are in process of surrendering to mine. Do you yourself as Commander formally give me your surrender?'

'I do,' said Ricarda.

'Thank you, Sir. Now I must ask you to hand over your personal weapons.' The Admiral picked up his sub-machine-gun which was lying on the table, and gave it to the man with the fierce moustache, who advanced to receive it. He then, with his good hand, took his revolver from its holster and handed that over too.

'Thank you,' said Captain Jenkins. 'Shall we sit down? I am sorry to see you are wounded; as you see, I am too. I find it rather tiring. My name is Jenkins, by the way. My superior officer, Major Wilkins, was killed a couple of hours ago. May I ask where you acquired your command of English, Sir?'

'London,' replied the Admiral. 'I was Naval Attaché a few years ago. I wish to God I still was.' Both men laughed, and sat down at the big table. During their exchange the Sergeant-Major had collected the personal weapons of the staff-officer and orderly: they stood irresolutely in the background.

'Admiral,' Jenkins said, 'we have horrible problems, chief of which is the very big number of wounded. I speak for my own side, but I have also seen a lot of wounded among your men. I am sure that you have a medical team here, and that they will do their best: we also have a medical team from the Stanley hospital, but quite frankly the resources at our disposal are

216

completely inadequate to cope with such numbers of casualties.

'I don't expect to have anyone look at this wound of mine for many hours – there are too many more serious cases. Now, Sir, you will appreciate that in a moment I am going to telephone the Governor, and that he will telephone London, and that a relieving force will then leave Ascension Island at once. They will bring some medical reinforcements with them, but even then we will be hard put to it to treat everyone properly. It strikes me, Sir, that you ought to tell your people on the mainland about this serious situation with the wounded, so they can make contact with the International Red Cross, and make preparations for some medical back-up. You will appreciate I have no authority to agree any arrangements – they'll have to do that with London through the intermediary of the Red Cross.'

'Yes,' said Admiral Ricarda. 'That is sensible. Shall I do that immediately?'

'Please. I hope you will forgive me if I tell you that I understand Spanish fairly well. Would you tell them one or two more things?'

'What sort of things?' asked the Admiral.

'I suggest you tell them that this camp is full of your men and mine, all mixed up, and that if any bombing attack takes place they will hit your men as well as mine. If they feel like making a gas attack like they did on Thursday morning, we now have your respirators, so it will be your men who get gassed.'

'I will certainly tell them that, but I can't take their decisions for them, as I am sure you will understand. Now, before I radio, is there anything else?'

'Only this, Sir. We are all going to be awfully hungry quite soon. I know this camp is full of food. I don't know whether your cooks have been much disturbed by the fighting, but I suspect they may not have been. Could your staff-officer here go with Sergeant-Major Hillier, and try and sort out some feeding arrangements? I don't see why any of us should go to bed hungry, whether we've won or lost.'

The Admiral laughed. 'You are certainly a highly practical young man, Captain.' He spoke rapidly in Spanish to the staff-officer, who nodded and then saluted, leaving the tower with CSM Hillier. 'We have indeed been enjoying excellent food since we arrived here, and like you I see no reason for anyone to be hungry tonight. Now I will try to persuade my side on the mainland not to bomb us. In my opinion there has been quite enough blood shed already.' And he went to the radio.

☆   ☆   ☆

Major-General Romera had had a difficult and frustrating day. He had not been able to leave the vicinity of his radio room in case Mount Pleasant came through, and he had indeed had several conversations with Admiral Ricarda, increasingly less hopeful in tone on the Admiral's side.

Now, after this final conversation, he laid down the headset, and looked at his Chief-of-Staff who had been listening in. Outside on the tarmac, an Air Brigade of Mirage fighter-bombers was lined up. The aircraft had been fuelled and bombed-up, as a precautionary measure, for hours. The bombs were high-explosive: all the gas bombs had been used on Thursday. The crews were ready and briefed: a word would launch them towards the Malvinas. There would be no Rapier ground defences, no Phantom heavy fighters to greet them. They could bomb the place to bits without let or hindrance, and other planes were waiting on other southern airfields to go in after them.

'What do you think?' he asked the Colonel. 'That camp is a sitting duck for us, isn't it?'

'I think, Sir,' replied the Colonel decisively, 'that you should not attack on your own initiative. Should you not consult with the other service heads? Personally, I do not like the idea of bombing our own men, and I ask myself what we would achieve by doing so, except to make a lot more dead and wounded men. However much we bomb the British, they will still be able to dominate the runway with fire. Even if they are down to their very last machine-gunner they will still be able to brew up our transport aircraft like they did this morning, and unless we can get some troops in we shall get nowhere by bombing. I calculate the British will be in there with more troops flown in from Ascension in about twelve hours. In short, Sir, all the factors which were operating in our favour are now operating against us. I hope I have not spoken too frankly, Sir.'

General Romera walked over to the window. Outside, the Mirages lay in the sunshine, attended by the odd mechanic doing last-minute adjustments. He looked at them for a full half-minute. Suddenly he felt very old and immensely depressed: he wondered whether they would put him in prison, and whether he would ever get his pension. How had it all gone wrong? But it had, and now he and his colleagues would have to face the consequences. No doubt the President would be back at his desk at the Casa Rosada by tomorrow morning: well, it was to be hoped he would make a good job of picking up the pieces, and perhaps something good for Argentina would be salvaged from the debacle. He turned round.

'No, Jorge, you have not spoken too frankly. I expect General Gonzalez will react exactly as you have done. Let us talk to him now.'

☆   ☆   ☆

Sir Hereward Gurney had also had an anxious and frustrating day. He had faced the dilemma which confronts many senior commanders – whether they will be better employed at the front seeing things for themselves, or at their headquarters. Not fancying himself at street-fighting at his time of life, Sir Hereward had chosen to remain by his telephone, and had been rewarded by a virtual absence of news from both his fronts for many hours.

In the middle of the morning, however, he had sent out scouts: the Commissioner of Police had visited Mount Pleasant, from where he reported that the assault seemed to be going reasonably well, but that there were already many casualties. His secretary had gone over to Major Revington at Hooker's Point, and was able to bring back a favourable report.

The telephone rang, and the Governor picked it up quickly.

'Governor, Sir? Captain Jenkins here, Mercians. It's all right, Sir, we've won. Admiral Ricarda has surrendered to me, and his men have also given themselves up, and are under lock and key. Their weapons have been collected and locked up, and I have also taken over all their gas-masks and given them to my own men, just in case they drop any more of that nerve-gas. Admiral Ricarda, Sir, has radioed his mainland headquarters in my hearing, and he told them that this camp is full of Argentines and British all mixed up, that any bombing

219

attack will cause more casualties indiscriminately, and that we've got the gas-masks.'

'Good,' said the Governor, 'that might deter them. What about Wilkins? Is he all right?'

'No, Sir, he's dead: that's why I'm calling you. I am slightly wounded myself, actually, but it's not too serious. I can remain in command for a bit, and I've got two subalterns and both Company Sergeant-Majors to help me. But, needless to say, we need reinforcements, but quick. Will you ring London, Sir? Tell them the chief problem is the wounded: there are scores of them, and lots of dead too, on both sides. We just must have more medical help: anything you can do here will be of assistance, Sir, but most of it must come from London. I did get Admiral Ricarda to tell his mainland people about the wounded problem: he asked them to get going with the International Red Cross. It's a really serious problem, Sir.'

'Yes, of course. I'll call London now, and tell them all you've told me. Now, how about the runway? Is it clear? I presume you can stop any Argentine plane landing, but can our planes land? This is absolutely vital, I'm sure you understand that.'

'The runway is clear, Sir. I have no-one who understands how to be an air traffic controller or speak on the air, but we'll fire white Verey lights when they arrive. I can guarantee that no Argentine aircraft will land: we brewed up one transport this morning, and we'll do the same to anything else that tries to land. What I can't guarantee is that there'll be no air attack while our chaps are landing. I think they should send the Phantoms in just before the transports, to maintain cover: they must have thought of it, Sir, but you might just mention it. One last thing, Sir, for the moment: could you possibly come up here yourself and see how things are? We might even give you some supper: I've got the Argentine cooks working, to feed everyone.'

'Yes, I will come, when I've called London.' said Sir Hereward. 'God bless you, Jenkins, you've done wonderfully well. I'll be with you shortly. Goodbye now.'

The Governor replaced the receiver, and found his young secretary standing beside him.

'Good, just the man I want. Go over to Major Revington, and tell him we've won. He should enter into parley with those fellows there, under flag of truce. The object is to persuade them to go back to barracks and stay there. They can keep their weapons, provided they promise not to try any more break-outs. We'll sort them out in a couple of days' time, and then they can march out with all the honours of war, drums beating and so on. The thing is, they must be made to understand we have won: Mount Pleasant is in our hands and large reinforcements will shortly be arriving from England. Got it?'

The secretary signified assent and prepared to leave.

'Oh, and one more thing. Before you go, get hold of the Commissioner. Tell him we've won at Mount Pleasant, but that there are very many wounded. There's a first-class medical emergency: all hands to the pump, anything he can organize will be of vital importance.'

'Now,' said the Governor, 'London.'

Company Sergeant-Major John Hillier was feeling on the top of his form. True, he was dirty, exhausted, and beginning to be hungry, but he was sustained by the elation of combat and victory: the adrenalin was still coursing through his veins.

Hillier was more or less monarch of all that he surveyed. The other CSM, Mineur, was some way junior to him: an excellent fellow, and a good colleague, with a good line of recitation in the sergeants' mess, but junior all the same. He had willingly taken over the entire job of guarding the Argentine prisoners, safeguarding their weapons, and appropriating their special respirators and distributing them to the Mercian and SAS men and the auxiliaries. He, John Hillier, was responsible for everything else, and the surviving company commander was wounded: to be sure, he was still in command, but he was getting quieter and it was a question whether he would last out until the TriStars came in with the spearhead battalion. Meanwhile, he as senior CSM would see to things.

His visit to the Argentine cookhouse had been a success. Despite language difficulties, the Argentine staff lieutenant had proved to be both sensible and helpful. They had found the main cookhouse undamaged, and had flushed the cooks out of various pantries and larders in which they had taken refuge. The master-cook had been quick to understand the staff-lieutenant's orders to get busy preparing six hundred-plus meals for all men of both nations, wounded and unwounded, and to be ready to do the same at breakfast-time in the morning. On their way back through the camp they had explained, in their respective languages, to all whom they met, that food was in prospect, and the news had been greeted with general acclamation.

Hillier knew that he had behaved with conspicuous gallantry when Captain Jenkins had been wounded. The captain had been cut down, like many others, while dodging across one of the camp's long, straight streets: the Argentine bullet, with high striking and stopping power, had caught him in the shoulder, spun him round, and dumped him on the ground a couple of yards away. Without hesitation the CSM had gone out into the roadway, ignoring the bullets kicking up the dirt all around him, to drag his officer back into cover.

'Thank you, Sarn't Major,' Jenkins had muttered. 'I'll see you get a medal for this.'

As he walked round the camp, a beguiling vision swam in front of Hillier's eyes. All his life he had grown up to revere and admire his great-uncle Bert, one of the most noted warrant-officers who had served in the Welsh Guards in World War Two. Three times, twice in Tunisia and once in Italy, the then CSM B. Hillier had had his company officers shot under him, and in every case he had gone on, at Fondouk and Hammam Lif in Tunisia to ensure his company's continued participation in the battalion's successful attacks, and at Monte Piccolo to help an unwounded subaltern to achieve the withdrawal of the shattered remnants: for these exploits he had been rewarded with the DCM, and eventual promotion to Regimental Sergeant-Major. Now John Hillier fleetingly saw himself in uniform outside Buckingham Palace, RSM J. Hillier, MBE, MM, flanked by a smiling wife and well-scrubbed children, displaying the two medals in their velvet-covered cases to appreciative press-photographers.

The vision faded: urgent tasks crowded in upon him. Here was Private 02 Jones, never distinguished for initiative.

'Sir, there's an Argie locked himself in one of the loos, and he won't come out!'

'Chuck a smoke-bomb in, Jones,' said the Sergeant-Major briskly. 'Smoke gets in my arse. Ha, ha!' And he strode away to his other manifold and pressing duties.

As the afternoon wore on, order began to be restored in the camp. Fatigue parties of Argentine prisoners, under British guard, were employed in collecting the bodies of those who had been killed, and transporting them to two separate resting-places by the runway's edge, pending decisions on the burial arrangements. There were twenty-seven British dead and thirty-four Argentine, excluding the large numbers who had been in the burnt-out Hercules, and those in the two shot-down helicopters, which no-one had yet ventured to approach. In wounded men, the casualty figures were forty-eight British and seventy Argentine. These large numbers of dead and wounded, very large indeed on the Argentine side, were shortly to cause horror and consternation all round the world.

After the surrender had become a fact, the British medical team from Stanley had moved forward to the regular camp medical centre which was well equipped, and in which the Argentine regimental medical officers had established their aid post. Thenceforth both medical teams worked together on all the wounded, but they had a desperately uphill task: it was apparent that many comparatively lightly wounded men would receive no attention for many hours to come.

At five o'clock, with darkness falling, a convoy of vehicles wound into the camp and approached the medical centre: it was led by the Commissioner of Police. As well as the three ambulances, which were all that the Stanley hospital could muster, there were a number of private cars and Land-Rovers containing ordinary citizens of Stanley and their wives: from the backs of these vehicles were taken bedsheets, disinfectant, painkillers, spare pairs of pyjamas, bandages, everything which the people of Stanley had been able to find in their houses which they thought could be of service in this emergency. If skilled medical and surgical resources were in short supply, there would be no shortage of unskilled but willing helpers and nurses, and now the less seriously wounded men of both sides began to be made more comfortable pending the attentions of the medical officers.

As night fell, notification was given from the main Argentine cookhouse that food was ready, and somehow it was distributed to everyone, to the prisoners under guard as well as their guardians. Everyone was tired out, and the security of the prisoners was a matter of great anxiety. These were not the sheep-like conscripts of 1982, but tough professional soldiers who outnumbered their captors: the possibility that they might cause trouble, or even attempt to overwhelm the British troops, could not be ruled out. CSM Mineur's arrangements, however, were well-thought-out and stood the test, and with the assistance of the Sappers and LDF men the surviving unwounded Mercian men were able to keep a tight grip. There would be no more than a couple of hours' sleep for any British soldier that night, and everyone was fervently hoping that relief would arrive in the morning. With regard to the possibility of bombing attacks, a strange optimism prevailed; no-one thought very much about it, and with the onset of night it seemed that this optimism would be justified.

In the control tower, Admiral Ricarda and Captain Jenkins kept each other company. Both men were in some pain now, but each was resolved to be at the back of the still-lengthy queue for attention. The radio set was silent, Jenkins having made it plain that there could be no more communication with the mainland for the time being. Ricarda's orderly, a friendly and unassuming young man from Mendoza in the foothills of the Andes, looked after both officers: when the time came he went out scouting for food and returned with a good meal for them both, plus a bottle of wine which he had obtained by the simple expedient of walking into the empty officers' mess and demanding it from the mess-sergeant, who was wondering what would happen next.

Sir Hereward Gurney appeared just as they were finishing their meal. He commiserated with them both on their wounds, and with the Admiral on the way the fortunes of war had treated him. He was able to assure them that he had had satisfactory communication with London, and that a British relieving force would arrive early next morning, with a substantial field ambulance element. He had also, he said, emphasized to London that arrangements should quickly be concerted through the International Red Cross for the Argentine wounded to be transported to the mainland and for arrangements to be made for the early repatriation of the other prisoners. His own office, he said, would act as the clearing-house for these arrangements.

So night fell on victors and vanquished alike, the latter

confined to their guarded hut-complexes, and the former snatching what sleep they were allowed, and which was compatible with guarding a larger number of fit and unwounded prisoners throughout the long winter night. In the medical centre and in the surrounding huts which had been turned into emergency wards, the doctors and their helpers worked on tirelessly. The bodies lay in neat rows, under tarpaulin sheets, by the side of the runway, and the blood congealed in the gutters under the pale light of the moon.

17

The House of Commons was over-crowded for Tuesday's emergency debate. The motion before the House, which had been put down in the names of the Leader of the Opposition and several members of his Shadow Cabinet, was clearly one of no confidence in the Government. From the outset it was clear that the Secretary of State for Defence, who made the first speech for the Government, would be under heavy attack, and would find it difficult to resist calls for his resignation. Not only were the Opposition persistent in making the point that the defence arrangements for the Falklands had been insufficiently well-thought-out and laxly set-up, but the point was now made that, on the fatal night, those on the spot had failed to take adequate precautions against the possibility that the aircraft which was allowed to land might be something of a Trojan Horse. These were difficult charges to rebut, but there was more to come. The Opposition motion contained a clear demand that the situation which had been allowed to develop should not be dealt with by way of a forcible response. Sir Henry Jones could not concede this, and when he did not do so it was pointed out by speaker after speaker that it was well-known throughout the country that some preparations were being made to mount a Task Force operation. The sudden clangorous pace of work in the dockyards; the abrupt departure of Royal Navy ships and the requisitioning of civilian ones; and the movements of commando and parachute units and the cancellation of leave for some other units – none of these things had gone unnoticed and they all pointed in the same direction: the intention to send, or at least to be in a position to send, a 1982-style expedition. And that was something to which the Opposition were in no wise prepared to consent. With a narrow overall Government majority, and an apparent marked lack of enthusiasm throughout the country

226

for a forcible solution, the Opposition scented victory and went after it hard: no-one really believed that an adverse vote would actually in the circumstances force the resignation of the Government and bring about a second General Election; but it would at least tie the Government's hands, and make it virtually impossible for it to pursue its intention of resorting to force. And, who knew? As well as procuring the resignation of the Defence Minister (an event which seemed fairly certain), it could even bring about the concession that in all circumstances the Government would be willing to accept the expressed feeling of the House and of the country, as well as that of the United Nations.

On this last point, a considerable degree of uncertainty prevailed. In the public debate which had raged for many hours every day and night since the preceding Thursday on the television and in the newspapers, there had been plenty of references to the developing drama in New York, and much speculation on what sort of resolution might finally emerge from the tall glass-clad building there. There had been a number of indications that Britain might get a rough ride. In these circumstances, the result of the Security Council's deliberations was anxiously awaited by both sides. It was expected to come in before the debate ended. A strongly-termed resolution would clearly help the Government to resist the motion, and to persist in its preparations for an expedition: the reverse result would make the Opposition motion almost irresistible.

The timetable of the debate had, for various technical reasons, been difficult to arrange: having started at two-thirty, it was expected to end at eight. The Government would have dearly liked a later end, but that was pronounced impossible. The Prime Minister and his colleagues could thus only hope that before the end of the proceedings news would be received, not only about the Security Council result, but also from the Falklands. As the evening wore on, it seemed that neither might arrive in time. For reasons of security and tactics it had been decided there could be no disclosure to the House that a desperate struggle was probably proceeding at Mount Pleasant at the very time that the House was debating the responsibility for the base's loss, and the admissibility or otherwise of mounting an operation for its recovery. After anxious consideration, the Prime Minister had decided that a firm result must

227

be available before anything could be said to the House: should it be favourable, and should it arrive before the end of the debate, the Opposition's motion would be in ruins. Since it was confidently expected that the result would be favourable, and that it would be received in time, that was the course that must be adopted. A premature disclosure might also be reported to the Security Council before its deliberations were completed, and might have a markedly unfavourable effect.

So, as the debate raged with high tempers on both sides, with speaker after speaker on the Labour side demanding the resignation of the Defence Minister (one of them even resurrected Aneurin Bevan's famous quip, and demanded that the organ-grinder should resign as well as the monkey), the Government front bench sat grimly on, hoping for something to turn up. Just after seven, something did.

A civil servant, dodging round the Speaker's chair, delivered to the nearest front bench Member a piece of paper, which was swiftly passed along the Government front bench until it reached the Prime Minister. A similar, but less official, process was taking place on the Opposition side.

The Prime Minister looked at the paper. He did not seem to like what he read. Across the floor, Mr Kinnock smiled encouragingly: he held up, conspicuously, his own bit of paper, to indicate that he knew what he did. He nodded resignedly, and handed the message to the Foreign Secretary, who was in full flood at the dispatch box. He was in process of emphasizing to the House the importance of the diplomatic process, of the all-important significance of the United Nations' attitude to the new Falklands situation, and of the strong likelihood that Britain would receive her due support from the Family of Nations.

Into this oration the message passed to him by the Prime Minister obtruded. He paused, while he read the message. A cloud passed over his face. The pause continued.

'Go on, read it!' a Labour Member shouted.

'Order!' decreed the Speaker. The Foreign Secretary held the paper before his spectacles, and clearly prepared to read from it: near-silence fell.

'I have to inform the House,' he intoned, 'that our representative at the headquarters of the United Nations Organization has informed the Foreign Office that the United Nations

Security Council has today passed a resolution concerning the situation which has arisen in the Falklands, which is the subject of our debate tonight.'

'Get on with it, you bloody twerp!' yelled the Honourable Member for a Midlands constituency. The Foreign Secretary did so.

'Our representative has informed us,' he continued unhappily, 'that the resolution which he had put forward to the Security Council, condemning in unequivocal terms the recent Argentine aggression against the Falkland Islands, was defeated by fourteen votes to one.'

Uproar, uproar, banging on benches, clapping, shouting. 'Order! Order!!' from the Speaker, and eventual near-quiet.

'Our representative adds,' said the Foreign Secretary, not less unhappily, 'that the Security Council subsequently considered and passed, by fourteen votes with one abstention, a resolution submitted by the United States of America, in the following terms:-

"That the Security Council deplores the recent resort to force by Argentina in connection with the Falklands Islands dispute with the United Kingdom, and calls upon both Argentina and the United Kingdom to refrain from the further use of force and to submit to the binding jurisdiction of a commission to be forthwith established under the authority of the Secretary-General in order to adjudicate upon the future political devolvement of the Falkland Islands."

'Our representative further reports that the Secretary General has established the commission with members as follows:- The United States of America (Chairman), Venezuela, India, Peru, and Malawi. Sittings are to commence immediately in New York.'

Uproar. Prolonged uproar. Cries of 'Resign, resign!' More uproar. 'Order! Order!! Order!!!' Gradually, a lower decibel-level of noise was achieved, whereupon the Leader of the Opposition rose, and asked:

'Will the Right Honourable gentleman kindly inform the House how the terms of the resolution, which he has just read out, fit in with what he has been telling the House for the preceding twenty minutes?'

Fairly prolonged uproar, after which the Foreign Secretary rose once more and did his best to answer the question, and then to continue his speech. He limped on, amid continuing noise and volume of interjection for another ten minutes, and then thankfully sat down.

The Leader of the Opposition rose to wind up the debate for the Opposition, and to administer the coup-de-grace. As he was speaking, the Prime Minister wondered whether he had been wise in concealing from the House the fact that a severe struggle for possession of the Mount Pleasant base had been in progress since mid-morning, London time. The Governor had of course been on the telephone early, with a cryptic message indicating that 'it' had begun, but then, in accordance with a pre-arranged plan, he had had the satellite telephone link disconnected in order to prevent any unauthorized person from telephoning abroad. The link would be replaced when he was in a position to call with the results of the fighting. There had thus been a news blackout all day, not a hint that anything was going on appearing in the world's radio news programmes: nothing had even come from Argentina, as General Romera had himself decided against a release of news while the outcome was uncertain, and his service chief colleagues had agreed with him.

As he sat with one ear attuned to the soaring cadences of Mr Kinnock's eloquence, the Prime Minister questioned himself as to whether it might not have been better to announce the attack at the beginning of the debate, and seek its postponement on grounds that no meaningful discussion could be held while the outcome was still uncertain. Still, he and his Cabinet colleagues had chosen the other way, and now they had to live with that decision. If good news duly came in before the end of the debate, the decision to withhold information might pay a very handsome dividend.

When his turn came to wind up for the Government, he was robust. He did not think that the British people would readily acquiesce in the Argentines getting away with the sort of aggression that had been so condignly punished in 1982. What had happened was aggression, and it never paid to give in to aggression. Whether the Argentines were really prepared to co-operate in a conciliatory spirit with the UN Commission was doubtful. He believed that they would be much more inclined to co-operate if they saw that we were prepared to use firm measures if we had to. For these reasons he was unable to accept the terms of the motion before the House. He sat down in an atmosphere of high tension, noise and excitement. He had not been able to make the special announcement which he had hoped to make. The House was crowded, and the public galleries were also full: there, the handsome profile of the Argentine Ambassador could be seen as he listened impassively to the debate.

In this highly-charged atmosphere the House divided, and the Members streamed into the division lobbies. In due course they came back into the chamber, many standing in the aisle and behind the Speaker's Chair to hear the result. Then it was seen that the four tellers, the Whips who had been responsible for counting the votes, were disputing among themselves and jostling for the right-hand position in front of the Speaker's Chair, from which the senior Whip for the winning side invariably reads out the result. This caused intense excitement and noise all over the House, but it finally fell silent as the senior Government Whip was conceded the right-hand position, and in a sudden deathly hush he read out

'Ayes to the right 301, Noes to the left 301.' A tie. The Speaker rose: the House was still hushed, and everyone knew what he was going to say.

'I cast my vote in accordance with precedent and with the customs of this honourable House. The Noes have it.'

To be saved from defeat only by the casting vote of the Speaker was a terrible humiliation. It was clear that, despite the efforts of the Whips, nearly twenty Conservative members must have abstained. The Labour benches emptied in an explosion of sound: everyone was on their feet. The Labour front bench crowded round Mr Kinnock, congratulating him and slapping him on the back. A loud chant of 'Resign, Resign!' arose and was taken up by everyone on the Opposition side of the House. The Government front bench sat impassively: behind them their back-benches, confused and angry, could find nothing with which to contest or refute the Labour chanting.

The Speaker was on his feet and clearly preparing to leave the Chamber, when he saw, once more, a messenger come in from behind his chair: this time he came right in and placed a folded paper in the Prime Minister's hands. He glanced briefly at it, then immediately stood up and, unable to make himself

231

heard in the still-continuing din, walked over to the Speaker's Chair: he bent down to hear what he had to say. Then he straightened and held out his hands, appealing for order: the Prime Minister went back and stood at the dispatch box, holding the paper prominently displayed. The Speaker sat down again, and gradually the noise subsided. Those Members who had seats sat down, and everyone prepared to listen.

'It's his resignation speech!' shouted a wag on the Labour side before the House once more fell silent.

'Mr Speaker, with permission I should like to tell the House of an important development with regard to the subject-matter of tonight's debate.'

This was not a usual situation. The Speaker looked enquiringly at the Leader of the Opposition: he nodded vigorously: the Prime Minister inclined his head briefly towards him, and started to read from the paper which he held.

'Mr Speaker, in the last few minutes the Governor of the Falkland Islands has been in telephone contact with the Ministry of Defence, and I am able to inform the House as follows:-

'At dawn this morning, British troops under the command of Major J.F. Wilkins, Royal Mercian Regiment, carried out an attack on the Mount Pleasant base with the object of recapturing it. After achieving initial surprise they encountered strong resistance, and very heavy hand-to-hand fighting ensued and continued for some hours.

'I am pleased to report that our forces were in the end able to overcome the Argentine resistance. The Argentine Commander and all his men have surrendered to the senior surviving British officer. The Governor tells us that the base is securely under our control, and that the Union Jack once more flies over it. Negotiations have also been successfully concluded with the Commander of the detached Argentine force at Stanley airfield, whereby that force has agreed to abstain from hostile acts pending a formal surrender to be arranged tomorrow.

'The runway at Mount Pleasant Airfield is clear, and a substantial British relieving force of fighter aircraft and ground troops is already on its way there from Ascension Island.

'I must express my regret, Mr Speaker, that because of security considerations I have been unable until now to tell the

House that these operations were in progress. I should tomorrow be in a position to provide a great deal more information upon the restored situation in the Falklands, and upon the progress of the arrangements, which are already under discussion with the International Red Cross, for the repatriation of the Argentine personnel to their own country and for the removal of all traces of their temporary occupation. My Right Honourable friend the Leader of the House will of course co-operate fully in arranging a suitable discussion tomorrow.

'Finally, Mr Speaker, I regret to have to inform the House that, by the Governor's account, very heavy casualties have been sustained by our forces, including a large number of dead of which the commander, Major Wilkins, is one. Casualties on an even larger scale were inflicted on the Argentine forces before their surrender. The Governor states that everything possible is being done for the wounded of both sides by the medical resources available on the spot, but that he is seriously concerned at the scale of this problem. I can however state that a substantial field ambulance element is included in the force now on its way to the Falklands: furthermore, the Government is already pursuing with the International Red Cross suggestions for the early provision, under suitable safeguards, of additional medical help from Argentina. I am afraid I cannot at this moment tell the House about numbers of casualties: those details will no doubt be available tomorrow. Further information on these grave matters will be given to the House as soon as possible.'

The Prime Minister sat down, to a buzz of noise and comment which was stilled when Mr. Kinnock rose to speak.

'Mr. Speaker,' he started, 'the statement which the Right Honourable gentleman has just made is extraordinary by any standards. We were not told that there were any more British troops in the Falklands capable of offensive action. Indeed, we were specifically told that there were none. We were not told that those troops were to make an attack, this very morning. The whole of the debate in which this honourable House has been engaged today has been a charade. There are many questions to be answered, many explanations to be made. The gravamen of our charge today against the Government, which is one of incompetence, is wholly unaffected. Above all, the whole of the main question about the Falklands remains to be answered: recent events have shown how vulnerable is our position there, and today's events have done little to dispel that impression: one minute we are down, the next minute we are up, and so it will go on, until we evolve a more sensible way of life. The thrust of our argument remains – the present situation in the Falklands, whether for the moment we happen to be up or down, is unreal and must be replaced by a better permanent solution. This must be further fully debated by the House, Mr Speaker, in the very near future, and I shall seek your help in arranging that.

'Meanwhile, as a Briton I can only welcome the news that seems to tell us that our control over the Falklands has been re-established. We on this side of the House honour the courage of our soldiers and lament the casualties we are told they have suffered. We look forward to receiving further and fuller information as to what has actually happened, and the way in which it has happened. On that note, I leave this honourable House tonight.'

A long, sustained burst of applause greeted the Leader of the Opposition's remarks. After a moment's hesitation, and amid a volume of audible comment and speculation, the members dispersed and left the Chamber.

☆   ☆   ☆

The Phantoms came first, just after dawn. A night arrival had not been considered wise or necessary. The F4 fighters had been refuelled three times on their journey from Ascension, the last time only a few miles from the Falklands, in order to give them near-maximum endurance after their arrival. The six aircraft spread out to cover the islands, searching visually and by radar for intruders: none were found, and they returned to Mount Pleasant. No word came to them from ground-control because there was no-one in the tower capable of speaking to them; but they could see the Union Jack flying over the camp, and the two white Verey lights which climbed into the sky.

The squadron-leader ordered the other aircraft to maintain a watch patrol while he landed. When he did so, and taxied to a halt on the apron in front of the control tower, he could see a number of British soldiers cheering, and waving at him. He gave them the thumbs-up sign, spoke into his UHF radio first

234

to the commander's TriStar which was only a few miles away (for the Phantoms' speed had been moderated throughout the journey to ensure a near-simultaneous arrival), and then to his own circling planes: he then took off again to join them while the TriStars came in.

There were five of them and they came in quickly, one after the other. Disembarkation was a rapid procedure, involving the use of the emergency chutes. Soon the men of 2 Para, ready for action but greatly relieved not to be in it, were swarming over the apron. Last to land was a Victor tanker aircraft full of aviation fuel, an insurance policy in case the refuelling facilities of the base were found to be out of order, or fuel in short supply.

Brigadier Leatham was the first man out of the first TriStar to land. He was met on the apron by a smart, well-shaven soldier with a military moustache, who saluted him. 'Company Sergeant-Major Hillier, D Company, 1st Mercians, Sir,' he announced.

The Brigadier returned his salute. 'Well, good morning, Company Sergeant-Major,' he said. 'Who is in command here?'

'In a manner of speaking, Sir, I am,' replied CSM Hillier. 'Captain Jenkins is in actual command, up in the control tower: he's wounded, Sir, and refuses to have his wound looked at until all the others have been attended to. I'm afraid he's getting rather to the end of his tether. Major Wilkins was killed, Sir, and Captain Jerman is severely wounded. We have two platoon commanders left.'

Leatham took the control tower stairs two at a time. When he got into the big glass-fronted room, he found Alan Jenkins grey-faced, slumped in the chair in which he had spent the night: his orderly hovered anxiously in the background. Jenkins attempted to rise, but failed to do so. But he could speak, and he made his formal report to the Brigadier.

'Where is the Argentine Commander?' the Brigadier asked him after their first exchange had been completed.

'He's wounded, Sir, rather like my wound, actually. I sent him off ten minutes ago with his orderly to the Argentine aid post: he wouldn't go before. He's a real gentleman, Sir, by the way, a Marine Admiral called Ricarda. He made formal surrender to me yesterday afternoon.'

'Right,' said Brigadier Leatham, 'now we'll get you looked at without any more delay. I've brought some medical back-up with me.'

And so began a very busy day for all the officers and men of the relieving force. It was not long before the radars were back in service, and Royal Artillery officers and men on their way to reactivate the Rapier batteries. All over the camp the weary Mercian and SAS men and the Sappers and Local Defence Force found themselves relieved by numerous, cheerful, red-bereted soldiers; and now they were able to go to sleep.

In the big military camp by the sea, in an upper room of the comfortable but well-guarded house which had been allotted to him, the President of Argentina was in bed with his wife. Although free to come and go, she had spent almost all the last five days with her husband. They awoke to the morning sunshine which was streaming in through the windows. A knock on the door heralded the arrival of the housekeeper who was looking after them with a tray of morning tea, an English habit to which the President was addicted. As she put the tray down, she informed the President that General Gonzalez and Admiral Vasquez were on their way out from Buenos Aires, and that they wished to see him as soon as possible.

The President switched on the radio. It was playing martial music, and when the news bulletin fell due at eight o'clock the announcer simply said that normal programmes were suspended for the time being and that a special announcement would be made later on in the morning. 'Something's up!' said the President, 'I'd better get dressed.'

Thirty minutes later, the General and the Admiral, both in full uniform, stood before him in a downstairs room. The President was composed and dignified, as he asked his visitors what their business was. It did not take them long to tell him of the events of the previous day in the Malvinas, and of their conclusion that no further naval, military or air action should be attempted at the present time in order to bring about a further reversal of fortune. Apart from anything else, they said, the whole theory behind their adventure had been that Argentina was taking up a responsible and non-violent position on the Malvinas question: to attempt further action now, after so many casualties had been sustained in the brutal and violent British surprise counter-attack, would fatally prejudice the country's international position at the bar of world opinion and, in particular, in the proceedings of the United Nations Commission of adjudication which was about to begin its work.

'I do not disagree with you, gentlemen,' said the President drily. 'But what do you suggest should happen now?'

'Mr President,' General Gonzalez replied, 'you may have heard your radio this morning. We have managed to impose a news blackout, but it can't hold for much longer: the media people are all going mad. We consider it essential, Sir, that you return to Buenos Aires and speak to the nation by television and radio. We have made some notes for what we think you might wish to say. There is much to do, Sir, in particular with regard to getting our men back home, both wounded and unwounded: there are, unfortunately, a great many of the former, and we understand facilities are completely inadequate at Mount Pleasant to deal with the numbers involved. The International Red Cross has already been in touch with us with certain proposals.'

'You propose, in short, that I should resume the duties of my office, and try to clear up the mess which you and your Air Force colleague have made?'

'With respect, Mr President, that is what we do propose. We realize that our position cannot be unaffected by what has occurred. The situation which has now arisen requires the full authority of your office. The armed services submit themselves to that authority. The game is over: the forfeits must now be paid.'

The President walked over to the window and looked for a moment over the sea. Turning, he said,

'Yes, gentlemen, I am afraid there must be some forfeits. Both of you, and Major-General Romera, must be suspended from your offices pending the appointment of a judicial commission to examine all aspects of your conduct of this affair. I suppose you understand and accept that?'

Both officers bowed wordlessly. The President went on.

'I am not a naïve man, nor am I a vengeful one. I understand full well what you tried to achieve and in particular why you temporarily deprived me of my functions, and why

237

you are now giving them back to me.'

He walked over to the bell and pressed it. When the housekeeper came in he said, 'Kindly give my compliments to my wife, and tell her I am leaving for Buenos Aires in ten minutes' time. I will send a car for her in two hours' time. I shall not be returning here. Please pack our bags.'

The President turned back to the two waiting officers. 'Gentlemen,' he said, 'after we have done our business in the capital this morning, you and General Romera will all hand over your duties to your deputies and will go to your homes: you will be under house arrest for the time being. I say this to you, you have gambled and you have failed. The nation will wish to know why so many of its sons have been killed or wounded in this adventure. And yet, I also say to you, what was done may yet prove to be of significant importance in solving this question of the Malvinas in a manner which is honourable and profitable to Argentina. After what has happened, things can never be the same again in Buenos Aires or London, or indeed in New York and Washington. Good may yet come out of it all.'

The news blackout of which the two service heads had spoken was in fact far from complete. Listeners to the BBC World Service had heard the news from the Malvinas the previous night: since then, telephone lines had been busy. It had only been possible to impose control over the main media channels, in the traditional way in which these things are done in Argentina, for a very few hours.

In the world at large, the sudden reversal of fortunes in the South Atlantic was a principal item of news. The news was not greeted with any particular approval, even in Britain itself. Public opinion in 1992 was not ready to accept heavy casualties. This had in fact been made clear ten years previously, but at least then the forces had gone into action with proper medical facilities. Now, it was clear that they necessarily had not, and the public reaction was that this was a reversion to the standards of the American Civil War and the Franco-Prussian War, if not of Waterloo. A frisson of horror ran round the world when it realized how many soldiers on both sides had been killed or wounded, and how difficult it was proving to give the wounded proper treatment. The statesmen of the world sprang to action.

Even before the British Chiefs of Staff had sent their message in to the House of Commons on Tuesday evening, they had alerted the Foreign Office about the need to mobilize international medical assistance. They were of course insistent that this should be done in a way which contained safeguards for the small British force in the Falklands.

President Bush was apprised of the situation almost at once. He made telephone calls to London, Buenos Aires, and Rio de Janeiro. Then the carrier *Eisenhower*, which was visiting Rio, hurriedly recalled her men from shore leave and steamed south at her very best speed. Next day her helicopters were able to start ferrying some of her doctors and medics, with essential drugs and dressings, to Mount Pleasant; and they returned bringing some of the more seriously-wounded men of both sides to the carrier's hospital quarters.

Next to move was Brazil herself. A planeload of surgeons and medics, also with equipment including blood plasma, set off for the Falklands. Later in the day Brazilian Army transport aircraft, having refuelled in Argentina, landed by agreement at Mount Pleasant to embark the unwounded Argentine personnel.

Also on Wednesday afternoon one of the burial teams, which had been out in the interior of East Falkland looking for crashed aircraft, returned to Mount Pleasant, which they found to their astonishment not to be occupied by their own forces. A British paratroop officer told them to add the six bodies which they had brought back with them to the row of other Argentine bodies which still lay, pending a decision on their disposal, by the side of the runway: then, he said, they had better go over to the burnt-out C-130 on the other side of the runway, and see if they could make some sense out of its contents. One of the team had a camera and took an instant picture of the inside of the Hercules: this picture, brought out by the pilot of one of the Brazilian transports, was shortly to appear on the front pages of all the newspapers in Argentina, and of many others throughout the world, adding very greatly to public horror and revulsion that two great and civilized nations could, in 1992, do such things to each other in pursuance of a quarrel over a place which mattered so little, and where so few people lived.

In London too it was clear that things would never be the same again, and that some new approach was needed.

The Prime Minister, although an instinctive follower of his predecessor and mentor, was nevertheless his own man. He had just won, against the predictions of the opinion polls and after healing the breaches of unity which in 1990 had surfaced in his party, a General Election. He had then survived, by the narrowest of margins, a vote of no-confidence in the House of Commons. During the course of the crisis it had been made very plain to him that 1992 was not the same as 1982, and the somewhat horrifying, albeit victorious, outcome in the South Atlantic had convinced him that the time had come to achieve a permanent and non-violent solution to the question of those faraway and expensive islands in the South Atlantic. Thus it was that the British Government now entered in earnest good faith into the deliberations of the United Nations Commission.

EPILOGUE

It was once again autumn in the windy city beside the River Plate. The leaves were falling steadily from the big plane trees in the park where Alicia Martinez wheeled her pram, as she did most afternoons.

Alicia sat down on one of the park benches. Her baby was asleep in the pram. He was a sturdy child, dark-haired like his father, and dark-eyed too. She adored him, of course, and in him she found fulfilment as a mother, and as much happiness as a young widow can ever have.

A man sat down on the bench beside her. He was white-haired, with an upright bearing which might indicate a service background. After a moment he turned to her and said, 'You are Señora Martinez, I believe?'

'Yes,' she replied, 'I am. But who are you? I do not think we have met before?'

'No, Señora,' the man said, 'we have not met before, but we have mutual acquaintances. Admiral Vasquez, for instance, and General Gonzalez. I should tell you that I am Luis Almira, and I am the steward at the Jockey Club, at the racecourse.'

'I see,' said Alicia. 'Yes, I see. But why are you talking to me now? What can I do for you?'

'The thing is this, Señora. When those great and terrible events of last year were being planned and discussed, the planning and the discussion took place at my club. Of course I know Admiral Vasquez well: he used to be my Captain when I was in the Navy. He's a very fine man, and the other two officers, the Generals, are fine men too.'

'Yes,' said Alicia. 'They're all fine men, and I know them all well.' One particularly well, she might have said, but did not. 'But go on.'

'Well, Señora,' continued Luis, 'I made full tape-recordings of their three meetings in my club. I intend to use them to write a book, which I am convinced will be a best-seller in Argen-

241

tina, and perhaps in other countries too, about those events. I have sold the serialisation rights to *La Prensa* and a senior journalist of theirs is helping me to write the book.'

'I see,' said Alicia reflectively. This all took a bit of taking in. It seemed at first blush to be rather disloyal and dishonourable; but let's hear more. 'Go on,' she said, 'how do I come into this?'

'Señora, the trouble is that the last tape of the three is pretty well useless. The three chiefs were getting a presentation in writing from their planning officers: they were reading, not talking. So, just when we were getting to the really meaty bits, what the detailed plan was, there was nothing. I need fill-in on the details. I happen to know that you were the person who typed out the planning report. You may even still have a copy of it.'

'No, I haven't got a copy of it,' Alicia said. 'Far too top-secret. But, I must say, I can remember most of it.'

'That's just what I thought. I will be frank with you. I need your co-operation to finish off this book, which I know well will be a smash hit in Argentina and all over South America. Then, it will be translated into English and it will go in America and Britain – particularly Britain. But I can't do it without you: will you help me?'

Alicia pointed at the baby in the pram. He was gurgling in an encouraging manner. 'He needs a bit of looking after, you know. He will need to go to school. Perhaps he will want to be a Navy flier, like his father. I am talking about money, you understand.'

'Yes, Señora, so am I: I am talking about lots of money. Enough money to help Admiral Vasquez over his defence at his court-martial. Enough to help his wife with their living expenses: he has his pension, it's not been frozen, but he's not rich. I should like to help him a bit, for old times' sake. With your help, I can fill in the blanks, and I'll see that that young man in the pram lacks for nothing. Please believe me, Señora, I really mean it.'

Alicia looked out over the park, the bicycling boys, the children running and playing. She looked at her son in the pram, gurgling and laughing, no longer asleep, the dark eyes darting and sparkling. Why not, she thought, why not?

'All right,' she finally said. 'I'll help. I have no copy, but I remember it all, every word of it. Let's write a bestseller.'